SEA LIO

ASCENDING

The Invasion of England, 21 July 1940

An Alternate History

Volume 1: Planning and Preparation

Alternate History Novel

By Harry Bold

Sea Lion Ascending, Volume One

ISBN: 9781796504231

Imprint: Independently Published

Editor: Michael Highland

Sea Lion Ascending is a work of historical fiction, a work of alternative history. Apart from well known actual people, events, and locales that figure in the narrative, all names, characters, places, and incidents are the author's imagination or are used fictitiously. Any resemblance to past or current events or locales, or to living persons, is entirely coincidental.

NB:
This is the first volume of the Sealion Trilogy:
Volume 1: Sealion Ascending
Volume 2: Sealion Boarding
Volume 3: Sealion Expanding- All available on Amazon.

PROLOGUE

1913
Vienna, Austria, 3rd District
"Darling isn't this picture lovely. Would you mind buying it for me, would you please?"

Lord Maitland knew that his wife's art expertise was not one of her more exceptional traits. Fortunately, she possessed other wonderful qualities. The picture was a watercolor and not very good, a view of the Saint Stephen`s Cathedral, accurate but lifeless.

"What would this picture cost, my good fellow?" he asked the artist who had a number of his painting spread out on the sidewalk.

The artist was young and undernourished, with shabby clothes and a distinctive but unfriendly smell. The artist had recognized that the potential buyer was one of those rich Englishmen.

"50 Kronen, your Excellency."

"50 Kronen! Quite ridiculous, good man. It's not even worth 20! Okay, I'll give you 10 Kronen!"

Maitland, who had spent about 20 years in Egypt and had acquired a lot of experience dealing with bazaar merchants, pulled a 10 Kronen coin from his pocket and offered it to the painter. He could see the struggle of pride versus hunger in the man's face. Then the man reluctantly offered his palm, took the coin, and handed over the picture.

"Well, dear, wasn't that a bargain?" his wife whispered.

Maitland offered his arm and the picture to his wife, nodding respectfully to the painter. He could see the hate flashing in the man's eyes.

When the English couple was gone, the painter turned to another street painter and said, "Did you hear what that English pig said? You would think that he had no money. Someday, I'll pay them all back."

"Rest easy, Adolf, and stay friendly. Otherwise, you won't get any money for your pictures."

1937
Chartwell, Kent

Would it ever be enough, painting pictures as the sole purpose of life? And anyway, he wasn't good enough. But his daughter and Clemmie applied a lot of pressure…and he had to do something. Just sitting, sipping whiskey, and brooding about that nincompoop Chamberlain wasn't enough.

God Damn, he thought. He was only 63 years old, but the damn Tories had shifted him to the scrap yard. But the time was decisive; England must prepare for the next war against the Huns. If only the government would wake up.

At least at Versailles in 1919, England and France had done everything they could to subjugate Germany and keep it small and powerless. Cheers to Lloyd George and most of all Clemenceau, even if he had removed him from any involvement. But he had to give them credit for the chains they put on the Germans.

What a perfect beginning it was at Versailles. It seemed impossible for Germany to revive and become a threat. The Allies had ignored the Kaiser, whom Lloyd George would preferably have hung from a rope, imposed stiff reparations, limited the size of their armed forces, and occupied the Ruhr, Germany's industrial center.

But then the bloody Commies appeared, providing Germany with a new enemy. Without them, maybe they would have fallen apart as a nation. That I would have liked, he thought.

Then the gold standard was sacked. Had Europe avoided that, Germany would be bankrupt by now. But no, the dumb Americans helped the Krauts get back on their feet.

Then this mustached Austrian, Herr Hitler, popped up and in a mere four years had undone everything, and no one wanted to stop him. Hitler was quite another type of politician, unlike anything they knew in Britain. Lloyd George, who had personally talked with Hitler, had returned cheerfully from

Germany, not concerned about Hitler's programs, arms build-up, mass rallies, and ranting against anything not German. Moreover, Lloyd George wasn't the only one with praise.

The hot summer sun burned through Winston's straw hat. Shortly past three o'clock and he felt in need of a drink.

Well, Herr Hitler's time would come. The man wanted more and more, and eventually, he would make a mistake. He had repeatedly warned the government, but nowadays after Baldwin, who had at least had some kind of spine, the appeaser Chamberlain reigned. These were hard times for him, someone who would never be quiet, who waited not so patiently for his time.

21 July 1940, 4:35 a.m.
Dover, England, over the Channel

The night wasn't completely dark. A sliver of moonlight gave the pilot of the German glider the necessary waypoints. The sun would rise in about 25 minutes, and the night was already fading in the east.

Two minutes prior, the glider had separated from the cable connecting it to its tow-plane. There would be no going back. That was fine with First Lieutenant Karl Ullrich von der Heyden and his commandos. They were ready and eager for the fight.

Heyden was born on 28 June 1919 in eastern Prussia, the very day that Germany was forced to sign the Versailles Treaty ending WWI. His family descended from the old Prussian nobility. His father, a major in the Imperial Army, had lost a foot in the Great War. On each of Karl's birthdays and anniversaries of the treaty, his father reminded him of the great injustice the Allies had forced on Germany.

He had explained to Karl that he would have to fight soon because Versailles was nothing more than a truce between wars. For Karl Ullrich, this was reason enough to follow the profession of his father and his ancestors as early as possible. He had joined the Army on his 18th birthday. Nothing else would even have been thinkable.

In his limited fighting in Poland, Karl had found out about death. After his unit's commando operation In Belgium, he became a national German hero. He had led his unit, Assault Group Granite (*Sturmgruppe Granit*) in the attack on Fort Eben-Emael, the main fortification the Belgians had built in the thirties. Military leaders proclaimed it the strongest modern fort in the world, a fort his unit had captured in minutes.

With great pride, he and his men wore their Iron Cross First Class awards for their boldness and bravery. The Führer had personally awarded it to him and all the troops in his unit, even posthumous awards to his 6 troopers killed in the attack.

"Touch down 20 seconds," called the glider pilot. Heyden and his men cocked their submachine guns. All the men in the unit had submachine guns, the ideal weapon for combat in close quarters.
He felt the excitement, anxiety, and anticipation rushing through his body as Dover Castle loomed ahead of him. At a young age, he was becoming an old pro. Unlike the attack on Eben-Emael, at least he hadn't pissed his pants.
Another commando unit, Assault Group Iron (*Sturmgruppe Eisen*) was landing on the other side of Dover to attack the coastal guns and AA batteries on the Western Heights. And a third commando unit, Assault Group Concrete (*Sturmgruppe Beton*) was landing to the northwest of Dover on the city outskirts, attacking the city from inland toward the sea. The 3 assault groups were under the command of Captain Harz, who with his small staff and commandos, was in a glider landing Assault Group Iron.
The glider hit hard, bumped along a few yards, and came to a standstill. It was eerily quiet, a silence that would not last.
"Get going," he commanded in a soft, confident voice. Leaving the glider with his submachine gun

ready, he could see that they had landed on target, near perfectly beside Dover Castle.

He could already see five other gliders, with their storm troopers quickly forming up. Now they would attack the bunker, destroy the coastal artillery, and capture the headquarters and Admiral Ramsay, the Royal Navy Commander for Dover and the Channel.

Heyden's unit had achieved complete surprise. Even so, he heard the first shots from a submachine gun. His troops had quickly killed the guards in front of the Command Center bunker and placed charges on the door. When he heard the first charge detonate, he knew he was at the right place at the right time.[i]

* * * *

Fact

In 1919 there were already contemporaries (e.g. Herbert Hoover, later US president, and David L. George, GB prime minister in the Great War), who considered the so-called Versailles treaty only to be a 20-year armistice.

"I was deeply disturbed. The political and economic parts were filled with hatred and revenge ... Conditions were created under which Europe could

never be rebuilt or peace returned to humanity".
Herbert Hoover, US President, 1919 (cf. Hoover,
H., "Memoiren", Mainz, 1951, p. 413)

Lloyd George, British Prime Minister and co-signer
of the Versailles Treaties, said in 1919: "We have a
written document that will guarantee us war in
twenty years' time". (Griffin, "The Descenders", p.
170)

They would be right.
For our generation today, the effect of Versailles in
1919 cannot be felt at all and can only be
understood with a certain amount of effort.
In order to explain the background in more detail,
one must make some digressions.
Continued after the glossary at the end of the book!

Part I

War is nothing but the continuation of state policy by other means. — Carl von Clausewitz

23 March 1939
Rostock, Germany, about 6 meters above the Baltic Sea

Captain Lindemann barked: "Are you trying to kill us, you moron? You must first pull up a little and then go into the curve. Otherwise, the wingtip will hit the water, and we are all fucking dead." Lindemann was seething and not only on the outside. It was ridiculous the inferior pilots they were sending him. No idea of mathematics or geometry. If this continued for another 50 years, they won't even know how to count to fucking 10. "Well, once again, we'll try it again," growled Lindemann. "Now listen. The torpedoes cost about 23,000 Reichsmarks apiece. That's nothing you just drop in the water like fish bait. It must be properly aimed, and it must be expertly sent on its way to hit its target. Only your flying can control all of that." "Yes, sir." Lieutenant Klaasen, a rather quiet young man from the East Frisian Islands, took a deep breath, heavily sweating and visibly shaking as he sat in the pilot seat next to Lindemann in the Heinkel 111. He wondered whether he regretted the day in 1936 when he entered basic flying school. But Lindemann, a very precise and strict instructor, was the best in the Luftwaffe.

"Okay, Captain, I'll do it again and remember to pull up."

Lindemann closely watched as Klaasen put his all into it. After the third run, Lindemann raised his thumbs up and said, "Okay, you have the basics."

14 June 1939
Freital near Dresden, Germany

He became a businessman because he liked earning money and enjoyed the lifestyle. Usually, the Luftwaffe, with whom he had been doing business since 1935, paid promptly and took all deliveries in due time. But they hadn't with this order. There had been 4,500 auxiliary airplane fuel tanks, so-called "drop tanks", sitting in one of his warehouses for more than six months.

That was annoying him. He could use that space, and the Luftwaffe would not pay rent on the area. And as he knew, even the brand new Me 109 "wonder bird" wasn't excelling at distance flying. Those 60-gallon tanks would be very useful.

The bureaucracy in Prussia wasn't the same as the

one in the old Kaiser's Prussia, thought Grabow. Maybe he should call the RLM, the German Air Ministry, in Berlin. Or he could travel to Berlin for a nice business trip with evening entertainment. He would have to go there anyway to discuss the new equipment contract for the Heinkel order.

And there was always a night with Emma, that delightful tart from one of his equipment suppliers. She had unique skills, including fitting a condom on your cock using her mouth. His groin tingled with anticipation.

He suddenly stopped. Of course, how could he be so dense? He would sell the gas tanks a second time. If the Luftwaffe were so dumb as to forget auxiliary gas tanks worth more than 180,000 Reichsmarks, well, that wasn't his problem. Grabow was suddenly excited. A trip to Berlin, a night with Emma, and a 100% profit! Then, again, the RLM did not seem to understand about excess profits. He'd think about it some more. But he'd still go to Berlin.

12 July 1939
Ventnor, Isle of Wight, England
Moira Devlin was very proud of her Irish-accented English, even if her English neighbors gave her peculiar looks. Sometimes she even exaggerated it.

John loved that accent, calling her his Irish seagull. Moreover, he loved her unrestrained sexuality when bedding her. They had been seeing each other for more than a year. John was a first lieutenant in a special outfit that operated the experimental Ventnor Radar Station on the island.

When John Harris opened the door to her tiny cottage, she hurried to him, kissing him warmly. They had to be careful about their liaisons; they couldn't make it too visible. He usually didn't stay the night but returned to the officer's billets. To John, that made their meetings more exciting and erotic.

"Hey, my big English warrior, how was your day?"

"Rather boring, darling, always the same issues."

"Oh no, I don't want to talk about your equipment problems." She waited for the right amount of time and, changing her facial expression to one of sympathy, softly said, "Okay, dear, tell me. What is the problem this time?"

John smiled: "Same-old, same-old. We have a lot of trouble getting range and height measurements right."

She teasingly said, "I thought you were the real expert on those problems?"

He smiled. Like all young men being cheered and uplifted by their women, he loved her naïve girlish ways that supported his ego. Not only was she great in bed, but she also seemed to be very intelligent for a woman.

"Well," he sighed, "whenever our target went below 500 feet, we'd lose it. Our equipment isn't able to track it, and we get a lot of surface echoes."

Even as he said it, he looked at her freckles. She had them everywhere, gorgeous. Sometimes he asked himself, what she saw in him. He was 28, already balding slightly. He thought of himself as a somewhat dull engineer, even as his thoughts turned to things other than work.

"Let's forget that dreary stuff," she said. "And think about something more exciting." Her hand slipped below his belt and gently rubbed the front of his pants.

Smiling, she kissed him, her hand rubbing and squeezing a little harder. Her thoughts were not on what her hand was feeling, but on the valuable information her ears had heard. She remembered her German mother. She had never met her Irish father. English troops murdered him at the Easter Uprising of 1916.

15 July 1939
Rostock Airbase, Germany
He tapped slowly on his typewriter keys using the two-finger style, very slowly to avoid errors, so he

would not have to type it another time.

Commanding Officer, Training
Division, Attack Aviation

I am very proud to report the
successful graduation of the
first torpedo attack course. 84
pilots participated in the
class; 4 have been killed during
training; 11 others dropped out
for various reasons. □

On behalf of the unit and the
new graduates, I respectfully
request that you ask our
commanding General to award the
torpedo citation to the new
graduates. The ceremony is next
Wednesday.□

Regards
Lindemann, Captain

Lindeman leaned back, looking at the letter. With the day's work done, he now would have time to relax. He thought about whether to call Marion or Louisa but then decided to call Gertrude, who was no fan of extended foreplay. He grabbed his keys, looked at himself in the mirror, and centered his Iron Cross First Class for service in Spain as a member of the Condor Legion. He had never really understood why women preferred uniformed men, especially pilots, but he had no qualms satisfying their preferences.

11 December 1939
Dublin Pub in the Temple Bar District

Leberecht enjoyed his draught bitter. Even after six pints, his thinking was reasonably clear and working smoothly. His drinking companion was a different story. Lochlin, the 6-foot 3 Irishman, drinking the much stronger Guinness, was already groggy.

Leberecht had supported Lochlin's IRA with a big cache of weapons that were on their way by ship. Not that he liked the IRA, but as long as they hurt the English, he would help them. And the IRA being in debt to the Reich was an added benefit.

Lochlin, a fanatical IRA assassin, was becoming loud, spewing hate against England. It took three nights and a lot of beer to discover the reason for Lochlin's hatred, but it had been worth it. The English-supported Irish constabulary had brutally murdered Lochlin's brother.

Learning a person's reason to hate was something his boss, Brigade Leader Hans-Heinrich Sixt von Armin, said was the window on a person's essence.

One should always search for the emotional weakness, for the catastrophe that had changed a person's life. It was what made him vulnerable to manipulation.

Lochlin glanced gloomily at his beer. "Fuck all the English bastards," Lochlin yelled and gulped down his pint. Three old men at the table next to them nodded and drank their beers, drooling slightly.

2 March 1940
Berlin, the Hotel Adlon

"Gentlemen, the Bordeaux, Chateau Lafitte 1933," the wine waiter quietly remarked and offered Bergmann's father a sip to taste. He pointed to his son, "He deserves the honor, it's his birthday." Michael Bergmann was 20 years old today and a Second Lieutenant in the Luftwaffe, a proud member of Fighter Wing 26.

His father had not wholly accepted his air force service, including the ludicrous name of his squadron: Devil Birds. Like many fathers, he wanted Michael to follow in his footsteps, to become an accomplished engineer, and continue in the family business.

His son had been accepted to one of the best engineering universities, attended a year, and then became excited about flying and not school or the family business. Bergmann Senior's company supplied essential electrical aircraft equipment to the Luftwaffe. As a result, he heard more than enough information about planes and their problems.

Even so, Bergmann Senior was proud of his son, even if he wasted too much time on women. He'd been doing that starting as a young teenager.

Though Michael was very intelligent, most of the time you couldn't see it. As his teachers often remarked, he had high potential, but only satisfactory achievement.

He was sociable and full of vitality and confidence. He was also the ideal Aryan — muscular, blonde, blue-eyed, and handsome, too handsome for his own good, his father thought. Instead of using his intelligence on productive work, he used his mind, good looks, and physique to chase women, play sports, and have a good time.

He was also tall, probably too tall for being a pilot thought his father.

Nevertheless, he loved his son, who loved flying. Michael wore a perfectly fitted blue flying uniform, and Bergmann Senior had noticed the admiring looks of an elegant woman sitting two tables away near the window.

"Excellent red wine," Michael nodded to the waiter, who then filled the glasses.

Senior knew that the Polish campaign had not been an evening walk in the woods and that the Luftwaffe had lost almost 200 killed and over 200 missing. Michael had only talked about his two air victories, both against outdated Polish fighters. He didn't talk about the losses in his squadron. "Since Poland, what is your squadron doing with all this downtime?" his father asked.

Michael smiled. The old man was always worried about leaving time unused, especially by his son. It had led to more than one intense argument.

"We have just completed our conversion to the Messerschmitt Bf 109," Michael proudly answered. "Quite an effort, but worth it. As you probably know, Dad, the plane has a completely new and more powerful engine. We have new performance parameters that we have to resolve. But I can tell you, with 40 % more engine power, I can fly in a new, different way."

"But the engine is much heavier," his father asserted. "Doesn't that make the cornering characteristics worse?"

"Well, yes, a little, but it doesn't have that much effect." He was always surprised by his father's knowledge of modern aircraft. "Here's the thing, the dogfight of the future will not be the dogfight of the last war. Flight tactics have and are changing to deemphasize cornering and tight curving. Oh, sure, we still train for it, but curves are too slow."

"And how are you going to avoid curving?" his father asked, frowning a little.

Bergmann Junior now grinned broadly. He was in his element.

"It's straightforward, Dad. We attack, preferably with the advantage of height, surprise, speed, and sun. We dictate the conditions; the opponent responds, usually too late."

"What if you don't have those advantages?" asked his Father.

"Well, we can evade and hope to gain the advantages…or we can vanish fast. The Me 109 even does that well. As far as we know, there's no other plane that's faster in a nosedive, which, God forbid, will stay that way for a while." He drank more wine and stole a glance at the attractive woman a few tables away. She had been looking at him, and Michael was reasonably sure he knew why.

Bergmann Senior hoped that his son was right about the superiority of the Me 109. He had been a chief aircraft mechanic in the first war and had seen enough pilots come back wounded or not come back at all.

"Doesn't your miracle plane have any quirks? In my day, every plane had its problems."

"Well, yes, a few. Dad, you know that all planes have quirks. The undercarriage is not the best. The wheelbase is too narrow and too weakly dimensioned; there have been some accidents as a result. The visibility is not particularly good out of the back. I keep looking around to spot anyone coming up in my blind spot.

"And when we fly over 650 km/h, the control stick can hardly be moved. And, aerodynamically and from the surface design, Messerschmitt could learn something from the Heinkel's design and speed. But that's been the case since the A version of the Me 109. Why nothing is improving is a mystery to me. I know that we have criticized it several times, but someone is probably running interference for Messerschmitt, the ingenious designer, and even more ingenious politician." Michael stopped, realizing his father had baited him, as usual, and he had talked too long.

"Well then write to the Führer, maybe it will help!" Bergmann Senior's smile grew as he saw the face of his son darken in surprise. No junior or senior officer in his right mind would write to the Führer, even if he thought Hitler walked on water.

"Let's not argue, Dad. We came here to celebrate my birthday. Let's do that without politics."

"Reluctantly..." said the elder, who knew that his son had known nothing but the politics of the Third Reich and the fanatical worship of Hitler. Next month, Hitler would celebrate his 50th birthday, and Bergmann senior could not deny that Germany had achieved an enormously positive economic expansion in the last seven years. He had also become a rich man through the growth and profits of his company.

But Bergmann Senior's loyalty was still with the old Emperor. Everything that followed the Emperor's abdication had convinced him that he was right about that. And whether it was right to start a war against Poland because of the German minority and the Polish pogroms and the question of Danzig, he asked himself that also!

That in September, after two days of war, England and France declared war on the Reich had been a great surprise to him. And so illogical!

He had never realized why Poland had pursued such a megalomaniacal policy in the years after the First War. After all, Germany had helped them to become a state again and then only got back ingratitude. Also, with the other neighbours, Russia and the Czech Republic, the Poles had had only unfriendly relations. Did they feel too strong with the support of the British and French?

But were British and French promises worth anything?

Not really, after the declaration of war to Germany on September 3, they had not lifted a finger, had not even reacted when the Russians invaded eastern Poland two weeks later and tore half of Poland under their nails. Of course, the Allied hypocrites had not declared war on them. Once again 1914, everybody against Germany.

He thought of the old saying, that those who do not live in peace with their neighbours should not be surprised if their neighbours respond with war.

No, Poland got what it deserved. But the English and French interfering was somehow weird. Those were the idiots who destroyed the good order in Germany and Europe with Versailles. The Führer would not have existed without Versailles.

"Who started this damn war — England, France, Germany, or Poland?" he asked rhetorically.

But his son just raised his glass with a friendly smile. "Cheers, Dad. May all our enemies get toothaches on Saturdays! Did you see the blonde at the window table?"

"Yes! And she saw you, son," smiled his father. He suspected how this evening would end for Michael, once 'the old man' left the hotel.

Michael politely declined his father's offer of a ride home. Instead, he went into the bar and, after looking around, found the woman he'd seen in the restaurant. Never shy around woman, he approached her. "Is anyone sitting here?" referring to an empty chair.

"No, not at all."

"May I join you?" he asked politely.

"Certainly, please do."

"Thank you. I saw you in the restaurant this evening. Did you enjoy your dinner?" He warmly smiled at her.

"Very much. And you?" She returned his smile.

"I did. It's a very nice restaurant. I enjoy its food and the view of the Brandenburg Gate. Are you visiting Berlin?" Bergmann's tone was casual and relaxed.

"Yes, I am. I just didn't want to order room service and eat alone. I enjoy the company of people." Bergmann smiled kindly and gently asked, "Would you like some company this evening?"

She paused just long enough before answering. "Yes, I believe I would."

And that was the end of the talking. Bergmann thoroughly enjoyed himself, and if her moaning and climaxes were any indications, so did she. It was the best birthday present he had ever received.

3 March 1940
Lisbon, Prahca de Comercio
Leberecht sat in a cafe in the old town of Lisbon and looked at the Tagus River flowing lazily by his table. After it became too risky for him in Dublin, the *Abwehr*, the German Intelligence Service, sent him to Portugal. Berlin wanted to see if he could entice a British MI6 agent at the British Embassy

with German classified documents. While he reported only to Berlin, it was through a discreete contact at the German Embassy.

His papers were a mixed bag of documents, depending on which country he was visiting. In Portugal, he was a Russian émigré and sometime a citizen of Ireland. He enjoyed the change in the climate from Ireland, and the fantastic Lisbon espresso. Not for a moment did he mourn the loss of English tea in Dublin. Maybe Guinness, but not tea. He was thinking of his last conversation with Lochlin. They had made a deal. It was amazing how little money it took to make the Irish happy, and how many problems they could cause the English. After the Reich had conquered the Czech Republic, whose armories were full, some of the weapons were a gift of God for the IRA. The first delivery was already on its way in a Turkish freighter and would arrive in Cork in a few days.

Lochlin, the IRA hero. Leberecht had to grin. It just always worked. He was curious to see if Lochlin would take it seriously. The First Lord of the Admiralty, Churchill, was a tempting target. Lochlin wanted the weapons first, and then he would give Germany something in return. That was how things were done in espionage when a country dealt with a single man or small group. But for some reason, the S.S. and not the Army had possession of the guns. Himmler, the former chicken farmer accountant, resisted giving up the weapons. It took some intervention by the *Abwehr* to convince Himmler.

Even if it didn't work out, it wouldn't be much of a loss to the Reich. The rifles they were delivering to the Irish were in a caliber that the Wehrmacht couldn't use. Moreover, the Czech taxpayer had already paid for them, which made the trade even sweeter in Leberecht's view.

The sun in Portugal was pleasantly warm, and the girls were even more so. Why would he go back to cold Berlin now? He thought about his assignment and how he could postpone his return to Berlin, and then ordered a *Vinho Verde* from the beautiful dark-haired waitress.

5 March 1940
Berlin, Norway Invasion Task Force
He stood next to General von Falkenhorst and Admiral Dönitz, looking at a map of Norway. He still marveled that he, General Colonel Erhard Milch, was invited to join the planning for the Denmark and Norway campaigns, Operation *Weserübung*. It was a joint operation of the Army, Navy, and Air Force. Von Falkenhorst had requested his assistance, and Göring, his superior, had reluctantly consented.

Maybe it was Göring's way of sidelining him. He and Göring had been drifting apart on several Luftwaffe issues. In addition to the lack of a heavy bomber, there was the problem of the changing roles for aircraft, the resulting technical changes, and the adverse consequences on standardized production efficiencies and training. It seemed to Milch and to other officers that Göring was not in step with a modern air force.

It also didn't help that Göring's obesity, drug addiction, and lifestyle – decadent was an understatement – were repugnant to Milch and many others, and affecting his mental skills. Still, Göring was his patron, he had saved his life and family, and paved his promotion to Deputy Commander of the Luftwaffe. Milch knew he would have to tread carefully.

The plan von Falkenhorst was describing was complicated but ingenious. Von Falkenhorst envisioned something that had never been attempted — a surprise air invasion and capture of critical locations by airborne troops. Milch was tasked with making it happen. Milch enjoyed complexity, in particular the effort to simplify complex challenges into actionable, coordinated steps.

"And so, gentlemen, that is the general outline of the plan. I should also mention that the OKH, the Supreme High Command of the German Army, will follow our lead in the planning. Given our short schedule, I don't anticipate any major objections from OKH," Falkenhorst forcefully asserted. The man was right to bear his name, thought Milch. He had a face as strong as oak with the features of a predatory falcon.

"And I understand, General Milch, that you have a recommendation for a chief-of-staff for our planning group?" asked Falkenhorst.

"General, I will without reservations recommend Colonel Terstegen. He is the best staff officer and planner I have in our office. After all, the air force must be able to keep up with the other branches," Milch joked.

"Indeed," retorted von Falkenhorst with a slight smile. "Then, that is settled. And you, General Milch, must get a little field experience. I've recommended to the Führer that you command Luftflotte 5, the air fleet for the invasion of Denmark and Norway. It will be a short tour but a valuable experience. The Führer seemed in favor." Milch suppressed his surprise and responded, "Thank you, indeed, general. It will be a great honor and privilege."

"What does the Führer say about the plan?" Milch asked.

"Oh, he's thrilled," answered von Falkenhorst. "When I suggested the concept of an air invasion, he became very enthusiastic. I get the impression the more unconventional a military idea is, the more he's for it. The man has little tolerance with the usual military skeptics who advocate conventional plans."

Both Milch and Dönitz nodded. They were also familiar with that variety of planning.

Fact
On March 28, the English war cabinet orders the occupation of Norway, Operation R 4 begins on April 8, 1940.
On April 9, the German operation "Weserübung" begins, the occupation of Denmark and Norway. This is remarkable, as actually the Second World War begins here, since the seven months before had essentially been a German-Polish war, while the clashes between Germany and the Allies had been reduced to a few naval war manoeuvres.
Both England and Germany had clear strategic interests here. Germany obtained about 50% of its iron ore from the Swedish ore mines of Gävilla, which could only be shipped all year round via neutral Norway and its port of Narvik, as the Baltic Sea, unlike the North Sea, was mostly frozen in winter.
English considerations were concerned on the one hand with the support of Finland, which, however,

became invalid due to the ceasefire between the Soviet Union and Finland in March 1940. On the other hand, England would have liked to shut down the German ore supplies in the course of this. Here, too, England was not concerned with rescuing any democracies, as German apologists like to say upfront.

After the war, General von Falkenhorst was first sentenced to death by the victors and then pardoned to 20 years. He was released in 1953 because of his poor health. That same year, Winston Churchill, a warrior of aggression not indicted and therefore not condemned for Norway, received the Nobel Prize for Literature, though the same prize was not given to Stalin (Poland and Finland!) an evil but not condemned aggressor who died in the same year. Why four weeks later France was so surprised by the German Blitzkrieg is not really obvious, given this context.

What is hardly discussed in the relevant publications, is the question why the German Reich attacked France in May 1940. Since September 1939, after the French and English declarations of war with Germany at the mutual border, which was protected on the one hand by the Maginot Line and on the other hand by the Westwall, both sides had established themselves with only marginal combat activity. There had been a series of German plans to conquer France since autumn 1939, but only the

Manstein Plan, which Hitler had to force upon his generals, seemed to give a chance to conquer France in a quick campaign.

Strategically, there are two arguments favouring a blow against France.

    a) the far superior naval forces of France and England had practically brought the import of raw materials and goods into Germany to a standstill. A reaction with German submarines, the only German weapon capable of threatening or even interrupting imports of raw materials and goods into England, could be made much faster and more effectively from French ports than from German North Sea ports or from the newly conquered bases in Norway.

    b) Since September 1939 there was a common border between Germany and the Soviet Union in Poland. It cannot have escaped the German leadership that the Soviet Union, beginning with its invasion of Poland and the attack on Finland, undertook a considerable reinforcement of its troops at its western border. From spring 1939 to spring 1940, the troop strength of the Red Army at the western border doubled to about 7 million men. If one did not want to be confronted with a war on two fronts in a reasonable time, it was essential to eliminate at least one of the main opponents in a one-front war.

9 March 1940
Lisbon

Jane Rossiter was fascinated with the man sitting opposite her, casually holding his red wine glass in his hand. She couldn't place his accent. There was some Eton in it, but also something that sounded harsh, coupled with some Irish. And his physique was very pleasing to look at — tall, muscular, dark-haired with a touch of grey at the temples, strong hands, and a masculine face that reminded her of a football player. He palpably transmitted sexual energy. As far as Jane knew, Leberecht was a Russian exile living in Lisbon.

She was in her early thirties, married to a dull diplomat who headed the visa department at the English Embassy in Lisbon. She rarely attracted the look of men, she was not self-confident enough for flirting, and she tended to shy away from conversations about diplomatic matters.
But she didn't shy away from this man. They were excitedly talking about Marcel Carne's new film, "The Day Rises", which they had just seen together. He had told Berlin he thought he could seduce Jane

Rossiter, the wife of the English Embassy target, the resident for British intelligence MI6. He observed her for three days, confident no watchers were tailing her. He approached her a few days ago, and they were now at a café in the old part of town. He looked warmly at the young Englishwoman sitting across the table. He had already noticed that under the polite, almost bored English façade, she bubbled like a teakettle. She could never hold her hands still and always formed strange figures with her fingers when she spoke.

She was telling him the story of the film. Leberecht nodded, knowingly smiled, and laid his hand on hers. She paused, looking at his hand, and swallowed, trying to compose her feelings and continue talking about Jean Gabin's role in the film. She didn't pull her hand away, and he saw red spots forming on her neck. He bent closer to her, pretending affection, and said:

"Don't you think Gabin's character is too rough with Clara?"

Jane looked startled and said with conviction, "But no … not at all!"

That started well, Leberecht thought. He smiled warmly at Jane and wondered if the affair would start today. Neither was disappointed.

10 March 1940
7th Panzer Division, near the Luxembourg Border

He loved his big Panzer IV machine. Twenty-five tons, 80 millimeters of armor at the front, and a 75 mm cannon. It was bigger and better than any French or English tanks…according to the briefings.

Well, all right, the English had the Matilda with its thick armor and 40 mm gun, and the frog eaters had the Char B1 with its 75 mm cannon. Worse for the French, though, the joke was the Char B1 ran out of fuel driving across the street. The French and English tanks were slow, lumbering vehicles, good at best for infantry support. On the other hand, his tank could run rings around both of those slower monsters, deftly positioning itself for the kill. The Panzer IV was a marvel of German engineering: fully rotating turret, powered by an electric motor; a gun that fired a variety of rounds, including armor-piercing; speed; mobility; 5 person crew; and intercom and radio communications. It outclassed any of the French and English tanks.

They had been practicing massed formations of panzers in cooperation with the Luftwaffe. In training, massed panzer units coordinating with the Luftwaffe were incredibly lethal, driving through enemy lines and formations with devastating effect. Artillery could not move fast enough to keep up with panzers. Consequently, the Luftwaffe had become their air artillery, capable of pinpoint targeting with devastating effects. The training was going very well, and he was eager to test it in a real battle.

Hans-Joachim Müller, Master Sergeant, opened his commander's hatch and spoke into his intercom. "Driver, advance to the edge of the forest." He enjoyed the speed and power and the feel of the 300 HP Maybach engine. He hoped the battle would start soon. Throughout the winter, there had been many false alarms and attack preparations, but each time there had been a stop order.

What a shitty way to fight a war. No wonder the French called it the *drole de guerre*, and the English called it the "Phony War."

But Müller thought that it wouldn't be phony for long. When the weather got better, the French and English would be in for a surprise, a big, fucking surprise. After all, it makes no sense to mobilize a panzer army as powerful as this and then not use it. He had already learned in the first days of the Polish campaign that wasted time was lost forever. Battle was like a brawl. Whoever landed the first blow and did not hesitate to continue or waste time, won the day.

He turned to the radio operator: "Order to the unit to travel back to the camp!"

Then he raised his head out of the hatch, satisfied

that all the Panzer IV`s in his platoon were turning and rolling back to camp.

10 March 1940
Lisbon

It had been effortless to seduce Jane. He liked women, and they liked him. From shortly after puberty, women were attracted to him. So much so, women and how to afford them became the overriding focus of his life.

His mother died when he was young, leaving his father to raise him. Unfortunately, his father had other pursuits, mainly gambling and his carousing. Left to take care of himself, Leberecht fell into the wrong crowd in Frankfurt.

It started as petty theft and ended up as grand larceny. Along the way, he learned all the tradecraft of casing a place, watching for usual and unusual activity, and stealthily breaking and entering. Because he was so good-looking and personable, he often played the part of diverting the attention of women whose homes were targets. He quickly found that in addition to his share of the loot, he had the full share of the women.

Being a strong man, he also learned how to take care of himself in a fight. By the time the police caught him in the act of stealing, he was in his mid-thirties and had killed several men. Even the first one wasn't that difficult.

As usual, the police roughed him up a little and threw him in a dirty cell. This time, the Duty Sergeant snickered, "Enjoy the time alone, asshole. We've got your balls in a vice this time. We're coming back, and when you leave jail, you're not going to look so good to the ladies and maybe not fuck so well."

Not one to fear the police, he replied, "No matter. I've turned down more pussy than all you assholes have had put together."

Instead of the police, two men in suits came for him. Was he interested in helping his country, in getting out of jail, in clearing his criminal record, in perfecting his skills?

So after signing a confession that was held as insurance, he joined an Abwehr special unit. Two weeks into the training, he came to two conclusions. First, he knew a fucking lot more than his teachers. Second, he was surprised to discover he had a talent and ear for foreign languages. As he told one of his classmates, "Who'd a fuck'n thunk it?"

Jane was in her early thirties, with no children, married to a boring diplomat for almost ten years. She had been entirely predictable in terms of her emotional situation. Yesterday, it had been almost frighteningly easy to get her into bed for the first time, with her hunger for tenderness, closeness, and sex, something she hadn't experienced too much of in the last few years. Now she wanted more.

A bonus was that she also volunteered one morning each week at the embassy. Bored Jane was utterly open to anything, especially romance that gave her life more color and excitement.

They had to be extremely careful. To ensure Jane was not watched by the British, German Embassy agents shadowed them. The embassy also recorded and filmed their sexual activities in a safe house in the old part of town. They'd furnished the apartment according to Leberecht's preferences, to include appropriate Russian personal effects.

Jane was so hungry for attention and affection that she pleaded with him to meet again, only one day after their first meeting. They met in the cinema, sitting in the back in a dark corner. They had begun to kiss and grope each other. She wanted to go down on him, to enjoy the thrill of public sex. Given how dark it was and how few customers there were, he consented with gentlemanly grace. As she was leaning over his lap, he slid his hand down her back and slowly hoisted up her dress. He was surprised to find that she didn't have on any panties. His hand slowly rubbed her between the moist folds of her vulva. It didn't take long for both of them to satisfy each other.

Afterward, they were still excited and rushed to his apartment. What followed in wildness and lust had even surprised Leberecht. Her slight hesitation and awkwardness yesterday when they first made love had vanished. She was passionate and intense, eagerly taking him inside her and crying in ecstasy when she came.

She still wasn't finished. Sitting on his lap, she wanted him to admire her beautiful breasts, all the while stroking his cock. She teasingly asked, "Do you like what you see?" Instead of answering, Leberecht pulled her to him, bit her nipple, and started making love again.

When they were finally satisfied and exhausted, and were lying entangled in each other's arms, he asked about her husband. She had no discretion and talked freely about what his real work was and what he was working on today. Leberecht thought, what a wonderful combination, great sex and great information.

19 March 1940
London, Admiralty Headquarters
His colleagues at the Admiralty gave him mocking looks. Why was an Army Intelligence major working at the Admiralty? Most thought he was an insufferable prick, and many understood why the Army kicked him over to the Royal Navy.

They called him "Newport with the Norwegian spleen." He had repeatedly warned of an impending German attack on Norway. It was clear to him and should be clear to every intelligence officer with a modicum of intelligence and reason. The Germans clung on to the Swedish iron ore like a baby on a wet nurse. Without iron ore, the Germans could not build tanks or cannons.

The British Navy was planning a landing in Norway. Even if the Germans knew nothing about this, they could not avoid securing their supply of ore. So they would have to invade Norway, not Sweden. It was possible to ship ore all year round via Norway's ports on the Atlantic, while the Swedish ports on the Baltic Sea were often frozen over in winter. And if you controlled Norway, you didn't have to invade Sweden. It was therefore not a question of "if" but only "when."

Newport briefly thought about the term "intelligence" in the military, which somehow seemed contradictory to him. But he rejected the thought. Such thinking would not help him. He almost wished that the Germans would attack now, to create clarity, but then he also rejected this idea as not expedient. What could he do to get Lassiter, that stupid Eton buffoon who ran the department, to convey his analysis to Churchill, First Lord of the Admiralty?

Avoiding the chain of command would be the only

way, but then he would risk putting his career and position at risk, resulting in a likely reassignment to a remote corner of the Empire. He did like the risk of a good poker game, but he preferred the subtlety of bridge. He would do it via Admiral Summerfield, who was certainly no admirer of Churchill but whose memos Churchill read with interest. Not directly with Summerfield, but through his good acquaintance David, the Admiral's son. He reached for the phone.[ii]

11 April 1940
Scapa Flow, aboard the battleship HMS *Rodney*
There was no sound from the assembled officers in the Admiral's cabin when he read the telegram. During the advance to Narvik, Norway, the Destroyers HMS *Hardy* and HMS *Hunter* had been sunk after a fight against the German invasion fleet. Most of them had friends on both ships. David, the Admiral's son, had been on board the *Hardy*. None of the officers had survived.

They waited for the Admiral's reaction, but all they saw was Summerfield's usual motionless, tanned and hard-looking face, which after 35 years at sea was furrowed by deep lines.

"A first-class performance by our Admiralty after receiving warnings of a German invasion a week ago," whispered Summerfield in disgust. "My son told me a senior Admiralty intelligence officer, a major on loan from the Army, even predicted such an attack in mid-March."

He threw the telegram on the table in disgust. "And we lie here in Scapa collecting mussels on our ships' hulls instead of entering the North Sea and cutting off the German supplies. You may step down, gentlemen." Almost relieved, his officers left the Admiral's cabin.

Fact

On 28 March 1940, the English war cabinet ordered the occupation of Norway under the codename Operation R 4. On 8 April, the English and French landed in Norway. On 9 April, the Germans attacked Denmark and Norway in a combined sea and air invasion. Germany prevailed. By the end of June 1940, all Allied forces had been evacuated.

Some historians argue that this date was the substantive start of the Second World War, the beginning of actual combat between the Germans and the Allies. Before 9 April, there had essentially been the German-Polish war, the air skirmishes, and a few naval engagements between the Germans and Allies.

Both England and Germany had clear strategic interests in Norway. For Germany, it was iron ore. Germany obtained about 50% of its iron ore from the Swedish mines of Gävilla, which could only be shipped all-year-round via neutral Norway and its Atlantic port at Narvik. Winter and its freezing temperatures closed many of the Swedish ports on the Baltic Sea.

For England, it was the blockade of iron ore to Germany and the support of Finland, which became moot due to the ceasefire between the Soviet Union and Finland in March 1940.

11 April 1940
London, Admiralty Headquarters

"Fetch up Newport!" barked Winston Spencer Churchill, First Lord of the Admiralty, as if calling a dog. Churchill did not like sitting at his desk. He preferred to walk back and forth in the room. It helped his thinking, and today, given the Norway mess, he needed all of the "thinking" help he could muster.

There was a knock on the door, and Newport was shown through. For a moment, Churchill looked at him and saw a tall, gangly, almost bald major in a neglected army uniform. Despite his bean-pole build and the appearance of his uniform, he had a very relaxed and self-confident presence. Churchill waved him to the chair in front of his desk and got immediately to the point.

"So you were right, and everyone else, including I, was on the wrong track." Churchill laughed grimly while still pacing. "I looked at your reports. In August of '39, you warned us that the Germans and Russians would sign a treaty and that soon after Germany would invade Poland. Two successes could be a fluke, but there's more to it after the prediction on Norway. I'm reassigning you to work on my staff. You will report directly to Admiral Winslow."

"With pleasure, sir!"

Churchill stopped pacing and looked at Newport, perceiving some arrogance in the answer. He had a better understanding of why Newport irritated so many at the Admiralty. "And what does your glass ball say now?" Churchill demanded. "What are you working on?"

"I am in the process of preparing a study on Germany's strategic possibilities and necessities from a time perspective. As I said, Norway was only a matter of time, a short duration of time before the Germans had to invade".

God, he is arrogant, thought Churchill, more arrogant than I.

"Like we, the Reich is subject to obvious strategic

constraints and cannot afford to lose time. Since Herr Hitler is unwilling to achieve peace based on the status quo before September 1939, and we are not prepared to sanction his invasion of Poland, Denmark, or Norway, he must act very soon. Otherwise, the Royal Navy will strangle supplies and sea trade to Germany. Besides, he has a mass of Russian tanks less than 200 km away from his main oil supply in Romania. The Soviet Union's intention is not quite clear at this moment, but Hitler must expect that he may have to fight them at some point. So it's only natural that he first takes out his current opponents one by one."

"And who do you think is number one in line?" Churchill would have been surprised if Newport didn't say the Low Countries and France

"France, along with the Low Countries, sir."

"Well, keep me posted…and clean up your damn uniform!"

"Yes, sir!"

Churchill nodded as Newport saluted and left. Walking down the hall, Newport smiled to himself and chuckled over Churchill's order to clean up his 'damn uniform.' This from a man who many said often worked in the nude! Aside from one's uniform or lack of it, he could see that the First Lord of the Admiralty had to digest that another person, an Army major no less, had made better predictions than he and his close advisors had made.

12 April 1940
Watton, England
The sun was sinking below the horizon when the Blenheims of the 82nd Squadron slowly started to land like big swans. They had spent hours flying over the North Sea looking to bomb German transport ships. Delaney, the squadron commander, switched off the ignition and climbed out of the cockpit. Fast as a cat, he jumped from the wing to the ground and pissed on the front left wheel. Even though each crewmember usually took their own "piss bottles" — beer bottles and the like — they filled up fast. Sitting on a well-filled bladder for hours without being able to empty it, was something they didn't tell the new recruits.

A moment later, Jameson, the Welsh gunner who had spent the last 5 hours trapped in the cupola, and Tommy Collins, the navigator, joined him. Together they watered the wheels. It was always good luck to piss on the front wheels.

"This is the best moment of this whole fucking day," Collins grinned.

Jameson, a medium-sized, black-haired Dublin Irishman with a scar on his cheek from a fight, sighed with relief. "Forget the bombs. With all this piss, we could have sunk a damn Kraut ship.

Imagine if we had all the money the five squadrons burned for gas today. We wouldn't have to worry about money. We could spend the next few years in the pub and the whorehouse. And a whorehouse is where I need to go. God, I need a fuck!"

"What else is new?" smiled Collins. "You're so fucking horny, that's why we isolate you in the back gunner's sling."

After a long flight, Delaney mused to himself that banter and insults about one's parentage and sexual prowess were all great forms of stress release and indicators of good morale.

They heard the siren of the fire truck. Looking up, they saw another Blenheim with a smoking right engine. It floated in, landed with three bumps, and rolled to the end of the runway. The fire brigade chased after it, but nothing started to burn out of control.

"That was Remington. Looks like at least everybody made it," Delaney said.

The unspoken fact was that the Blenheims were now too slow and too weakly armed against German fighters. A few years ago, Blenheims were faster than fighters. Not any longer.

Collins broke the silence and said, "Yep, they made it. This is a clear reason to celebrate."

Delaney thought of Joyce for a moment. He missed her. Maybe he'd call her later. Maybe he could get his wing commander to give him a little leave.

"Well then, boys, let's get the bloody hell out of here before some idiot wants another mission report. First round is on me."
He waved to the corporal, who placed the brake shoes in front of the main landing wheels, and then Delaney and his crew ran laughing across the airfield towards the pub.

Fact

Blenheim Mk 1
As the prototype aircraft took flight in April 1935, it was realized that the prototype flew faster than any Royal Air Force fighter in service at the time. In production since 1937, in 1940 it was outclassed by modern fighters, but continued in production until 1942.

17 April 1940
London, at the Savoy

For them, she thought it was a special evening, a first-class dinner in the restaurant of the Savoy, later the dance in the ballroom, and then a night of sweet sex. She felt as if her cheeks were glowing, but her husband, Major Terence Tremaine, had just made a grumpy face.

Later, he relaxed and looked like the man she had married 15 years ago. He was a dark-haired but exceptionally elegant looking lieutenant back then. Now he was a major and looked even better.

Terence wasn't exactly happy to be in the Savoy while some of his friends fought in Norway.

"Could you do anything with your tanks in Norway?" she asked to get him to talk and maybe change his mood.

"Actually no, that's why they sent French mountain troops; there is hardly any terrain around Narvik where tanks could be used. But still, I find it somehow inappropriate to dance here."

"Come on, darling, don't spoil the evening. We have so little time. I already hate that you have to go back to France the day after tomorrow."

Terence shrugged his shoulders in the French way and said with his muddled French accent, "C'est la Guerre, Cherie."

They both laughed and Helen tenderly laid her hand on his arm.

"We're here, now, Terence. It doesn't matter what tomorrow brings. I want to enjoy the day and night with you."

This time she didn't blush. Strangely enough, she was not afraid for Terence. The war, which was over half a year old, did not affect her other than the annoying blackout at night. She even understood that the Germans had replied to the British attempt to occupy Norway with an attack.

But the Germans in France...no, that was unthinkable! She knew Terence's huge contingent of tanks and artillery were stationed in France. He had Matilda II tanks, massive monsters with enormously thick armor that he said no German gun could penetrate. With inferior tanks, the Germans wouldn't attack France. The Germans had not managed to subdue France in the last war. Why should they succeed this time?

2 May 1940
Mannheim-Sandhofen, Germany
After hanging up the phone, Merkle was excited

and anxious. The Duty Officer told him his leave was canceled and to immediately report to his unit at Trier, Germany near the French border. This had to mean that the attack against France would begin soon. But the start of the operation had been postponed so often since winter, that he didn't wholly believe it. But this sounded different. He could hear the excitement in the duty officer's voice, and it was infectious.

The anxiety was with his wife. With each alert, she had become more agitated and even hysterical at times. Ellen was furious this time, offering no help as he hurriedly packed.

She had tears in her eyes and screamed so loudly that he was afraid she would wake up their son. "I just can't stand it. It's so awful when you are gone, and I'm so alone. Every time you leave, I sit here for hours crying, just incapable of doing anything. During the Polish campaign, I spent days listening to the radio to hear something about you. If I didn't have to care for our son, I don't know what I'd do." She was close to crying now.

"Please visit with the other officers' wives. They are in the same situation, and together you all can cope."

She turned away in disgust. "I want you, not those other wives. You must stay here and take care of me."

Merkle sighed. When had she become so needy,

and how many times had they argued about this? Only God knew. She didn't seem to understand that he was an officer in the Luftwaffe. He had responsibilities and duties.

"If you loved me, you'd stay here." She wiped away the tears.

"I do love you. But that doesn't change my obligations to the Luftwaffe."

Merkle had been born in the beet winter of 1916, and he had witnessed the agony of the last Weimar years. His father had gone bankrupt in the Great Depression following 1929.

Then everything changed very quickly. Within a short time, the Brown Shirts, which most of his friends supported, had changed the situation. Above all, they had awakened hope in the people that the economy could improve. His father started over again and soon produced parts for air force bombers. Merkle — like everyone else — became intoxicated in the wake of the positive changes.

He had always been interested in flying, so it was a logical decision to volunteer with the new German Air Force immediately after graduating from high school. As a high school graduate, officer candidate school accepted him. The months of training flew by, and even the many burials of fellow candidates who had died in training accidents, could not slow down his enthusiasm for flying.

Graduating as one of the best pilots, Merkle was

free to choose which aircraft he wanted to fly. Of course, he became a fighter pilot, the elite.
Although Merkle came from a middle-class family in Hanover, belonging to the German Air Force's elite was the most significant thing he had ever achieved. You could even see it in the way he took care of himself. His parents sometimes made jokes about how well dressed and tidy their son appeared now. A boy they knew throughout his life as a slack, loose, and distinctly untidy youth.
Then the Spanish Civil War broke out. Merkle had no idea what it was all about, but he was enthusiastic about the prospect of fighting and wanted to know how good he was. So he volunteered for the Condor Legion.

The six months in Spain had changed him. He became a successful aviator, with four kills, one short of an ace during those times. He was awarded the Iron Cross First Class and promoted to First Lieutenant.
But he disagreed with his superior, Captain Daiber, about flying tactics. After a heated disagreement over Daiber's flying, Daiber sent him back to Germany with a poor evaluation report, a report that would hurt his advancement and promotion. Worse, Daiber, who knew how much Merkle loved fighters, had recommended that he be transferred to the newly formed Me 110 Destroyer units as an

instructor. It was pure revenge.

The Destroyers were advertised as the new elite, to which only the best were assigned. But Daiber knew that the transfer would hurt Merkle. Merkle had protested in vain. The personnel office couldn't understand all the complaining. Besides, they were happy to send an experienced and successful pilot to the elite Destroyers.

He didn't like his new workhorse, Germany's new heavy fighter, the twin-engine Me 110. It flew well, but in terms of speed and handling, the things that made a fighter so unique, it was no comparison to his lithe Me 109.

With Ellen still yelling at him and sobbing, he closed the door and headed for the train station.

Part 2

The envelopment strategy which won the 1940 campaign was revolutionary only in its technical aspects, armor, and air power. — Anonymous German Officer

10 May 1940
Lulworth Cove, England

In the afternoon sun, Joyce's long hair was tousled from the wind as they walked along the trail overlooking the water.

Adoringly he looked at her, her beautiful red hair and soft, china-ivory complexion. Sean Delaney thought he was the luckiest man in the world. He still could not understand why she had married him and not his friend, James. James was a dashing, tall, and movie-star handsome Black Irishman. Maybe she married him because they were both redheads. Whatever the reason, he knew he loved her dearly. Joyce knew why she loved Sean. Underneath his military exterior, she had discovered pleasant surprises, qualities, and traits she admired, even adored. He was self-taught and enjoyed literature, music, and paintings, things she dearly loved. Moreover, after you got to know him and his shyness faded, he made her laugh. He was reliable and dependable. Average height and build, a little curl in his red hair, and gorgeous, dark, deep blue eyes. The more she knew him, the more she thought he was handsome.

And unlike his friend, James, he didn't jump from bed to bed. On the contrary, he was adoringly shy. Under a beautiful tree in the country during a warm summer afternoon last year, she had to take the initiative.

"Are you trying to seduce me?" he smiled when her hand lightly brushed against his pants. They had been kissing and hugging for some time, and it was clear they were aroused.

"Well, Sean Delaney, someone has to do something about that bulge." She laid her hand on his pants and gently rubbed.

He lifted his head a little, swallowed hard, and stared earnestly at her hand movement. "Wow, I hadn't noticed. Honestly, Joyce, I don't know where that came from! Remember, I'm a boy from a middle-class Irish background. We don't know about such things."

She laughed. "That's not been my experience with middle-class Irish boys."

"Really! And how much experience do you have with Irish boys?" He could feel his wet underwear, and if she didn't stop rubbing him, his penis would tear a hole in his pants.

"Obviously, more experience than you."

"Well, I hope so! I'm not really interested in boys." She laughed and withdrew her hand. "How can I seduce you if you make me laugh?"

He nestled next to her, lightly kissing her neck, and whispered, "You can start by putting your hand back." As her hand moved, he gently slipped his under her dress. She moaned and closed her eyes. She was wet, as wet as he was.

Later in the afternoon, after the beautiful sex, she felt an incredibly warm and satisfying glow. She wondered why she waited so long to take the initiative.

Yes, as she walked along the path, she knew exactly why she loved him. With all their hiking today, she was ready for some rest and refreshments.

"I think there's a pub down there on the beach next to the boat dock. Let's go down," she remarked.

He leaned carefully over the stone wall and looked down. They stood on top of the hill above Lulworth Cove, where only a few fishing boats bobbed. The sun and wind were at their best this afternoon, and no other hikers were about.

He playfully pulled Joyce to him. "Let's make love first. We can go behind that stone wall over there. I promise I'll make it worth your while."

"You silly man. I'm not going to make love on this rock-strewn ground. You'll have to provide much better accommodations than rocks if you think you have any chance with me, Sean Delaney." She nestled up to him, slipped her hands below his belt and gently massaged. "Well, maybe…I might do it on the rocks, if you were a famous movie star and extremely well-hung."

"I'm becoming one of those conditions," he answered.

Joyce passionately kissed him, giggled, turned quickly, and ran down the steep footpath. "You'll also have to catch me."

He sighed and smiled, wondering again why he was so lucky? He slowly walked down the path. As a 24-year-old squadron commander, he didn't want to stumble and injure himself. Besides, running with an erection was never a good idea.

The pub was open, and two fishermen were sitting at a table in it. The landlord nodded briefly to them and then concentrated again on the radio. Sean could hear something about France and heavy fighting, so he went to the bar.

"Good day! What's going on with the frogs?"

The bartender looked up: "The Germans attacked this morning. The radio reports fighting in Holland and Belgium". The landlord, a middle-aged man who moved slowly with a pronounced falter, moved over to them and stared into emptiness. "I was in Flanders in 1916. We should have really fucked up the damn Krauts back then, so they'd never attack us again. Cost me my leg and most of my mates."

He pointed his hand at yellowed pictures hanging on the wall behind the bar. "Those were my mates, we were with the artillery, and we even had tanks at the end. Most of my pals in those pictures didn't survive."

As a squadron commander, Sean Delaney made a dark face when it became clear that his leave, which he had just started two days ago, was over. "I need to call my squadron in Watton and return to my base. Is there any way to get to Wareham today?"

The bartender shook his head. "There's no bus tonight, no bus until 7:20 a.m. tomorrow. Tommy can take you with him in the morning; he takes fish to the market."

"Can I stay here with my wife?"

Joyce had rested her head on his shoulder, sensing his concern and anxiety. She was regretting they hadn't made love behind the stone wall.

"Yes, if you are satisfied with a small room." Joyce laughed nervously. "We are at home wherever we are together. Thank you very much. We'd like something to eat, too."

The bartender looked at them with evident enthusiasm and nodded. "I'll tell my wife, we still have some lamb and beans, but first, you should drink something to warm yourself. And we have wonderful scones. Would you like some cream tea?"

The phone was next to the bar, and the landlord was

already calling the telephone switchboard.

13 May 1940
Trier, Germany

It was strange. He had achieved his first Me 110 kill, but he didn't have any feelings about it. There was only emptiness, like a battery that only produces a glimmer of light in the lamp and fades away.

The kill wasn't due to superior flying, just luck. He was lucky he had been coming out of the sun and lucky he was the first to shoot. Fortunately, it was a Blenheim and not an English fighter.

"Well, Lieutenant, how did the flying work out?" Walzenburg, the group operations officer, led the debriefing, an annoying after-action ritual to confirm whether a kill could be claimed.

Merkle pulled himself together. "We were already on our way back north of Reims. There was a Blenheim bomber, not a fighter, about 300 meters below us. We came straight out of the western sun. The gunner in the Blenheim's upper cupola only saw us when we were 100 or so meters above him. We fired a short burst from the two guns and the machine guns, and bam, parts detached from the left engine. The cockpit glass was shattered, and the Blenheim went down in a left loop. Nobody got out.

It exploded on impact in a large fireball. Time was 2:22 p.m."

"Were there any witnesses?"

"Yes, my Number Two, Sergeant Ferkinghoff." Walzenburg beamed at him, knowing it improved the Group's kill numbers. "Well, then, congratulations. That was your first. That means…no, wait. You were in Spain and Poland, right?" Without waiting for a reply, he continued, "Please submit your report by tomorrow!" Merkle saluted and left. All he wanted was a shower. It was pure chance he was coming out of the west with the sun behind him. The Me 110 was too heavy at the controls, too slow, and too unmanageable. It just didn't match up to the new English fighter planes.

Fact
Me 110
The first prototype was delivered to the German military in May 1936 and production began in the summer of 1937. The Me 110 participated in the fighting after the European War broke out, but the large size and weak maneuverability soon led to a high loss rate especially in the Battle of Britain. With a speed of 560 km/h (C 4 Model), about 120 km/h faster than a Blenheim, and about as fast as

contemporary one-engined fighters.

Bundesarchiv, Bild 101I-382-0211-011
Foto: Wundshammer, Benno I Mai 1940

Source: Photographer Benno Wundshammer ; German Federal Archive;
Identification Code Bild 101I-382-0211-011

14 May 1940
London, 10 Downing St.
It was disturbing. The front in Belgium was
relatively quiet. The Germans had captured the
Belgian Fort Eben-Emael on the morning of 10
May, had accomplished an operational victory after
the tank battle of Hannut on 12 and 13 May, and
had reached Rotterdam yesterday. Why the lull in
attacks? The Low Countries were where the Allies

expected the main German effort. It was where all of the best Allied divisions were holding the line. The other disturbance was what was happening to the south of Belgium. The front at Sedan, France was in turmoil. It appeared the Sedan front was where the Germans were also making a big push with lots of panzers, troops, and planes. Sedan was not the place the Allies expected the main German attack — certainly not out of the Ardennes forest! Was Sedan a German feint or the primary focus of attack?

Admiral Graham Winslow looked again at the report in his hand. General Gaston-Henri Billotte, commander of the French First Army Group, desperately pleaded that the Allies destroy the German bridges across the Meuse at Sedan. He adamantly believed that "over them will pass either victory or defeat!"

The third disturbance was what was happening at the end of the conference room. Instead of reviewing the military situation, Churchill was still arguing with the Socialists about who should have which positions in the new cabinet.

Admiral Graham Winslow had been honored when Churchill, the new Prime Minister, had asked him to continue working for him at 10 Downing Street. He wondered if this was an advancement.

He could see Churchill turning red over the arguing. As always, the PM felt things were not developing fast enough, as he considered most of the other participants to be limited and incapable. Winslow got up and went to Churchill, bent over and softly asked if he should let the attendants serve a round of drinks.

"Thank you, Graham," Churchill sighed, nodding, hinting at the height of the whiskey with two fingers.

Winslow did not understand politics. Why had they fired Chamberlain over Norway, then elevated Churchill to PM, the man who had been the driving force behind the Norway operation and fiasco? That he couldn't understand! On the other hand, Churchill was everything that Chamberlain wasn't. A bull, a fighter, a man of energy who was able to energize others. Chamberlain was serious and respectable but did not radiate any discernible energy, except that required to carry his umbrella. Nevertheless, it was very annoying that it seemed the Germans had managed such a thorough strategic surprise at Sedan, if it really was one. Newport had advised that the Germans could attack through the Ardennes. As usual, nobody listened to him. Maybe they should spend more time listening to Newport, even though he was an arrogant Army prick.

15 May 1940

Dyle Line, Belgium

Sergeant Savage was pissed off. It was early evening and for days they had been building, with hard work and a lot of sweat, a first-class hull-down position with two alternates per tank. Now Lieutenant Horrocks, who looked so young he needed written permission from his mother to be here, had passed on the order to retreat to a new defensive line. They had seen very little combat. Where the hell were the fucking Krauts?

What Horrocks explained had something to do with Sedan to the south. But it wasn't until Savage looked at the map, that he realized what the lieutenant was chattering about. If the Germans had broken through the French front at Sedan, they could threaten the Allies' right flank. But it didn't look like that was what the Germans were doing. Instead, as Horrocks excitedly exclaimed, they seemed to be driving west down the Somme River valley towards the Channel.

This was way above his pay grade, but Savage wondered if the German drive to the Channel could cut off the British Expeditionary Force and the northern French armies from southern France. Somewhere in his distant memory, he recalled something called 'envelopment.' He wondered also if the ones with the polished boots had once again fucked up royally.

After he had explained to his crew what was going

on, the Matilda was ready to go within short order and without the usual cursing from his crew. With Horrocks commanding, the five tanks of the platoon in a cloud of dust rolled towards the French border, soon surrounded by trucks and marching columns of infantry. More and more civilians were fleeing from the Germans, mostly on foot, or with heavily loaded cars or carts. Savage kept looking for German aircraft. What he had heard so far sounded worrying. The Stuka`s had an unpleasant reputation. But still, everything was quiet, although the clear weather cried out for German airplanes!
Then he heard loud explosions behind them. German artillery was pounding the rear guard covering the rest of the division's withdrawal.

16 May 1940
Montcornet, France

"God loves the infantry," said Company First Sergeant Albach, sweating but happy that the company was riding on the hot engine covers of a group of the panzers. Lieutenant Gademann, who sat next to him, eagerly followed the path of the panzers on his map. He knew that the "taxi ride" would last only about 2 more kilometers. Then they would have to continue towards Marle, France on foot. He saw the crossroads coming in the distance.

It was very considerate of the French not to remove the road signs. He patted the commander of the tank on the shoulder, signaling him to stop.

After his company had dismounted, the Maybach engines roared, and the panzers moved forward.

With regret, they watched the tanks vanish in a trail of dust. One would like to have such friends around all the time.

"No rest, let's go," he ordered, and they marched off. He almost wished that they had more contact with the enemy coupled with some rest time. Some of his men, after 8 days of forced marching, had bloody feet. But so far, not one of them had given up.

And so far, his infantry company had not caught up with the panzers of the 2nd Panzer Division. Guderian was pushing the panzers forward as fast as he could, stretching the tip of the salient ever closer to the Channel.

He looked up at the sun, which had made May hot so far.

Great weather to race to the Channel and trap the English and French in Belgium, he thought. Their infantry division, which supported Guderian's 19th Tank Corps, had little contact with the enemy to the north. Even at Sedan they came too late to fight. They saw only destroyed French equipment, a lot of it abandoned without a scratch.

"Could be a worse way to wage war, what do you

think Biegi?" asked Lieutenant Gademann.

The Sergeant Major, a weather-tanned, medium-sized, bald man from Baden, who had joined the Army just before the end in 1918, nodded and said in a broad Mannheim patois, "One can well say that, Lieutenant. Last time I was in the area, there was a lot more going on, mostly retreat. But not that I'm complaining, walking in the sunshine without artillery fire aimed at us is quite nice."

Gademann laughed, turned around, and shouted, "A song!" Schulz, who led the first platoon, promptly begin singing the Tipperary song they had heard so often over the BBC during the *drole de guerre*. The company sang enthusiastically. They would have about three more hours to walk to the day's objective if nothing happened.

18 May 1940
Above NW France

The attack came out of the sun, with no warning until the first Me 110 flew apart in an explosion even audible in Merkle's cockpit. A second one folded its wings upwards and fell to earth like a comet. Merkle saw brown-green camouflaged fighters with pointed wingtips flash past his plane. "Spitfires!" he yelled.

"Engage in a Lufbery circle!" Lenz's voice came

calm and measured over the radio.

Instinctively Merkle pulled his plane into a steep curve to stay in line.

"Do you see anything?" he asked his gunner, but only heard the fast staccato of his machinegun, the scattered short bursts of fire through the air. He looked desperately all around for the Spitfires. At the same time, he had to keep his place in the horizontal Lufbery circle.

Theoretically, the Lufbery was a sure thing, which led to the entire squadron circling a one-kilometer radius over the same place. The circle permitted overlapping fields of fire from each plane, increasing the defense of all the aircraft. One might even get lucky and shoot down an enemy plane. Or the Spitfires might get lucky and shoot down one of the circling Luftwaffe planes. But hopefully, it would result in a draw, and the enemy would lose interest. Only now four Spitfires kept a whole squadron of twelve Me 110`s in a circle.

The English tried to break the ring twice but were quickly deterred by the concentrated firepower. They circled the flock a few more times like hungry wolves. When they ran out of either desire or fuel, they disappeared in a steep roll downwards.

Lenz cleared his throat and calmly ordered: "Well, extend your dicks and let's go home."

Spitfires were not Polish or French fighters, thought Merkle; Spitfires were in a completely different, higher class of fighter aircraft.

21 May 1940
Le Crotoy, France on the English Channel
The men threw their helmets in the air, stripped, and ran into the surf. Standing on the dune, Lt. Gademann winced! The water was too cold for bathing, but most soldiers didn't care. This was not exactly "German Order" for Army soldiers, he thought.

But what the hell, after the exhausting, never-ending marches, his troops deserved it. In just 11 days, they had marched from Germany to the Channel. His father had fought for four years in the same general area in trenches against the English. Papa wouldn't believe it. Neither French nor English soldiers could be seen far or wide.

On 18 May, a reconnaissance unit of the 2nd Panzer Division reached Noyelle sur Mer, France, 1 km from the beach with a view of the Somme River flowing into the Channel. Gademann had heard that the panzers were moving north, with orders to attack Boulogne. The British Expeditionary Force was north of them, trying to make an orderly retreat to the coast. The trap was now closing. All you had to do was complete the envelopment and squeeze. To the south, reports were coming in of disorganized French forces. In support of 2nd Panzer's attack on Boulogne, Gademann's regiment was to hold the line at the Somme against any French counterattacks.

"Sergeant Albach, get the men out of the water and dressed. Then immediately establish a defensive line to the south with good fields of fire for machine guns. Also, put some troops overlooking the beaches."

He turned to the runner. "Runner, look for the battalion or regiment command post, report where we are. We're establishing our defensive line, waiting for new orders. Understood?"

The corporal nodded and ran back towards the east.

21 May 1940
Folkestone, England

Mrs. Tremaine walked along the beach of Folkestone with her dog. She was tall, slim, and dark-haired, and she didn't show her 40 years. She looked out to sea to France. Her husband Terence was over there with his tank battalion, part of the 3rd division of the BEF under General Montgomery.

She was worried about him. The news from France was not good. She hadn't heard from Terence in two weeks, and the news said the Germans had reached the coast and cut off the BEF from Southern France. The wind made her shiver when she stopped. Her dog nudged her with his nose; he wanted to play but sensed that his mistress was restless. Without thought, she threw a piece of driftwood for the dog to chase and began to go back to her house.

Terence served under Lord Gort, which didn't improve her concern. She had seen His Lordship several times on social occasions and was not impressed. Indeed, he was brave, very sociable, and friendly, but he seemed too old for the task.

21 May 1940
Near Arras, France

Major Tremaine was cautiously hopeful. Out of 6 Matilda II tanks, 4 were still operational and advancing; those damn Stuka`s had destroyed 2 in the fields between Mercatel and Tilloy.

He had hoped to attack with all 16 Matilda II tanks, emulating the concentration of armor used by the Germans. However, General Franklyn, commander of the combined English and French forces, left 10 Matilda`s to defend the garrison at Arras.

Nevertheless, the battle group of assorted English and French units had made good progress. They had advanced almost 10 km into the German salient. He was genuinely surprised how quickly the invincible

Germans fled from them, and how ineffective the German 37 mm anti-tank guns were against the Maltilda's heavy armor. Granted, they hadn't encountered any tanks yet.

He had to smile. Finally, General Gort did something right. For the first time, they attacked the exposed flank of the German tank thrust from Sedan to the Channel. The attack's goal was to cut it in half and isolate the German tanks to the west. That was more than urgently necessary. The German thrust had cut their supply lines, and Allied units were running low on petrol and ammunition.

He looked around, instinctively searching for enemy armor and cover for his tanks, but the area was flat fields. There was hardly any place to take cover. But no matter, as long as the attack charged forward, cover was secondary.

He looked through his target eyepiece again, taking care not to hit his head on the cupola in the heaving and shaking tank. About 1 km ahead of him stood some houses in the middle of the wheat fields. He could see some movement, but he couldn't see clearly what it was.

He ordered the driver to stop.

He pulled himself up and began to search the village with his binoculars, saw some soldiers, but no tanks. Then he noticed a large grey steel shield next to one of the houses. It looked like a German anti-aircraft gun, a German 88, with its barrel pointed in their direction. "Driver, left turn...Now!" he shouted.

He saw a flash from near the houses and immediately heard a hissing sound, which terminated in a thunderous hammer blow to one of his tanks on the right. As he turned his head, he saw the tank's turret explode into the sky as if a giant had snapped it off with the flick of its finger. What the hell had hit it? He clung anxiously on the edge of the cupola. As he was giving the order to turn again, he saw another flash from the village. The round struck the front of his tank between the hull and the turret, slicing through the steel and violently exploding inside. All the shells stored in the tank exploded, throwing the four-ton turret several meters high before it crashed to the ground, a smoldering shell of steel next to the burning hull. No recognizable remains of Major Terence Tremaine or his crew were to be found.

Fact

The 8.8 cm Flak, although heavy, was still designed to become mobile relatively quickly, though requiring a large half track vehicle for towing. They were designed with a high rate of fire (15 rounds per minute) in mind, with the guns automatically ejecting spent shells so that the crews were spared this task. While they fired high explosive shells against aircraft, they were also given anti-tank shells so that they could be used in an anti-tank role.

As can be seen, the gun with its shield was not much higher than the men.

Bundesarchiv, Bild 183-B27411
Foto: Lachmann | Juli 1942

Source: *Photographer: Lachmann; German Federal Archive; Identification Code 183-B27411*

21 May 1940
Near Arras, France
The whole panzer shook and resounded like a bell when the two-pound shell struck against the front

armor and bounced off. The loading gunner was already pushing an armor-piercing round into the breech of the 75 mm gun, as Sergeant Kreisler looked through his gunner's telescope and strained to spot the source of the shell.

But panzer platoon commander Sergeant Müller was faster. He had seen the firing flash and quickly gave the gunner the target values.

"Got it," Kreisler said and pressed the fire button. The shell left the barrel with a loud pop and struck the English cruiser tank almost 800 meters away. Initially, there was only a small flash. But moments later, a large column of fire and smoke exploded out of the hatches of the hull and turret.

Müller stuck his head out of the commander's hatch, looked around with his binoculars, and then over the radio ordered his four panzers to move forward. Bernhard Venske, his driver, already knew what his commander expected of him, putting his foot down full-throttle and driving in a zigzag pattern to the group of trees, where a fat cloud of smoke billowed above the English tank. The panzers in the 7th Panzer Division had circled back to Arras from the west when the English and French attacked the infantry and artillery columns of the division. Along with 88`s, the panzers had stopped the attack.

23 May 1940
Trier Airbase, Germany

That evening there was a pervasive silence in the officer's mess. Four pilots and their crews had been killed today, and more than one of the remaining pilots silently thought about his will. Even the most ardent realized their twin-engine Me 110`s had no real chance against a single-engine Spitfire or Hurricane. The realization covered the pilots like a heavy, wet blanket.

Merkle watched Captain Lenz, the Squadron Commander, come in. Before all of the officers could stand to attention, he gave an "as you were" order. As quiet as he always was in the air, he was now vocally pissed off.

"What crap. How will we destroy the English in Belgium and France when we have to fly around in circles like a pack of canaries when some Spitfires show up?"

An orderly started serving everyone champagne. It was a tradition to toast and honor the dead, a tradition that started in the Great War.

Captain Lenz looked at his glass and raised it in a toast. "Here's to our lost comrades, going down with the flag raised. At least we're still alive." Lenz drank the champagne in one gulp.

Then on a more cheerful note, he said, "Do you guys realize that we've only been at this campaign for 13 days, and the French are almost finished?

That's amazing! And the English troops are encircled at Dunkirk."

Some of the younger officers nodded enthusiastically. The history of the Great War had been implanted in them from birth. Fathers describing again and again how enormously difficult and long the fights on the Western front had been, with little to show for it except trenches, mud, and dead comrades.

Merkle, however, always quick at arithmetic, had already calculated that the squadron at this loss-rate would be wiped out by autumn. Suppressing that thought, he raised his glass: "One more reason to drink, because we will never meet again so young as today."

The young and inexperienced laughed. They had learned the saying in flight school when drinking to honor their comrades killed in training accidents. Now it was comrades killed in combat.

The fact that there were more missions the next day did not prevent anyone from drinking. Tomorrow, some of the aviators would take Pervitin tablets to increase their performance. The pressure was so great for most of them, they needed some kind of security blanket.

Merkle took a bottle of champagne and sat on a couch next to the cold fireplace. Strange that he hadn't even thought about Ellen and his son for days. How insignificant those everyday domestic problems were when it came to survival.

Being eight years older than most of the other pilots, he seemed to have a more vivid perception of life than these easy-going boys. They had landed here immediately after graduating from air warfare school, optimistic young men, unencumbered by family and children, and reality.

Merkle was annoyed that he had so little political knowledge and too little strategic understanding. The feeling of being just a small drop of oil in a big gearbox didn't match his pride and success. The champagne ran wonderfully dry and tingly down his throat. Maybe someone feeling similar had invented the stuff. Given what his unit faced, it was a good thing they had a lot of it.

25 May 1940
Near Dunkirk

Still stiff from a night on the ground beneath his tank, Sergeant Savage stood in the commander's hatch of his Matilda II, looking for Stuka`s as he and other British troops lumbered down the road in the early morning. He heard his driver swear just as the right tread jammed, the Matilda pulled right, and slipped into the ditch with a jarring stop. Savage climbed out of the hatch and jumped down next to the tank. The rear pulley, which had been damaged two days ago by enemy activity, had finally given up. The track was now slack and useless. Irreparable, as Savage immediately saw.

Meanwhile, Walker, the driver, and Phelps, the gunner, along with Scott, the loader, had climbed out.
"We have to walk," said Phelps with a facial expression that showed a distinct aversion.
"All right, boys, get your gear out," ordered Savage. "Scott, unscrew the oil drain plugs in the engines."
In less than 2 minutes, they were ready to start on foot. Walker turned on the two Leyland diesel engines and they waited until both froze up from lack of oil. Phelps threw the breech of the two-pounder cannon into the next meadow. Then they joined the train of refugees and exhausted soldiers heading for Dunkirk. Far away he heard the bells in a village church, calling for early mass. Better than howling Stuka´s any morning, he thought. Then, replacing the church bells, he heard the distant sounds of artillery behind them.

27 May 1940
Berlin, Luftwaffe Headquarters
They were looking at a map of France displaying the successes of advancing German forces and the

less than glowing results of the air attack on the English at Dunkirk.

"Colonel Terstegen, the campaign in Northern France is as good as won. However, I'm not convinced we can destroy the English at Dunkirk. Maybe we should not have halted our panzers," stated General Milch.

When Milch learned of Göring's boast to Hitler that the panzers were not needed and that the Luftwaffe would destroy the English at Dunkirk, he and the Reich Marshall argued about it. Voices were raised. Göring finally stopped the heated discussion, insinuating that Milch had lost faith in his creation, the Luftwaffe.

Milch returned to thinking about the unfolding situation at Dunkirk. With each passing hour, more of the BEF escaped to England. "Terstegen, it's time to think about the next steps against England."

"Yes, sir. What do you want us to investigate, an air war against the Royal Air Force?"

"A little bigger than against the RAF. I want you and the staff to look at an invasion of England. The Navy did some preliminary work last year, I believe. Did you review it?" Milch was now looking at the Channel and the Dover coast.

"Yes, sir, but I'm vague on the details now."

"I remember reading it," Milch casually remarked as he shifted the map for a better view of the English coast across from Calais, France. "It was a very conventional plan, an invasion on a broad-front against the east coast of England. Two of the prerequisites were the defeat of France, and Luftwaffe air superiority over England, after the refitting of airfields and ports on the west coast of France."

Milch tapped the map with his pen. "No, a broad-front invasion will not work. It will take too much time, at least two months, maybe more before we are ready to begin the air war. By the time we are ready, the English will have had two or more months to recover."

Milch walked restlessly up and down the room. As the organizer of the Lufthansa commercial airline and the German Air Force in the 1930`s, he had solved many complex problems. He was a visionary who prided himself on anticipating the next steps. Still, none of those steps had been as urgent and complicated as the situation he believed Germany now faced. Germany not only had limited resources; it also had limited time.

"If the English evacuate their troops from Dunkirk, we'll have to attack England as quickly as possible. If the English are on the run, we must use our momentum in pursuit. This is a chance we'll never get again in this war." Milch returned to the map table.

Terstegen suppressed the surprise on his face. He'd learned that Milch could see many moves ahead.

And he had learned to work hard to keep up. "But what about the rest of France and her armed forces, and what if England sues for peace?"

Milch continued looking at the map of the Channel and SE England. "France is finished. All of her best forces are trapped in our envelopment. England, maybe she will seek peace, but I doubt it. Churchill is an English bulldog in more than looks."

Milch paused and tapped his finger on SE England. "Even so, Germany must plan for the worst case. Terstegen, you're going to prepare a plan for the invasion of England as soon as possible. But not under the Navy's plan. Given England's supremacy in naval strength, it's not realistic for our Navy to support a broad-front sea invasion of England or defend against the Royal Navy. Even Grand Admiral Raeder acknowledged Germany does not have the sea power to defend against the RN." He took a closer look at existing Northern French airfields.

"But we do have superior strength in the air. Remember what we accomplished in Spain in 1936. Therefore, plan it from the standpoint of a massive air invasion over a narrow front in the sky and on the ground in Kent, England. We've learned a great deal from our air invasion of Norway. Let's apply it to invading England. Place a premium on invading as soon as possible."

"Yes, sir. When do you want the plan, General?"

"Have the preliminary plan by 4 June at the latest. Read the Navy study. It will have addressed some of the issues you will face."

Milch smiled. "We must do today what the others will think of tomorrow, as that ingenious whiskey-boozer Churchill says." Milch gave Colonel Terstegen a nod indicating that he was dismissed.

Fact

At the beginning of the Spanish Civil War, the insurgent nationalists faced the problem of transporting troops from Morocco to Spain. The Republican Spanish Navy had blocked the Straits of Gibraltar. The Nationalists called the Germans for help. In response to a personal order by Hitler, 20 Ju 52 transporters were sent to Spain. In a few days, these few planes had transported the Spanish Foreign Legion to Spain. The best daily transport was 3,000 men in 20 planes. Up to three dozen legionaries were squeezed into a Ju 52. There was no defense or attack by Republican fighter planes.

27 May 1940, 3:10 p.m.
English Channel near Ostend

Merkle held his breath in shock. It was harder and harder to keep his plane in the air.

After a nerve-wracking aerial fight over the Channel attacking English ships in the Dunkirk evacuation and fending off Spitfires, the flight home had become a nightmare. The RAF was out in force, and the Luftwaffe provided scant cover. With only one engine working, his Me 110 had slowly crawled over the Channel at a low height. Merkle had radioed his situation and heading as the rest of the squadron flew ahead of him.

As if by some miracle, neither he nor Karl was injured, although the glass canopy had more than enough bullet holes to say otherwise. Merkle was sweating despite the airstream whistling through the holes. It was all he could do to keep the plane in the air.

Then it all happened so fast. Fountains of water spraying from bullets suddenly splashed in front of the plane. Merkle heard his gunner return fire and then felt the plane tremble under staccato hammer blows.

Karl screamed, "Fucking Spitfire!"

As if in slow motion, he could see from the corner of his eye the smoldering Spitfire splash into the water. "Good shooting, Karl," he yelled.

Then his second engine sputtered and failed. He desperately tried to lift the plane's nose.

Instinctively, he stiffened and shouted: "Attention,

Karl." The water smashed into the windshield.
He was jerked around in his safety harness and sat
quietly for a moment, completely perplexed and
rigid, tightly strapped into the cockpit. Then his
training took over.

He was prepared to free himself underwater, but the
plane floated sluggishly with rocking movements.
Probably the near-empty fuel tanks functioning as
flotation chambers, he thought.

With an experienced motion, he opened his seat
belts, folded the rest of the mostly fragmented glass
canopy to the side, and pushed himself up. He
looked back. Karl had sunk to the side in his seat
and made only small helpless movements to release
himself. The glass around him was shattered and
Karl was bloodstained.

"Karl, what's wrong?" Of course, the question was
ridiculous. Karl was badly hurt. He moved his lips
but could not speak. Merkle crawled backward
along the plane's surface and began to unbuckle
him.

The water was already washing around Karl's knees
as he lifted him out. He pulled the trigger on his and
Karl's life jackets and removed the rubber raft out of
the plane storage compartment and inflated it. He
pulled Karl into the small dinghy, which hardly
offered enough space for one man.

Karl's shoulder and belly were covered in blood. He
stripped Karl's leather jacket upwards and saw two

dark red holes in his upper abdomen. Merkle froze when he realized what it meant to be wounded and adrift in a rubber boat in the Channel.

Without thinking, he took the first aid kit out of the pack in the boat, unpacked the morphine syringe and injected it in Karl's thigh. Then he slid into the water and pulled the raft away from the plane. Slowly, with gurgling and hissing sounds, the plane sank lower. All of a sudden, the tail went steeply upwards and after a last whistling of escaping air, they were alone in the water with the silence surrounding them.

The water was pleasantly warm at first, but Merkle knew that this sensation would soon change. He was already losing body temperature.

Then he remembered the Spitfire. He looked around and discovered a head bobbing in the water about a hundred meters away. He could hear a subdued "Help" and thought how little it helps to call when seagulls and two enemy flyers are the only ones who hear you, and how nonsensical the term enemy was in such a situation.

Merkle was an experienced and good swimmer, and the Channel was almost calm. He turned on his back, pulled Karl's inflatable raft in tow and began swimming to the Spitfire pilot. It seemed like an eternity to get to the drifting Englishman. A large seagull curiously curved overhead.

"Looking at your dinner? Forget it, not with me!"

growled Merkle, although he had trouble keeping his head above water.

The Englishman had at least managed to inflate his lifejacket halfway with the old-fashioned tube attached to the top. Again and again, the man's head kept falling limply backward, only to be straightened up again with great effort. Merkle let go of the raft and swam the last two meters to the Englishman. He heard the man mumble vaguely but did not understand him.

When he was next to him, Merkle saw his face. It was so terrifying that nausea choked his throat. The man had looked unharmed from a distance, but up close, he saw that half of his face was almost burned to charcoal. He knew there was a gas tank in front of the cockpit on the Spitfire. When the engine caught fire, the cockpit usually caught fire, and the pilot was fried. How could engineers construct something so stupid?

The man must have been in terrible pain. Merkle carefully pulled him to the raft. He loosened his web belt and tied the man to the rope running around the raft. There was only room for one in the raft. Why didn't somebody come up with the idea to buy a two-person raft for a two-seater plane?

For a moment, he was filled with the hope that they might be near land or one of the Luftwaffe rescue buoys. He looked around, pulled himself up on the edge of the raft, but he could see nothing except water and a hazy horizon. They floated in the Channel, hoping someone would rescue them.

27 May 1940, 11:18 p.m., English Channel near Ostend

"I'm sorry, no more pills," Merkle said to the pilot in his halting high school English. He could see the man's uninjured eye for a moment showed understanding. He carefully examined the man, looking for any bandages, but only finding that his chest and left leg felt greasy and encrusted. The Englishman had endured Merkle's awkward touch in silence. How did the man get out of his plane?

"What is your name?"

"Pilot Officer Holborne," came back weakly after some hesitation.

Finally, the English pilot slept and moaned only occasionally. It was a ghastly situation to drift in the middle of a mostly moonless night in the almost windless Channel. His fingers and hands were numb and he could barely see Karl and the Englishman, which only made their moaning worse.

28 May 1940, 3:25 a.m.

English Channel, north of Ostend

The darkness lay over the sea like a heavy envelope. Merkle was cold and thirsty. He had confused thoughts, an argument with his wife and suddenly a woman appeared from another room. She pulled him from the room in which he was locked up with Ellen, pulling him into her arms. And Ellen raged and struck the door with hateful force. Then he saw no exit from the room into which the other woman had pulled him. He heard his son screaming. The torment of the nightmare faded, but not the screaming. It wasn't his son, it was the English pilot.

The Englishman bobbled in the water, his lifejacket colored by his blood. From time to time, he tried to talk, but Merkle could hardly understand anything. Something about Mary, or Mary Ann, maybe his girlfriend or his wife. Probably a girlfriend, as young as the rest of the face looked.

Merkle wondered if Ellen knew anything yet about his disappearance. Unlikely, there were a miracle, she would not receive the ominous telegram for two or three days. Maybe Lenz would write some kind words about him.

He checked on Karl. "How goes it, Karl?"

"Cold, so cold," he weakly mumbled.

God, they were all cold and thirsty. They had been warned not to drink seawater. What a joke it would be, to die of thirst in all of this water. Merkle was dehydrated and fatigued. Slowly he fell asleep.

28 May 1940, 6:19 a.m.
The English Channel, north of Ostend
The morning sun burned through his closed eyelids and woke him. Merkle felt his lips, chapped already by the heat and lack of drinking water. Why was there no water supply in the raft? He cursed quietly about the usual inability of people to think beyond the simplest requirements.

He looked at the English pilot. He didn't move at all, just bobbed in the water with his head on his chest. Merkle pulled his head up and saw only blind white eyes. Holborne's skin was white and swollen. Merkle closed his eyes and took one of the dog tags from him.

"It's all behind you now," Merkle mumbled quietly to himself and awkwardly loosened the belt he had used to tie him to the rubber raft. Feeling in his fingers and hands was almost gone. Slowly Holborne drifted away from the boat in the weak swell.

Turning to Karl, he saw the same white skin and distant look in his open eyes. "Karl! Karl! Wake up! God Damn it, wake up!"

Karl blinked and his eyes moved slowly.

"Karl, hang on. Don't give up. We shall not

surrender," insisted Merkle. Karl smiled ever so slightly.

Merkle started shivering uncontrollably. He knew that was a sure sign that his body temperature was too low. He was frightened. He felt terribly alone and helpless in the vastness of this sky and water.

He was damned to wait for death or for someone to find and save him. He thought for a moment of his wife and his little son, but then closed his eyes because it was too painful, but he couldn`t stop thinking about them. It was strange to have a little son, and he often thought about what it would be like to watch him grow up. But since the war began, he had resigned himself to the fact that he would have virtually no chance of surviving. The odds were against him.

Around 7:00 a.m., Merkle and Karl were found by a Luftwaffe Air Sea Rescue plane, which had been alerted by Merkle's squadron. They were pulled out of the water into the plane. Karl was dead.

29 May 1940
Dunkirk, France

The worst thing for Savage was the smell, a mixture of burning oil, rotten fish, and human decomposition. Nobody bothered to bury the bodies anymore. They had joined an infantry unit shortly after their Matilda had broken down. Although they had participated in several rear-guard actions, none of his men had been harmed.

But now they had been waiting for two days to get on board one of the evacuation ships. There were still at least 20,000 men in the queue in front of them, moving slowly like a large flock of sheep, only ducking during air raids but not leaving the line. Nobody wanted to give up their place in the line, even on pain of injury or death.

The number of dead and wounded on both sides of the snake line was correspondingly high. Some of the wounded were dragged along by their mates, but many simply remained lying down. There were hardly any paramedics left. Even at night, the line moved slowly, with most of the men sleeping standing up, bunched up against each other for support.

The gunning and bombing by the German planes, it seemed never to stop. Fortunately, the sand absorbed bullets and bombs. If the ground had been hard, the casualties would have been much higher. Also, the number of troops, thousands and thousands of them, and the number of boats off the coast, were too large for the Germans to kill or sink all of them. Not even the Germans with all their methodical efforts could kill everyone and prevent ships, small boats, yachts, and everything else that was floating, to transport troops westwards to England.

He noticed with pride that some men still had their rifles and sometimes even machine guns. Savage and his men had acquired Lee-Enfield carbines days ago, which they used diligently during every air raid. But to their regret, without success. However, by the morning of the third day, Savage was sure they would make it to England.

29 May 1940
Near Falmouth, England
She had studied philosophy at Oxford when women were still exotic and a unique phenomenon at the university. She had met her husband there, when Terence visited his friend, Lawrence, at college. It was a chance meeting in a book store. Terence wasn't her type, this young Royal Tank Officer from Cornwall.

But, for some reason, she agreed to see him. And soon she realized that there was more behind his very elegant but superficial officer uniform and military bearing. She was impressed with his modesty, humanity, and tenderness, especially in bed. For a nobody from Cornwall, he was the most exciting and, at the same time, the most sensitive lover she had ever known.

She had asked many times where he learned to be such a great lover. He only smiled and flippantly remarked that Cornwall had a lot of secret charms. She never thanked Lawrence for inviting Terence to Oxford. Unfortunately, she had only seen Lawrence on his motorbike once from a distance, just before he had a fatal accident. Terence had later taken her to the Moreton cemetery and laid flowers on Lawrence's grave. Now Terence was dead too, and there wasn't even a grave on which she could lay flowers.

Yesterday in Bovington, she took his personal belongings from his officer billet, which only deepened the pain of his loss. It wasn't philosophical; it was real. In her head was a piercing emptiness, an absolute refusal even to think beyond the present moment.

30 May 1940
Near Dunkirk

What fucking craziness. On 24 May they halted in place, mere miles from Dunkirk, a halt order that no one understood and everyone had just shaken their heads at. Then bad weather, then the order on 26 May to resume the attack! Except the English and French had used the two days to dig in and prepare a defense-in-depth around Dunkirk. Then the order to halt, again. Then the order to move south in preparation for the invasion of the rest of France. Fuck'em thought Müller, as he sat on the top of his panzer and enjoyed the late May weather that had returned. If they wanted to let the fucking English escape, it was above his rank as a sergeant to worry about.

In front of and behind him were dozens of tanks of all types and countless trucks, all in a long column. He diligently watched the sky for air raids, but the only thing he could see were the contrails of their planes.

"It's a shit time for the Tommies," he said to his gunner, who stuck his head out of his hatch and looked at the planes.

"Sarge, we could have done them English a lot worse than those flyboys done. Why the hell did we stop?" They both sighed and then laughed at the unfathomable decisions of their leaders.

1 June 1940
Brussels, Kesselring's Headquarters
Merkle could see that Lenz was nervous. They were both dressed in formal service uniforms with all their medals. Through an old school acquaintance working on the general's staff, Lenz had arranged a

meeting with Colonel-General Albert Kesselring, the Commander of Luftflotte 2, one of five Air Fleets in the Luftwaffe.

After Merkle's rescue from the Channel and his recuperation, he and Lenz decided to take their concerns about flying bomber escort to a higher commander. Their wing commander sympathized with them but was getting nowhere. Lenz and Merkle thought going to the top was the best approach. They didn't tell their wing commander what they planned. And they knew it was a risky endeavor, probably resulting in facing death from a firing squad. But if they didn't do something, they would surely be facing death from Spitfires. Merkle felt completely calm, in contrast to Lenz, who was nervous around higher-ranking officers, especially the senior General of their Luftflotte. Merkle was not intimidated by senior officers, only impressed by ones with competence. They had decided that Merkle would carry the discussion due to his fighter and Destroyer combat record, and his two Iron Cross First Class awards. The phone on the adjutant's desk rang.

The adjutant picked up the phone and said, "Yes, sir," and nodded to the door. Kesselring's headquarters were in an old castle with five-meter-high ceilings and floorboards that loudly enhanced each of their steps. The adjutant opened the door, and they went through and stood before

Kesselring's desk, with a Hitler salute.

Kesselring remained seated at his desk, nodded, smiled a little, and then pointed with a gesture to the two chairs positioned in front of his huge oak desk. Apparently, he attached little importance to military ceremonial or to a Sieg Heil!.

"As you know, this is completely unorthodox, completely circumventing to the chain of command," Kesselring stated in a stern voice but relaxed a little. "Alas, my personnel officer recommended that I see you. So go ahead, Captain Lenz."

Lenz cleared his throat and reminded himself not to rush. "General, we sought this conversation outside the usual official channels to talk openly with you about the situation with the Destroyers and because we need your help. I've asked Lieutenant Merkle to join me. He was a 109 pilot in Spain before joining the Destroyers. He is the best pilot in the squadron. It's his observations I'd like to begin with, sir."

Kesselring looked at Merkle. He presented a confident demeanor, in contrast to Lenz's obvious nervousness in the presence of his commanding General.

"Sir, the 110 is not a defensive fighter escort. As a fighter escort, it's a flying coffin. In effect, the escorts need an escort."

Kesselring almost smiled in amusement. Direct, forceful, and articulate. Merkle reminded him of another lieutenant he knew many years ago, who was also direct and forceful. Now that Lieutenant was a Colonel-General commanding *Liftflotte 2*. On the other hand, Lenz almost fainted. After hearing Merkle's words, he was sure both would end up in a coffin, but as a result of a firing squad.

"Sir, the 110`s have many good qualities, but speed and agility are not two of them. The plane is slow compared to fighters and heavy at the controls. Worse, the 110 cannot defend the bombers and we know they have also suffered.

"Those shortcomings have resulted in losing over 60% of our crews since the beginning of the mid-May fighting. We haven't even been able to replace half of these men with new crews for the 110 losses. And the new pilots are falling even faster than the men with whom we took up the fight against England."

Kesselring's smile had disappeared in the meantime, but Merkle continued to talk.

"The only thing stopping us from being slaughtered by the English is Lufbery's defense circles. We must take refuge in that defense almost every time we go out but we still lose planes. Without that defense, we would be destroyed by now.

"Sir, the plane is at its best when it attacks ground or marine targets. If we don't start taking the initiative, i.e., attacking, it's merely a simple task to calculate when the squadron will be destroyed. It also looks similar for the other two squadrons of our wing."

Kesselring interrupted him. "And how is it, that some of your comrades nevertheless shoot down English fighters? I recently gave an award to Lieutenant Jabs, who has downed multiple fighters with an Me 110." Kesselring had chosen an extremely formal tone.

The general's tone did not intimidate Merkle. "Yes, sir. General, I know Jabs. I spoke to him three days ago. His successes were all achieved in surprise attacks. In surprise attacks, we are the aggressor and have a chance. From my own experience, if we can surprise the English and get off the first shots, it's usually a kill."

"Yes, Lieutenant, I'm aware of both of your records. Please continue."

"Yes, sir. But as long as we are chained to the bombers and only react to attacks, we have no chance."

At this point, Lenz spoke. "Sir, this conversation is very difficult for me as a squadron commander. Our wing commander also shares our concerns but feels his hands are tied, even though the morale of the crews is now on the rocks."

Kesselring was still sitting silently with his unemotional face. Lenz found it very difficult to endure this silence and that look. Checking his watch, Kesselring's face relaxed. "What are you proposing, Captain Lenz?"

"The only type of operation in which we have a chance is what Rubensdörffer's unit has successfully carried out in recent weeks — low-altitude attacks with onboard weapons and bombs against English ground or naval targets. With the element of surprise that we can achieve in low-altitude flight, we have a chance to achieve high-performance battle results. The plane carries a lot of firepower and bombs."

Kesselring looked from Lenz to Merkle, remembering his record: a service ribbon of past service in the Condor Legion and two awards of the Iron Cross First Class. "Lieutenant Merkle, aren't you the Merkle who floated in the Channel with two wounded, one a British pilot, a few days ago?"

Merkle nodded: "Yes, sir. And I was shot down over the Channel by a Spitfire and lost my crewman. We were returning from escorting bombers looking for English shipping.

"One thing we noticed, sir, was that we always had the element of surprise with the few attacks that we made in the low-altitude runs. We also saw this during the first Channel Battles when we accompanied Colonel Fink's Dorniers. All those attacks took place at low altitudes, and the English fighters, if there were any at all, only arrived after a long time. During this time, we had good results and few losses.

"If we fly normal escort protection at 3-5,000 meters, we have no kills and plenty of losses. The English fighters are always already there, and attack us with the advantage of altitude and maneuverability, Sir. I once learned a rule that one is best if one imposes the rules and situation on the opponent. But close escort means that we fly according to the rules and dictates of the English." Lenz remembered something else. "Sir, one of our pilots knows Captain Knemeyer from the Lindbergh visit in 1938. He thinks that Knemeyer can accomplish flight maneuvers with an He 111, which most pilots of an Me 110 cannot do. Knemeyer is also a very good engineer. He suggested that we consult with him to see what else we can do, both aeronautically and technically, to reduce the performance gap with single-engine fighters." Lenz bowed slightly, indicating they were finished, and then remained silent.

Kesselring said nothing for a long time, looking at both of them. He then rose, went to the window, and looked outside with his back to Lenz and Merkle. "Gentlemen, you and the Destroyers are the elite of the German Luftwaffe. Reich Marshall Göring feels strongly connected to this weapon and the elite crews. We are all bound by his orders. Of course, the Luftwaffe leadership and I are aware of your losses. We are also aware of the improved results from low-altitude versus high-altitude flights and are giving it a great deal of study. But the Destroyers make up almost a third of the available fighters, which, by the way, are not enough to protect the existing bombers. Should I leave half of the bombers on the ground because I have no escort fighters? Furthermore, your Destroyers are the only ones with the range to escort the bombers.

No, I do not see any official way of helping you, gentlemen. As far as I am concerned, you were not here and this conversation did not take place."

Kesselring turned around. Lenz and Merkle immediately got up and stood at attention, regretting that they had come. Kesselring nodded as they saluted, and escorted them to the door.

"Thank you for coming, and I wish you a safe trip back to your base. By the way, I will instruct my staff to submit reports to me about the effects of low-flying attacks, especially from Destroyer units, even if this happens against existing standing orders. Operational data is always being evaluated and can become the basis for proposing policy changes. I consider this type of attack to be very interesting and will continue to observe it.

"As regards bomber escorts, there is increased discussion of using auxiliary gas tanks for Me 109`s, but headquarters has made no decision. As far as regards Knemeyer, the 'Mad Max,' I know him well. I will quietly see what he has to say.

Goodbye, gentlemen!"

A slow smile graced his face. Lenz and Merkle saluted again. If nothing else, Lenz and Merkle had a better understanding of the subtleties of senior commanders, and breathed a sigh of relief that they wouldn't be facing a firing squad.

Kesselring returned to his desk. Indeed, he thought, perceptive officers, ones taking the initiative and thinking about the effective use of aircraft and personnel. There's a hell lot more to this business than following orders. He decided to alert his personnel bureau to keep an eye on these officers, in particular First Lieutenant Merkle, despite Daiber's unfavorable review written in Spain. An impressive officer, well-spoken, and showing some strategic thinking.

Fact

On 3 June, the Germans launched Operation Paula, an attempt to destroy the remaining French Air Force as a prelude to the invasion of the rest of France. Based on Ultra intercepts, the English warned France of the planned attack. Unlike the air attacks at the beginning of Case Yellow on 9-10 May, Operation Paula failed to achieve its objectives.

4 June 1940
Berlin, Luftwaffe Headquarters
"Good morning, Colonel."

"Morning Miss Otte. Beautiful weather today. How about hanging out with me on the Havel River?"

She blushed. She knew Colonel Terstegen liked to joke a little, but he was all business. He had already opened the door to his office in the new Reich Aviation Ministry.

"Please come in for dictation, Fräulein Otte. I want to write the cover letter to General Milch on Sea Lion."

"Yes, sir." She hastily followed him and sat down ready to take dictation.

```
To: Colonel-General Milch (address
as usual)□
From: Colonel Terstegen
Date: 4 June 1940
Subject: Case Sea Lion


Pursuant to your order, I am
enclosing the proposed Luftwaffe
plan for the invasion of Britain:
Case Sea Lion.

As you requested, because of time
constraints, the Luftwaffe plan
for Sea Lion departs from the
```

current strategic thinking involving the prerequisite of air superiority over the RAF and then once attained, a broad-front invasion of Britain.

Instead of the conventional strategy, the Luftwaffe proposes the new strategic concept of *Schwerpunkt,* the "concentrated focus" of air, navy, and ground forces in a specific "invasion zone" of Britain, an arc from Dover to Folkestone on the SE English coast. This new strategic concept was approved and successfully implemented by our Führer in Case Yellow, the invasion of the Low Countries and Northern France. It will be further implemented tomorrow in Case Red, the invasion of the rest of France. ☐

For Sea Lion to have the highest chance of success, the pre-invasion air attacks against the RAF must begin immediately and the invasion must begin no later than mid or late July.

The main features and assumptions of Sea Lion are discussed in the following subtopics:

1. <u>The strength of British and German forces</u>.

<u>RAF</u>. Based on intelligence estimates, the RAF has the following combat-ready aircraft: 600 to 650 fighters (60 percent Hurricanes, 40 percent Spitfires) and 200 to 250 bombers. Based on the same intelligence reports, the RAF is weak in terms of experienced pilots and pilots in training.

<u>Luftwaffe</u>. The Luftwaffe has the following combat-ready aircraft: 800 Me 109`s, 250 two-engine Me 110`s, and 875 two-engine bombers, 316 Stuka`s, and 171 reconnaissance planes. The Luftwaffe has a nearly 2 to 1 advantage over the RAF in experienced fighter pilots and, equally important, a significant numerical advantage in pilots in

training.□

The Luftwaffe also has the following operational transport aircraft: 550 Ju 52`s and 8 Ju 90`s. Additional transport aircraft may be available, depending on the salvage of downed planes in Holland and Belgium, and planes recovered after our victory over the French.

The Luftwaffe has the following operational Fieseler Fi 156 Storks: 315.

The Luftwaffe has the following operational gliders: 160 DFS 230 gliders.

The Luftwaffe has 1 parachute division, including 1 glider battalion, and 1 air landing division.

Air Fleet staffs insist that we desperately need airfields closer to the invasion area for 109`s. This problem can be overcome by using auxiliary fuel tanks (drop

tanks) on Me 109`s using forward
German airfields and refitted ones
in Belgium.

English Army. Based on
intelligence estimates, the 1st
London Infantry Division is the
only division deployed in the area
of Ramsgate-Dover-Folkestone-
Dymchurch, with its headquarters
at Ashford. In addition to the
defense of airfields and possibly
radar stations, the division is
also assisting in reorganizing an
unknown number of troops evacuated
from Dunkirk without their
equipment or sufficient arms.
Intelligence also estimates that
infantry troops in all of England
are short of ammunition and
equipment.

German Army. The army has
numerical supremacy over the
British Army in infantry
divisions, panzer divisions,
artillery, and materiel. After
deployment of Luftwaffe units in
the initial invasion, the
following army units will be

airlifted to the invasion area: 2-4 infantry divisions. ☐

All Luftwaffe and army troops airlifted to England will be equipped with submachine guns, mortars, and enhanced machine gun squads. This will ensure that they always have superiority in firepower versus equivalent British units. ☐

Depending on circumstances, all other army units will be transported to England by sea transport.

Royal Navy. Based on intelligence estimates, during the Dunkirk evacuation, the British lost about 40 ships, including 6 destroyers lost and 20 destroyers damaged. The RN's current strength is estimated as follows: Home waters: 4 cruisers and 70 destroyers; Scapa Flow: 4 battleships and an unknown number of other heavy ships and destroyers.

German Navy. The Kriegsmarine currently has the following surface and undersea strength: 2 modern heavy cruisers, 2 pre-WWI battleships, 5 medium cruisers, 8 destroyers, 20 S-boats, and 29 U-boats.

After our victory over France, treaty terms must provide the surrender of all French naval vessels. However, for planning purposes, it is assumed that no French vessels will be available.

2. The pre-invasion operations by air, army, and naval units. Before the invasion, the Luftwaffe must initiate selective attacks against the RAF, its infrastructure, and radar systems, under conditions favorable to the Luftwaffe. The RAF must be degraded as much as possible before the invasion.

As soon as possible, commando units transported by Fieseler Fi 146 Stork planes will attack and destroy radar towers and stations on the east coast of England.

The German Navy will develop plans for: (i) the assembly of transport ships for sea delivery of heavy equipment, including panzers and their crews, troops, and supplies to England; (ii) the designation of a sea lane from France to Dover and Folkestone; and (iii) the mining the flanks of the sea lane and other areas to defend against the RN.

3. <u>The initial invasion operations by air, navy, and army units</u>. The Wehrmacht will conduct the following operations during the initial phase of the invasion: (i) Luftwaffe commando units will attack and destroy radar towers and stations on the east coast of England; (ii) the Luftwaffe will conduct maximum efforts to achieve local air superiority or supremacy over the invasion zone and sea transportation lane from France to England; (iii) the Luftwaffe will destroy railway junctions in Hastings, Canterbury, Ashford and Faversham; (iv) the Luftwaffe will

destroy phone and electrical power lines and substations in the general Kent area; (v) glider units will land and destroy key English shore batteries, command headquarters, and any remaining radar towers in Dover and Folkestone; (vi) glider and paratrooper units will land and secure two airfields: Hawkinge near the port of Folkestone and Swingfield near the port of Dover; (vii) air transports will deliver troops and supplies to the two captured airfields during the daylight hours; (vi) navy S-boats will deliver commando units to capture the harbor of Folkestone; and (vii) Luftwaffe bomber and fighter units will attack the London and regional headquarters of the PM, the Admiralty, the RAF, and the British Army.

Just as in Case Yellow and Red, the Luftwaffe must function as the air artillery for ground troops. Stuka`s and Destroyer Me 110`s are best suited for this role, supported by Me 109`s flying cover against the RAF. The use of Me 110`s for this role would be a change from their current role of bomber escort, which has resulted in unfavorable results.

As soon as the Folkestone and Dover harbors are secured and operational, the navy will deliver equipment, troop and panzer units, and supplies during daylight hours.

4. <u>The defense of the landing area and sea lane by the Luftwaffe and navy</u>.

The Luftwaffe has the main task of defending against the RAF and Royal Navy.

The army will develop heavy coastal artillery positions in France and Belgium to attack the RN and to defend German ports in France, Belgium, and Holland.

The navy will reposition available submarines north and south of the Channel. S-boats will attack RN ships in and on both sides of the Channel.

In summary, Sea Lion's success depends on the efficient implementation of the *Schwerpunkt* concept, surprise and creative use of air resources, and lightly equipped paratrooper and ground troops during the initial phase. Until the navy can deliver artillery, heavy equipment, troops, and panzers to England, the airborne troops will be at a high risk of destruction. Fortunately, with high risks also comes the opportunity for high rewards.

"Got that Miss Otte?"
" Yes, Colonel."
"Add the usual closings and signature block, make six copies. Send the original and three copies to General Milch, the other two copies to me, and put the highest security classification on this letter, the same as for Case Sea Lion."
"Immediately, Colonel!"
"And Miss Otte, you look lovely today." She blushed and could only lower her head in shyness. Hastily she left Terstegen's office.

Terstegen smiled, lit his pipe, and reached for the telephone. "Connect me with the Führer's headquarters, the Führer's adjutant, Colonel Schmundt, please".

Schmundt was an old friend and a direct voice to Hitler. As General Milch said, this report was too important to entrust it only to the chain of command. Milch had reminded Terstegen how important von Manstein's staff had been in presenting directly to Hitler von Manstein's revised Case Yellow and the *Schwerpunkt* strategy for the invasion of France through the Ardennes.

Funny, thought Terstegen, Sea Lion was developed and promoted by a German general who was once rumored to have Jewish ancestors. He was saved and protected only by the intervention of Göring. General Milch is probably one of the Wehrmacht's greatest strategic thinkers and surely the smartest and most efficient organizer in the German armed forces.[iii]

Fact
"Do you realize that for the first time in a thousand years, our country is in danger of invasion?"
June 1, 1940 Chief of Staff Sir John Dill to General Montgomery

4 June 1940
Dunkirk, France

The smoke of the burning oil storage tanks was still polluting the air. And the ruins of a beaten army were polluting the white sandy beaches and dunes of Dunkirk: Guns, rifles, thousands of trucks of all colors and designs, many of them from private companies still with advertisements, and a few tanks. Imaginative officers had even built landing piers out of trucks. It looked like a gigantic scrap yard.

General Milch and General Otto von Waldau of the Luftwaffe thoughtfully walked along the beach with their security guards. The army had secured Dunkirk only this morning. The invasion of France (Case Red) was scheduled to start tomorrow. But the generals wanted to see Dunkirk and the result of the round-the-clock air attacks.

"Have you noticed how few dead there are, Otto?"

"Yes, unfortunately, General. I guess we weren't as successful as we had hoped."

"Indeed not!" Milch stopped and squinted his eyes together against the sun's brightness to look towards England.

"Otto, we must invade England and soon. A mere 40 kilometers over water. I think we've dealt with

problems more difficult, but we have to be quick."
Waldau just nodded, thinking the Dover Channel
was not a river. He pointed to a mountain of
whiskey and wine bottles. "The English must have
had a strong desire to calm their nerves."
"Don't underestimate the British," said Milch. "I
met a number of them in 1937 in Britain. Their
officers may be old fashioned, but they are also
professionals. But fortunately for us, their senior
officers are at least as conservative as ours."
Milch laughed. "Otto, these whiskey bottles foretell
the future. I predict that soon we will drink from the
whiskey cellar of Mr. Churchill."

Fact
*During Operation Dynamo, the English evacuated
over 350,000 British and allied soldiers, but largely
without weapons or heavy equipment. The
Wehrmacht subsequently counted around 50,000
abandoned vehicles of all kinds, including over 400
tanks. However, the German Air Force, which had
not yet been deployed close enough to the front, was
not able to prevent the evacuation. Nor had the
RAF fighter command been able to stop the German
air attacks, even though some of the RAF airfields
were less than 50 km away. Neither air force had
superiority over Dunkirk. However, more than 200*

mostly British ships were sunk. Even so, British and French troops escaped en masse to England.

Due to poor weather conditions, the German air force could not fly on several days. Nevertheless, the Luftwaffe attacks were increasingly effective. During the last days of Operation Dynamo, the evacuation took place entirely at night.

This suggests that the RAF was not as strong as believed and would not have been able to stop a German invasion fleet. The RAF had no plane comparable to the tactical dive bombers, the Ju 87 and Ju 88. They had a few naval planes, Blackburn Skua, with dive bomber capabilities. In addition to effective support of ground troops, the German Stuka dive-bombers were very effective in bombing targets in Dunkirk and evacuation ships in the Channel.

5 June 1940
London, Cabinet War Rooms

Captain Hunter nervously twisted his cap in his hands. He waited to report to the Prime Minister. Admiral Ramsay, whose staff he was on in Dover, had sent him. He felt the deep depression that prevailed here in the command center. Everyone who met him radiated that feeling. He had yet to see anyone smiling or laughing.

He had a success to announce. Operation Dynamo, the evacuation of troops from Dunkirk, had been completed. Unfortunately, of course, they had brought back more than 300,000 men without heavy equipment and vehicles.

Three days ago, he had been at Dunkirk with the destroyer *HMS Havelock*. He was depressed over the enormous amount of materiel left lying around on the beach, with no dock facilities or ships to salvage any of it.

There was also the Luftwaffe. They were attacking the harbor, beach, and shipping in the Channel. The *Havelock* had been attacked four times on its way back to England.

Havelock had brought back 550 army troops. The men had been quiet with sullen expressions, but amazingly disciplined. Even at embarkation, the soldiers mostly had boarded together with their respective units.

The door of the operations room opened, and a sergeant from Churchill's guard invited him in.

"Captain Hunter on behalf of Admiral Ramsay, sir."

Churchill looked tired with red-rimmed eyes and a pale face. He smoked a cigar and a general he didn't know smoked a pipe. The pipe was a good smell, much like Navy Flake, but the cigar and pipe's smoke was thick.

"I hear you were in Dunkirk. Report, Captain!"

Churchill listened with concentration and without

questions.

Hunter's nervousness quickly subsided, and he limited his report to the essentials and came to an end after a few minutes. Churchill sucked intensely on his cigar.

"Captain, how's the mood in the Navy? I'm sure you realize the Navy is the only thing stopping the Germans from visiting us."

Hunter took a deep breath. It was unusual that a lowly navy captain was asked for his opinion by the PM. But at least he had been present at Dunkirk, unlike the members of the war cabinet.

"Yes, sir, I realize that. The morale onboard the ships I have been on in recent days is excellent. People are eager to fight back against the Germans. Even many of the evacuated soldiers are not demoralized. A few even made jokes on the crossing. Some of them still had their weapons. In Dunkirk, I could see that almost all the men were gathered with their units. We were attacked several times by German planes during the crossing. The soldiers fiercely fought back with their Bren`s and rifles, sir. I think we lost a battle, but we are not defeated."

Churchill nodded and then turned to the general sitting next to him.

"I heard the same thing from General Brooke. At least some good news."

He turned to Hunter again. "Give my heartfelt thanks to Admiral Ramsay and your men. You've done a great job planning and implementing Operation Dynamo. Thank you, Captain."

Hunter left the room encouraged.

5 June 1940
Vlissingen, Netherlands

She was finally his, an S-boat (*Schnellboot*). She had a 21-man crew, weighed 115 tons, was armed with two large torpedo tubes, and cruised at a top speed of 37 knots. It was too bad that the former Captain had to die before he could take command. Meyer was a good man and officer.

Meyer had died under a low-flying attack the day before yesterday. They were moving the boat from Wilhelmshaven to Vlissingen, Holland when a Blenheim bomber spotted them, probably completely by accident. The plane made only one attack pass. That was enough for a devastating salvo from her guns. Meyer and Lüders were killed immediately, and the boat had over 60 bullet holes. Fortunately, the small rifle-caliber bullets had not caused structural or engine damage.

Last night, by order of the commanding admiral, Hans Georgson was promoted from First Officer to Captain of the boat. He had been waiting over three years for this opportunity, carefully learning all he could about S-boats and leadership. He was 23 and thought about how far he had come.

He was an only child from an old working-class family in Wilhelmshaven. Unlike his parents and relatives, he was taller and huskier than average, had soft brown eyes, according to the girls, and dark wavy hair that the girls liked to run their fingers through. His grandfather teased him about those physical traits, joking that a Tartar must have snuck into the family bed when Attila the Hun attacked Europe. His father laughed at the kidding; his mother didn't. He loved sports and excelled at soccer.

High school (*Gymnasium*) studies were a challenge. It wasn't that he was stupid. At school, they said he was above average in intelligence. But he wasn't interested in studies unless it involved mechanical equipment and ships. Even so, he was just able to graduate from high school.

After graduation, he went to work with his father, who was foreman of a machine shop at the docks. He loved the work, fascinated with marine equipment, how it worked, and how to keep it working.

His mother, however, wasn't pleased. He was too young to be around sailors and rough men; he should go to university and study marine engineering. The docks were no place for her teenage son. She had scolded him more than once about speaking "filthy" language, and she worried about what else he might be learning around the harbor.

He learned a lot more than filthy language. The other workers at the shop made sure he tried all of the temptations, some more than once. After thinking about them, he decided he didn't like smoking, gambling, or fighting unless he had to defend himself, but he did like drinking and fucking, especially fucking.

Since he also liked ships, service in the navy was an easy decision. Because he was a high school graduate, the navy accepted him into the Naval Officers program in 1934. And now he was Captain of his own boat.

Boat S-28 had not taken part in the Norwegian campaign because of a complete engine overhaul. Most of the other boats of her flotilla were still in Bergen and would not return for about a week. The boat bobbed slowly at its mooring in the Schelde River estuary. It was shortly after 6:00 a.m. and quite foggy. From behind him, he heard the muffled voice of Boatswain Schell, who explained to a working group how to repair the bullet holes at the stern.

"Come on men, hurry up, before we start the repairs, the camouflage nets must be rigged before the fog clears," ordered Schell.

Georgson put on his white Captain's cap for the first time and had to grin, his pride was palpable.

"Boatswain Schell to me," he said to the bridge guard.

Schell came immediately. "Yes, Captain."

"I have an idea. We can't have another mess like the one with the Blenheim. The Oerlikon cannons simply didn't react fast enough. I want to have some machine guns on board, on both sides of the bridge." He looked at Schell, waiting for a response.

"It's doable, Captain, but we need a welding machine and material to build the gun mounts."

Georgson looked at his watch.

"Okay, Schell, we'll take two men with us and see what the Dutch in Vlissingen left for us."

The day before, they had requisitioned a small car, and now drove from their berth to Vlissingen for other supplies. He retrieved his submachine gun from the rack in the small cabin. The crew had finished camouflaging the boat. As he stepped off on to the pier, he was satisfied that his boat, S-28, couldn't be seen a few meters away.

Part 3

Let your plans be dark and impenetrable as night,
and when you move, fall like a thunderbolt. — Sun Tzu

6 June 1940
Berlin, Führer Headquarters

Colonel Schmundt had been the Führer's military adjutant for years, knew his habits, routines, and leadership style. So he was surprised to see Hitler in the office so early in the morning. Hitler liked to work late into the night and sleep late into the day, but not today. The Führer was at the office before Schmundt arrived. Schmundt was one of the few military men from the inner circle whose opinion Hitler carefully listened to, or so Schmundt thought. One was never sure with the Führer.

"Schmundt, did you read the translation of Churchill's speech on 4 June, what the English press is calling the 'We shall fight on the beaches' speech?"

"Yes, my Führer, I have." Schmundt knew Hitler had been bothered by Churchill's address to the English House of Commons. It contradicted his belief that the English were finished and would sue for peace.

"Well, what do you think?"

"I tend to believe him. Churchill has been against Germany since we came to power, calling us barbarians and a threat to Western Civilization, and calling for our destruction. Now he is the PM, with all the power of England and its empire to fight us. He'll fight on." Schmundt was always reluctant to give his opinion to Hitler, never knowing whether it could result in a quick transfer to a remote outpost.

"Yes…I tend to agree. I hoped England would seek peace after its catastrophic defeat in Northern France and at Dunkirk, but now I'm not so sure. In part, my hope was based on my deep concerns about our broad-front invasion thinking and planning. I had my share of frontal assaults during the last war. They were a huge waste of men and materiel, and usually not successful."

A quiet came over Hitler. He stood and gazed out the window of his Chancellery office into the garden. During Hitler's silence or agitated periods, Schmundt knew it was best to wait quietly. Hitler was deep in thought. Finally, whatever he was wrestling with was resolved.

"This invasion plan of General Milch and Colonel Terstegen intrigues me. An air *Schwerpunkt* invasion of England, and executed within weeks. What do you think of Terstegen, Schmundt?"

"Colonel Terstegen is one of the best planners I

have ever met. Even General Manstein admitted so at the war game in November 1938."

Hitler turned from the window. "Well, Manstein! That's impressive. It seems that our conservative Supreme High Command of the Army (OKH), has missed something in their planning. My dear Commander-in-Chief of the Army, General von Brauchitsch, favors a broad-front landing, spreading out troops all along the English coast. Keitel avoids any commitment and just shows up to the briefing. Göring believes all military problems can be solved with planes. That did not work at Dunkirk. None of them, or it seems any other senior Army generals — except Manstein, Guderian, and Rommel — has learned the lessons of *Schwerpunkt* or*Blitzkrieg*."

He took a sip from his teacup. "And our Grand Admiral, Herr Raeder, says we can't even dream of landing in England because the Royal Navy is so incredibly strong. It seems these experts have not consulted the Luftwaffe, at least not General Milch. Well, Schmundt, clear this evening's schedule and invite Göring, Milch, and Terstegen for dinner. Let's find out more about this Luftwaffe plan."

"Yes, my Führer!"

6 June 1940
Trier Airbase
Merkle stood with the rest of the squadron on the

parade field early in the morning. The English had loaded their last soldiers in boats on the evening of 4 June. On 5 June, German forces attacked the rest of France. The squadron would be supporting the ground forces after this parade formation. He wondered why they were standing on a parade ground instead of getting ready for the mission. Lenz had promised him a home leave, but with the new French campaign, he didn't hold his breath. Captain Lenz, the squadron commander, called the men to attention. The heads of the men flew with the usual jerk to the left. Merkle was mildly surprised. Colonel Stahlmüller, the Group Commander, was joining them. He was surprised a second time when Stahlmüller called Merkle and four other officers to the front and presented them with an Iron Cross First Class, Merkle's third decoration of the award. After the awards presentation, the colonel addressed the entire unit. "Gentlemen, the current situation is favorable and our prospects are excellent for defeating the French. I am proud of your achievements. Keep up the excellent work.

"As you know, your previous Wing Commander was shot down over Amiens a few days ago. Two new commanders have been approved for the wing. Will Captain Lenz and First Lieutenant Merkle please step forward."

He didn't know if Lenz was surprised, but Merkle

was dumbfounded. Coming to attention in front of Colonel Stahlmüller for a second time, the colonel read the orders.

"By order of the Commander of the Luftwaffe, Captain Lenz is promoted to Major.

"By order of the Commander of the Luftwaffe, First Lieutenant Merkle is promoted to Captain.

"By order of Luftflotte 2 Commanding General, Major Lenz is appointed as Wing Commander and Captain Merkle is appointed as Squadron Commander."

My God thought Merkle, he'd never complain about a parade formation again.

6 June 1940
Berlin, Luftwaffe Headquarters
Milch looked at Terstegen with a devilish smile.

"The Führer's headquarters just called regarding Sea Lion. Tonight we have dinner with the Führer and discuss our Sea Lion plan. Göring will also be there. Are you prepared, Colonel Terstegen?"

Terstegen pretended to look concerned, picked up his pipe, and started to stuff it.

"Well...? Keep in mind that the Führer will be less patient than I for answers to his questions."

"Yes, General, I am not only prepared but eager to explain and discuss Sea Lion. You and I have not

131

had time to discuss it. What are your thoughts, sir?" Milch grinned at him, "I like it Terstegen, I like it very much. You've followed my instructions very well and done excellent work explaining its risks and benefits. The plan is very unconventional, which I believe will be a major advantage to Hitler. I also believe the other services will see its merits of an air *Schwerpunkt* invasion over a broad-front invasion. But that discussion will come later after Hitler approves it."

He remained silent for a moment, and Terstegen used the break to ask: "What about the Reich Marshall, will he support the plan?"

"I sent a copy of the plan to him this morning. He will advocate precisely the solution that the Führer supports. He is very perceptive in determining which way Hitler is leaning. And remember, he is not exactly in the good graces of Hitler. He didn't destroy the British at Dunkirk. No, he let them escape!

"I suspect Hitler has already approved the plan, at least in concept. It's only been two days since Hitler's adjutant received the plan, and Hitler is now commanding us to explain it to him. Warlimont and others from OKW will support us. And also, in the army, there are some generals, namely Manstein and Rommel, whose opinions Hitler listens to. They will also support us." He paused for a moment and stood with his eyes closed at the window as if in prayer.

"Yes, Terstegen, our Sea Lion will prevail, not only against the conventional Germans but also against the English."

6 June 1940
Berlin, Führer Headquarters

The dinner was over, if you could call it dinner, thought Terstegen. A good schnitzel would have settled better on his stomach than all those boiled vegetables.

He had the strong impression that Hitler's mind was indeed made up in favor of Sea Lion. As Milch had said, the Führer loved the unconventional. He had spent a large part of the dinner talking about the success of his *Blitzkrieg* and *Schwerpunkt* from the Ardennes. Nevertheless, Terstegen was ready for a complete briefing about Sea Lion. Hitler nodded that he was ready.

"My Führer, Case Sea Lion is a very unorthodox and daring strategy compared to the conventional thinking of a broad-front invasion against England. Our naval forces are too weak for..."

Hitler interrupted. "Yes, yes, I know all that. Stick to the essential points. How long will it take to plan and invade?"

"Yes, my Führer. We have a detailed plan now. If

we adopt it, we can implement it within the next four or five weeks. Sea Lion allows us to keep time on our side; it maximizes our current resources in a narrow-front invasion within the four to five…"

Hitler interrupted again. "Yes, you've answered my question, Colonel. Move on."

"Certainly, my Führer. Today the British field army is still shocked and disorganized after Dunkirk and almost without heavy weapons. Crossing the 40 kilometers of the Channel is still an enormously difficult task on the water, but not as difficult in the air. To quote General Guderian, 'We use a big bat concentrated on a small area.' Sea Lion is the air *Schwerpunkt* against the weakened English."

Hitler showed no reaction, and Terstegen continued. "That 'big bat' is an air invasion as the first phase of Sea Lion. The Luftwaffe is capable of maintaining air superiority in the invasion zone, a limited arc of about 50 kilometers from Dover to Folkestone. We have superior numbers of planes and experienced pilots. Assuming good flying weather, our Stuka`s and torpedo bombers will also be able to close the Channel to the Royal Navy during the day.

"But it will be crucial that we use our air transport fleet almost around the clock, to transport troops and equipment. As a protection for the Ju 52`s, massive fighter protection will be staggered over the invasion area, the likes of which have never been seen before."

Terstegen knew as soon as he said that last statement that he had overstated it. Hitler interrupted him immediately and impatiently.

"Yes, I hear you, but I'm not sure I believe you. Doesn't your plan leave the current fighting in France without air support and, overall, place too much faith in the Luftwaffe…alone?"

There was total silence. Without directly saying so, Hitler was reminding the Luftwaffe officers of its recent failure over Dunkirk. All eyes were on Terstegen.

"No, my Führer. Sea Lion is a combined operation of all the services. In the initial phase, even before the invasion, the main burden lies with the Luftwaffe. And I believe it is a fair statement that we will be victorious over the French, with or without air resources in the battle." No one disputed that statement. "So moving air resources will not change that result, but it will improve the chances of success invading England."

Hitler thought for a moment and then waved him to continue.

"At the time of the invasion, the initial supplies will have to be flown into the invasion area." And here Milch had told Terstegen that Hitler had an almost encyclopedic memory for minute military details. "Given that the unloading capacity of the harbors at Folkestone and Dover, which is at best around 1,400 tons a day — without any interruption by the

RAF — and that each infantry division needs a daily requirement of almost 300 tons, it is clear that the main burden of supply in the first phase must be with the Luftwaffe."

Hitler thought, then nodded. Terstegen wondered if Hitler had checked on the numbers before the dinner.

"When the harbors are open, sea transport must first concentrate on transporting panzer troops and heavy materiel, such as tanks, guns, and fuel, presumably in small, fast, and well-protected ships. However, the main burden of transporting ammunition, food, and soldiers will have to be borne by the Luftwaffe during the first phase of the invasion."

Hitler still did not show any response. He got up and started pacing. "You've talked about the first phase. How do you imagine the entire process as a whole?"

Fortunately, Terstegen and Milch had given this some thought today and Terstegen was prepared to answer. "In the first phase, we will only be able to build a very strong bridgehead. After we have neutralized the RAF and RN in the invasion area and decreased their effectiveness overall, the second phase will be the breakout and invasion of the rest of England by the army, supported tactically by the Luftwaffe.

"The main goal of the first phase is not an immediate advance inland, because we could not supply that effort. The objective is to destroy or severely weaken the RAF and RN before the breakout of ground forces. Since we are at least twice as strong in the air and qualitatively better, we will win the first phase. With supervision of the Sea Lion staff, the planning of the second phase, including the build-up of troops, is the army's prime responsibility in cooperation with the Luftwaffe. The British are fierce fighters, but our troops and equipment are superior. We've demonstrated that fact in France."

Hitler nodded and looked away, which Terstegen took as a sign to stop. Hitler had also fought against Britons in the First World War and still remembered how tough the English were.

In a relaxed voice, Hitler said, "Actually, I would much rather work with the English than fight against them. What possibilities we would have. But Mr. Churchill wants to fight on. I think Britain is a serious problem, one we must resolve sooner rather than later. We must defeat England this year to focus on other matters."

He continued pacing back and forth in the room and seemed to talk himself into a near rage. "The problem of Britain has to be solved. Throughout my life, and probably most of all since last autumn, I have been faced with crucial issues that had to be resolved. Again and again, so-called experts and men actually in the leadership explained to me:

That is not feasible, that is not possible. I cannot accept such defeatism. Some problems absolutely must be solved.

"Where the right leaders are available, they have always been solved. It is not always possible to enforce it with peaceful means. But I don't care about kindness, just as I don't care what posterity will say about the methods I had to use." For a moment, he remained silent and paused. His dark blue eyes looked into emptiness, and then he began again in a measured, serious tone.

"For me, there is only one question that must be solved, that is: We have to win this war against Britain, or Germany faces a prolonged, destructive war. And the greatest task is still ahead of us after our victory over England."

Everyone waited for his decision. He looked at Milch: "You, Colonel General Milch…I believe you are someone who does not know the word impossible. You proved that with the organization of Lufthansa, the Luftwaffe, and the Norway operation. Your plan convinces me. Colonel Terstegen, I'm impressed with your staff accomplishments and ability to remain calm and responsive under my scrutiny. Milch and Terstegen, you have my approval and trust."

Nobody dared to say anything. Hitler went to the window of his large office in the Reich Chancellery and looked into the garden. After a few minutes of silence, he asked: "Reich Marshall Göring, how do you see the chances if we land in England within the next 4 to 6 weeks versus an invasion in 2 to 3 months?"

The Reich Marshall wore a magnificent white uniform and held his Reich Marshall baton in his left hand. "If you command my Führer, we will land in England tomorrow. But I think a few weeks of preparation to station our fighters and bombers closer to the Channel would make sense."

Göring was seething with blind rage and hatred at Milch for his betrayal and for not telling him about Sea Lion until this morning. This treachery would not go unpunished. Well, at least it would be a Luftwaffe operation, and when Milch and Terstegen were dealt with, he would be in command.

"My Führer, since the operation begins mainly as an aerial attack, I believe it would be best if the plans were worked out by the Air Force General Staff. Reassigning Colonel-General Kesselring from field duties to staff would be helpful in the planning." Göring had risen and looked at his Führer expectantly.

Adolf Hitler looked at Göring without expression, remained silent for a moment as he contemplated Göring's Dunkirk failure. "It is my will and order that Colonel-General Milch will lead the planning and implementation of the entire operation, Mr. Reich Marshall. I have complete confidence in him." He turned to Milch, "I expect us to invade England within 6 weeks at the latest. You will report to me every week about Sea Lion's progress." Milch was impressed by the audacity of Hitler and surprised at the blunt decision. Hitler had a reputation for dividing responsibilities and playing the services and senior officers against each other. But not this time. He saw that Göring tried to hide his disappointment from Hitler.

Reich Marshall Göring in his resplendent white uniform could only suppress his rage at the decision and against Milch. He was pleased that his Luftwaffe had the assignment, but displeased beyond measure with Milch. But if the Führer had decided, there could be no other alternative for him at present.

6 June 1940
Berlin, Führer Headquarters

Führer Directive No 16
To: Supreme Command of the Armed Forces (OKW), Supreme Commands of the Army (OKH), Navy (KM), Luftwaffe (DL), and Departments of the Reich.

The French campaign is in

progress, but there is no doubt that Germany will prevail. The German Army, Navy, and Luftwaffe will take part in the further campaign against France with appropriately limited forces. With immediate effect, our resources and forces will be used to defeat our main enemy: England.

Despite its hopeless military situation, England still shows no signs that it is ready to negotiate a reasonable peace. I have ordered the preparation of plans for the invasion of England, code-named Operation Sea Lion.☐

With immediate effect, the following officers are assigned to Sea Lion: Colonel-General Milch is appointed overall Supreme Commander of Sea Lion; Colonel Terstegen is appointed the Chief-of-Staff; Lt. General Manstein is appointed Commanding General of Army operations; Admiral Dönitz is appointed Commanding Admiral of Navy operations; and Colonel-General Kesselring is appointed

Commanding General of Luftwaffe operations.

With immediate effect, the Wehrmacht and all Reich departments are ordered to support Sea Lion and Colonel General Milch. Colonel-General Milch is granted all powers. The Wehrmacht will arrange for the immediate transfers of the officers involved. The planning for the implementation of Sea Lion shall begin immediately.

With immediate effect, Colonel-General Milch will prepare and, upon my review and order, implement the strategic and tactical operations of Sea Lion.

Signed: A. Hitler

6 June 1940
Göring's residence at Karinhall north of Berlin
He was seething with rage over Milch's betrayal and disloyalty. He paced his bedroom, kicking furniture and slamming his fist down on the ftable. Milch

142

would not survive the week. He would strip him of his rank and position, and destroy him and his family, every last one of them.

Göring still had friends, powerful friends, who would support him. Moreover, as the founder of the Gestapo, he had the contacts to permanently end Milch's life. He laughed at the redundancy of the phrase "permanently end." Must be the morphine shot he'd just injected to calm his nerves.

He would first leak to the press and public all of the secret papers on Milch's Jewish ancestry, his father, grandparents and distant relatives generations back, the documents he kept as insurance. Milch would rot in his cell in Gestapo Headquarters for the rest of his life, as short as that life would be. Then Hitler would have to return to him. Nobody else was available.

He shakily sniffed a large line of cocaine into his nose and felt the effects immediately. He'd finish it off with another morphine shot, but couldn't remember how many vials had he loaded into the needle, one or two? His vision was becoming blurry and he couldn't see clearly or remember. He didn't see the two empty vials on his dresser. Well, one more won't hurt, he thought. He was a big man and could take two doses. He loaded another vial of the drug and found his vein.

Yes, very soothing. He needed to lie down. On the bed he felt the soothing rush and relaxing effect of the morphine. Suddenly, there were spasms in his stomach and intestines, trouble breathing, a rapid heartbeat, and then a flash of darkness as his heart stopped.

7 June 1940
Berlin, Luftwaffe Headquarters

Milch couldn't believe Göring was dead, a massive overdose of cocaine and morphine. They had been friends for a long time, professionals working together to build the Luftwaffe into the world's greatest air force.

Göring had saved his life, family, and career over the rumors about his Jewish father. Over the years, they had grown apart, Göring becoming more dependent on drugs, which fogged his thinking and actions. Others were also concerned.

Then it struck him. He'd better secure Göring's home, his office, and papers. No telling what Milch would find in Göring's many safes. Why hadn't he thought of this earlier? The confusion of sudden death. He called his aide and instructed him to immediately secure Göring's office and residences. When finished with the instructions, he thought back to his time as an observer in a Roland reconnaissance airplane in the First World War and later as a wing commander. He knew Göring and greatly admired him. No drugs then. A dashing guy, a real German hero with lots of air victories, awarded the *Pour le Merite* (the Blue Max), German's highest award for bravery. And now, just 22 years later, a wreck full of cocaine and morphine. Sad, very sad.

Hitler had already called him and told him that he was Göring's successor, with a promotion to Field Marshall and a promotion for Terstegen to Major General. Perhaps his death wasn't so bad after all, thought Milch, definitely a positive for him, Terstegen, Sea Lion, and the Luftwaffe.

7 June 1940
Biggin Hill, England
The fighter Group Commander sat in front of Admiral Winslow. Churchill had sent Winslow on a tour of field operations. The Commander had noticeable dark rings of fatigue around his eyes and was contemplating an answer to the Admiral's question.

"It's not so much the planes, we're building them fast enough. It's the pilots, we're losing them too fast. Is the PM aware that we've lost over 200 experienced combat pilots in the last four weeks, but only train 200 a month with barely 12 flying hours and with no combat experience? Fighter

Command has just 600 fighters, with only 460 of them operational. If Air Chief Marshal Dowding hadn't resisted, the PM and the War Cabinet would have thrown away another 10 squadrons in France. Dowding has always told the Prime Minister that we need at least 45 to 52 squadrons to defend Britain, but he doesn't seem to have understood that."

Admiral Winslow, who had spoken to various army division commanders, had to work on not becoming depressed. First, the disastrous situation with the army and now it appeared the same situation with the RAF. Churchill had repeatedly told him that 25 squadrons would be enough to defend England.

"How long will it take for the Germans to attack us in strength?" Winslow asked.

"Hard to say, the French have not yet been defeated, and who knows how effective the new Luftwaffe commander is? And we don't know what reserves the Luftwaffe still has to use against us. Moreover, they have to move their bombers and especially their fighters much closer to the coast. That will take weeks, maybe a month or more."

"What do you estimate, how long?" asked Winslow.

"Well, when we transfer a squadron with the necessary personnel and spare parts to a new airfield, and it goes smoothly, it takes about 2 weeks at most until the squadron is fully operational. We estimate the same time for the

Germans. But they also have to refit the bombed French airfields. Say, add 2-3 weeks for that work. So a total of 4-5 weeks. But remember, missions can be flown earlier out of airfields that are not 100 percent operational."

Winslow nodded, "So we don't have much time. Thank you, Group Commander."

Fact

During the daylight attacks on German warships near Wilhelmshaven by RAF Bomber Command on 14 and 18 December 1939, the RAF bomber losses were 62 percent. The War Cabinet prohibited all further daylight operations by Whitley, Hampden, and Wellington bombers, the strongest and most numerous aircraft of Bomber Command.

Over the Channel and Low Countries in 1940, daylight bombing was a disaster for Bomber Command. Not only were their machine guns inadequate for protecting bombers and fighters in 1940, but the German fighters were also numerically greater than the English and their cannon armament was superior. German fighters were equipped with 2 mm cannons. These cannons had a longer range than the small rifle-caliber of the British machine guns.

Another factor was the German development and

deployment of radar. Beginning in June 1940, the Germans installed a Freya Radar System at Wissant, France, to monitor the Channel. During the war, Germany built individual radar systems for many locations. However, Germany never integrated the individual systems into a unified command and control organization.

8 June 1940
Berlin, State Funeral of Göring
The horse-drawn carriage slowly pulled the coffin. It had been specially reinforced to hold Göring's weight. Hitler and Field Marshall Milch, the new Luftwaffe Commander-in-chief, proceeded at a measured step directly behind the carriage. Behind them, General Terstegen also marched with a group of senior officers and staff.

With difficulty, Terstegen stifled a grin and maintained a somber demeanor. He had been promoted from Colonel to Major General, all because of Göring's drug addiction. Fate worked in mysterious ways.

8 June 1940
Berlin, Luftwaffe Headquarters

The assembled senior officers of the Wehrmacht had all attended Göring's funeral in the morning. They had no idea whey they were still in Berlin. Some expected to see Hitler address them. Instead, Field Marshall Milch, the new Commander-in-chief of the Luftwaffe, confidently strode into the conference room. The officers came to attention. He was followed by General Terstegen, and by General Keitel, Chief of the Armed Forces High Command (OKW), General von Brauchitsch, Commander-in-Chief of the Army, and Grand Admiral Raeder, Commander-in-Chief of the Navy.

Milch smartly saluted the assembled officers. "Gentlemen, the Führer." Hitler strode into the room and all officers quickly raised their arms and voices in saluting him.
"Thank you for attending Göring's funeral this morning. Your condolences are appreciated. Reich Marshall Göring was my close friend and Commander of the greatest air force in history. He was also my close colleague in the struggle for National Socialism. He will be missed.
"However, the struggle of National Socialism continues, must continue until Germany's enemies are defeated. France will fall soon. England fights on. As we continue to defeat France, we must also plan to defeat England. To that glorious end, I have approved Operation Sea Lion, the planning and

implementation of the invasion of England. I have appointed Field Marshall Milch as Supreme Commander of Sea Lion. I have the highest confidence and trust in Milch. I expect no less confidence, trust, and service from you." With that, Hitler came to attention, the officers saluted again, and he left the room.

The officers were both surprised and stunned. Sea Lion would be the Reich's first unified command, eliminating inter-service rivalries and enforcing cooperation.

After an appropriate silence, Milch spoke. "Please take a seat, gentlemen. The purpose of today's meeting is to present a summary of Sea Lion, the role of each of the branches of the Wehrmacht, the inter-service cooperation that must be achieved, and the appointment of key officers.

"Colonel Warlimont is appointed security officer. Everything you see and hear today is secret with the highest classification. Communications will only be made to those officers who have a need to know. Before the date of the invasion, all communications about Sea Lion are to be made only by couriers – no postal, no telephone, and no coded radio! Violation of this order will be considered a leak of classified information, punishable by death."

Terstegen knew Milch had made this unusual decision based on the unsuccessful surprise attack to destroy the rest of France's air force on 3 June

1940. It seemed to him that the French knew about the planned surprise attack. No hard evidence, but if there was a communication breach, he decided to take no chances with Sea Lion.

"Gentlemen, forget Douhet and his concept of winning wars by destroying civilian morale through the bombing of cities. The Führer has canceled the planning of any air war against British cities.

"In its place, he has issued Führer Directive No. 16, dated 6 June 1940. It orders a new plan to invade England, Operation Sea Lion.

The Luftwaffe is responsible for organizing and implementing it as a unified command of Army, Navy, and Luftwaffe services. As you heard from the Führer, he has appointed me overall Commander of Sea Lion and General Terstegen as the operation's chief of staff. Hitler has further ordered that all departments of the Reich must support Sea Lion, effective immediately.

"The invasion date is 21 July 1940, subject to favorable weather. As you can see, time is of the essence. We have a little more than a month to pull all of this together, implement it, as well as complete our victory over France."

Usually, Milch would now turn the meeting over to his chief-of-staff. However, given all the senior officers present, he had decided to continue with the presentation himself. He would reinforce Hitler's order that he was the Supreme Commander of Sea

Lion.

"Behind this curtain is a map of the Channel and the invasion area." He nodded to the officer standing at the large veiled wall map, who pulled the curtain. "As you can see, we will not, as the English currently believe, land in East Anglia. However, we will continue that false belief as long as possible. We will feed misinformation to the British, indicating a German build-up in Holland to invade East Anglia. We understand Mr. Churchill does not like to be contradicted or proved wrong." There were smiles and muffled laughter.

"Nor will we, as the current plan envisions, make a broad-front landing. Neither the Luftwaffe nor the Navy can support the troops while also defending against the RAF and RN.

"Most important, we would have to wait too long to refit the French ports and airfields that we do not yet control. We estimate that the refitting would take one to two months after the end of the French campaign.

"Sea Lion will allow us to invade England much earlier by concentrating our resources in a narrow-based invasion, an 'Air *Schwerpunkt*' in the designated 'invasion zone.' As you can see on the map, our invasion zone or focal point is in Kent County, England, the area in the arc from Dover to Folkestone.

"The shortened timeframe gives the English less

time to sort out their confusion and to reorganize and refit RAF, RN, and British Army units after the Dunkirk evacuation. From an inventory of equipment abandoned by the British Army, they left behind thousands of guns, hundreds of tanks, hundreds of thousands of other vehicles, and significant supplies. We also estimate that up to this point, the RAF has lost over 400 fighters.

"Military Intelligence estimates one English infantry division in the invasion area, poorly equipped and combat inexperienced. The division is currently guarding radar stations, and helping with the reorganization and refitting of those 'Dunkirk Troops'." Some more smiles and snickers. The officers were warming to the presentation.

"Intelligence also estimates that the British Army has between 11 to 17 infantry divisions and only a partial armored division, the 2nd Armored Division. All of these units are undermanned, ill-equipped, and short of ammunition and supplies.

"So you can see why the Führer wants to invade as soon as possible.

Sea Lion will precede in four phases, each a combined arms effort. In the first phase, the Luftwaffe will attack radar stations, the RAF, and the RN before the invasion of troops.

During the second phase, the Luftwaffe will achieve air superiority over the invasion zone and deliver Luftwaffe paratroopers and Heer infantry troops to capture airports and to secure the invasion zone on the ground, a airhead inland about 14 km from the English shore in an arc between Dover and Folkestone. The Navy will assist with the transportation of storm troopers to Dover and Folkestone to capture the harbors, shore gun sites, and the towns.

"In the third phase, panzer and infantry troops will be transported by the Navy to build up the bridgehead. The invasion will be supported by ports we currently control: Ostend, Calais, and Boulogne, and from airbases in the area. The Luftwaffe will maintain air superiority and continue to attack the RAF and RN.

"In the fourth phase, after the build-up of infantry and panzer divisions and supplies, the Wehrmacht will break out from the beachhead invasion zone and conquer the rest of England.

"General Kesselring is appointed Air Commander of Sea Lion." For many, this was a surprise. Given the animosity and history of disputes between the two officers, one would expect Kesselring to be sidelined. However, as would later be evident, Milch put aside his disputes with Kesselring, recognizing his excellent field leadership.

"Air Fleets 2, 3, and 5 will be consolidated under the unified command of General Kesselring. Before and during the invasion, an aggressive air reconnaissance will be conducted.

Before the landing and during the invasion, the Luftwaffe will attack the RAF and the RN over the Channel and SE England. These attacks will begin with limited encounters and build to a maximum effort during the first phase of the invasion. During the invasion, the Luftwaffe will achieve air superiority over the invasion zone and the sea lanes. Stuka Ju 87 and Ju 88 squadrons and the Heinkel 111 torpedo units will attack the RN. The Heinkel 111 torpedo planes and Stuka`s must become proficient in working together in attacking naval vessels. The new tactic is a two-prong attack on ships, a simultaneous bombing and torpedo run. During these operations, 109`s will provide escort cover against any RAF fighters.

At first light on Day 1, a special air unit will destroy power lines and electrical facilities in the Kent area of England.

Also at first light, a special bomber unit with fighter escorts will clear barrage balloons over London and bomb the headquarters of the Admiralty, RAF, British Army, and the Prime Minister's command bunker under Whitehall." Some doubtful looks were expressed. "I realize this is a very risky endeavor. However, I can also assure you we have a plan to obtain the location of these key targets and will be working on how to disable the barrage balloons without losing our aircraft.

Coordination and communication are essential

among these units.

Starting immediately, communication training will be increased among Luftwaffe units and between air and ground forces.

General Student, who has recovered from his injuries in the battle for Holland, is appointed Commander of the new 1st Air Landing Corps. He will serve under General Kesselring. The 1st Air Landing Corps is composed of the 7th Air Division, the 22nd Air Landing Division, the Assault Detachment Koch Battalion (ADK), and the supporting units of Fieseler Storks.

On the morning of the invasion, ADK will attack and destroy key British radar installations on the coast. These installations appear lightly defended. It is possible — and I know some of you in the Luftwaffe believe it very strongly — that these installations are central to the RAF's effective responses to our air raids. To date, we cannot verify or dispove that belief. To eliminate whatever capability these radar stations provide to the RAF, the storm troopers will destroy them.

On the morning of the invasion, ADK will capture or destroy essential British shore batteries and capture the Citadel of Dover, the British naval headquarters for the Channel.

On the morning of the invasion, paratroopers and ADK storm troopers will attack and take possession of the RAF bases of Hawkinge near Folkestone and

Swingfield near Dover, and establish an initial defensive perimeter around the invasion zone.

All troops will carry sub-machine guns. This will increase the individual soldier's firepower to the maximum. All troops must be trained in the effective and efficient use of sub-machineguns. In addition, units will receive additional machinegun crews and mortar squads.

"Some of the air units will be given new missions, a change in their current operational role. In general, one-third of the fighters will cooperate and provide cover for the Stuka`s, Destroyers, and bomber units. The remaining two-thirds will have the task during the invasion of forming an in-depth air cordon in a rolling operation. Their mission is to intercept the English fighters and the RN attacking the shipping, bombers, and the Ju 52 troop transports.

Me 110 Destroyers will change their mission from bomber escort to direct air support of our troops in the invasion area.

The task of non-torpedo Heinkel 111 squadrons will be to attack tactical targets near the invasion area. Railways and rail intersections, road networks and intersections, and bridges must be destroyed to impede the movement of British forces.

The Do 17 units, which have achieved special success in low-level attacks against French airfields, will primarily attack the RAF airfields in the Kent region.

Mission command or free hunting will no longer be allowed without the consent of General Kesselring. General Löhr is appointed commander of all air transport units for Sea Lion. He will serve under the command of General Kesselring. Air transport will include troops, supplies, 88`s, and lightly tracked vehicles. The production and repair of further Ju 52 transport planes will be done with all available means. Also, the machines lost in Holland shall be salvaged or scraped.

We will also be developing a method to air deliver 88`s and possibly light tracked vehicles. Units of 88s will be under the Heer's command and will continue their air defense and ground defense role of artillery and anti-tank support in the landing zone."

Most of the officers listening raised their eyebrows in disbelief. To some, it seemed like a feat of magic to disassemble an 88 and reassemble it across the Channel. And one would think the Luftwaffe would resist putting 88 units under army command.

"General von Manstein is appointed Army commander for Sea Lion. After the airfields are captured, the troop transport planes will begin immediately landing, averaging three sorties a day. Under optimal conditions, we will be able to deliver one infantry division along with supplies every day at each airfield.

The following army units will be transported by

ship: the 7th Panzer Division under General Rommel, and other infantry and panzer divisions as recommended by General Manstein.

General of the Artillery Trettwitz is appointed artillery commander for Sea Lion under General von Manstein. As part of the pre-invasion actions, German, and if time also permits French, heavy artillery will be placed near Calais for the defense of the port, sea transports in the sea-lanes, and bombardment of the RN and the Dover area.

The heavy anti-aircraft batteries of the 1st, 3rd, 5th, and 6th divisions will also move to the Calais area to shield the artillery. The 2nd, 4th, and 7th anti-aircraft divisions will move to protect the ports of Ostend and Boulogne. The light anti-aircraft batteries will prepare to move to England with the invasion. General Trettwitz will also command those units.

Admiral Dönitz is appointed Naval Commander for Sea Lion. All available submarines and surface units of the navy are to be kept on standby from 10 July forward in the maritime area north and south. The navy will immediately send three U-boats to the Central Atlantic for weather reporting. The boats must be able to stay at sea for long periods. At first light on the day of the invasion, concurrent with paratrooper and commando landings, S-boats will land commando troops at Dover and Folkestone to capture the harbors and the cities."

Commodore Engelhard is appointed commander of all sea transport ships and will serve under Admiral Dönitz. The Navy will procure all transport ships, ensure their operational readiness in appropriate ports by 10 July to transport tanks, heavy 88`s, ammunition, materiel, infantry, and necessary supplies not transported by the Luftwaffe. Gentlemen, those are the main features and orders of the first operational directive of Sea Lion. Specific orders are being prepared and will be distributed at the end of today. I will now introduce General Terstegen, who will continue the discussion with the staff officers. If all general and flag officers will join me in the adjoining room, we'll continue the discussion of the scope of Sea Lion and inter-service planning. I'm sure you also have questions."

Although many of the senior officers were skeptical about Sea Lion at the beginning of the briefing, those doubts seemed to be changing to acceptance. It was clear why Hitler had entrusted Milch with the planning and execution of Sea Lion. His drive, creativity, and understanding of the Wehrmacht's capabilities and limitations had impressed everyone. Terstegen looked around the room and saw that most of the staff officers were excited about the plan. Despite the immense additional workload, they had broad grins of satisfaction and eager anticipation. Ever since Hitler had let the British escape from Dunkirk, the Wehrmacht was concerned about how to conduct the war against England. Now they had their answer.

Fact

"However desirable it may have been to win air supremacy before the invasion began, sober consideration of all factors should have prompted the top German leadership to use the Luftwaffe for the decisive strike only in the immediate context of the invasion... The fate of the operation depended on the outcome of a great air battle that would have taken place over the Channel or over southern England from the moment the army and navy invaded. In this battle, however, the battle conditions for the German Luftwaffe would have been much more favourable than for the attacks into the interior of England." Erich von Manstein (1955:168/169)

8 June 1940
Deal, England
The men had slept the last three days, taking short breaks for the bathroom and for eating and drinking something. Only about half of the battalion had

been evacuated. The rest had died in Dunkirk or during the crossing from the air attacks. At least many of them still had their weapons, but all they had in clothes was what they wore. They were billeted in tents on the outskirts of Deal.

Captain Ferguson, the surviving officer with the highest rank in the battalion, stood on the promenade in the early morning, smoked a Player cigarette, and looked out to sea towards France. It still seemed unreal what had happened in the last four weeks. There was the comfortable crossing from Dover to Le Havre, the hasty move to Belgium, the first battles with the Germans, the continous retreat with many endless long marches to reach Dunkirk. Then the wait with tens of thousands more, all hoping that somehow they could escape. It had gone so fast, and they had not once managed to force the Germans to react but instead had lost the initiative and were forced to react to their opponent's moves.

Morale had improved with the news that Göring had died. It was reported to be a heart attack. Given how fat he was, the report might even be correct. Even so, Ferguson didn't like inaction and knew it was terrible for the battalion. He threw his half-smoked cigarette on the pavement, turned, and walked quickly to the camp. "Sergeant Major, full battalion assembly, quickly if you don't mind." He positioned himself, took up a command posture, and watched the lieutenants and non-commissioned officers roust the men.

8 June 1940
London, Cabinet War Rooms

Admiral Winslow sat at his desk, thinking about everything he'd heard over the last few days of his trip, including Göring's death. That exhausted RAF Group Commander was convinced that the Germans wouldn't invade until they had air superiority or supremacy over the RAF. It was a tall order for the Luftwaffe. Degrade not only the RAF but also the radar system, which the Germans didn't understand or seemed concerned about. Thank God for small favors.

The army was not as convinced. General Dill and most division commanders flatly stated that the Germans could invade at any minute. Dill believed after Dunkirk, the best starting date for an invasion was "immediately".

Winslow, trained to analyze in navy terms, didn't think much of Dill's belief. But he had been struggling for days with a gnawing feeling.

What if Dill was right? Except for naval forces, the Germans had air and ground capability to invade. Of course, he couldn't advise the Prime Minister based on a gut feeling, but they would have to think about all options.

On the other hand, what an enormous logistical effort such an operation would entail. Even the Germans could not provide hundreds of ships within days. And the loading of troops and materiel, which had then to go immediately into the fight. It was a logistical nightmare.

He had been present at the landing in Gallipoli as a young ensign on a destroyer and could well remember the chaos. Troops landing in the wrong place, their equipment elsewhere or lost. And the damn Turks had turned a supposed leisure stroll into a bloody killing field. They had underestimated the Turks.

Were they underestimating the Germans, who were so much more dangerous than the Turks? But talking to Winston about Gallipoli, what a nightmare! So far, the Prime Minister didn't seem to take the subject of invasion seriously, although he exploited it politically.

10 June 1940,
Bovington Tank Camp, England
They had been waiting days for a promised new Matilda tank, but no one in the 2nd Royal Tank Regiment knew when or where it would be delivered. Sergeant Savage and his crew were first

given new clothes, which was an improvement over the tattered uniforms they had been wearing since France and the slog to Dunkirk. To a man, they thought another improvement would be some leave. Even though there were no decisions on leaves and no new tanks, there were plenty of rumors. German paratroopers were falling out of the sky, commandos were raiding at night, fifth columnists and saboteurs were destroying bridges and key buildings. The rumors didn't stop with news of Göring's death. If anything, they increased. So everyone was pretty nervous. And despite Göring's death, every day there seemed to be plenty of German planes overhead, sometimes they could even hear distant machine guns rattling from aerial battles.

To keep them busy, they had been sent to the tank workshop where they repaired useless A10 tanks. Savage never understood why they had built hundreds of these tin cans that couldn't travel 20 miles without a total breakdown.

"Take a break, guys," said the Regimental Sergeant Major, who had just come into the workshop. He handed his cigarette box to Savage. "You'll have to be patient, guys. Right now, six tank regiments are waiting for new tanks. As you know, not one tank came back with the evacuation. But there's also something good about that because we've dumped a whole lot of scrap metal on the Krauts."

The men laughed, but they knew a lot of good equipment was abandoned. Besides, some good Matilda II`s, Vickers, and Carden Lloyd little tanks had been left in France. After they had experienced how fast and well-armed the German tanks were, and then the killing power of 88`s, everyone secretly hoped for a new miracle tank.

Savage asked, "How about some leave, Sergeant, repairing the A10 is more annoying than useful?" The RSM nodded, "Sergeant Savage, you and your crew will get a few days next week."

10 June 1940
Scapa Flow

As far as Summerfield could see, Churchill as Prime Minister had brought no significant improvement in the leadership of the English war effort. Two German heavy cruisers had just sunk the aircraft carrier *HMS Glorious*, which had only been protected by two escort destroyers. The Admiralty had overruled his direct order that the aircraft carrier be escorted by *Renown* and *Repulse* and a complete destroyer flotilla. He could only speculate about the motives, probably U-boat danger. But then the solution was more destroyers, a British ship in abundance.

He took a bottle of Haig from the lower desk

drawer. He thought sadly of his son David, who had died two months ago at Narvik. Fortunately, his wife was not alive to experience her son's death. David's death would have destroyed her. He wiped a tear from his eye.

As he opened the bottle, he thought about the next battle, one that was sure to come. Either the Admiralty played hardball with the Krauts or they would have to find another admiral to go along with their bullshit.

11 June 1940
Church in Worth, England

The young boy rang the bell of the old church of Worth with a great fervor this evening. The priest had told him this afternoon that tomorrow the bells would be silent – unless the Germans came. Paul Michaels, his friend, always said, "The damn Huns!" But Mama had looked at him quite angrily when he had called the Germans by that name. Would they come? He was 13 and had an air rifle, and he was not afraid of them, those damn Huns!

12 June 1940
Vlissingen, Belgium

It was a miracle that anyone on board was able to keep the boat on a straight course after last night. With the increased pace of training and maintenance, and the continued good news of German advances against the French, the whole crew had stormed into the tavern to celebrate, as if France had surrendered.

Throughout the night, his young crew had drunk the tavern's entire beer supply. Nothing like a bunch of happy teenage sailors — loud, drunk, and demanding beer and women. The owner finally surrendered and shooed out the few remaining locals, letting the crew run wild. Many of them ended up at the local brothel. Shore patrol had to round up those that didn't return to barracks. This morning, the boys could hardly walk. It's a good thing that the rest of the Flotilla wouldn't be here for a few more days, thought Georgson.

At first light, with the help of the boatswain, he rousted his sailors, sent them to the boat, and slowly motored around some islands. Now everyone was awake from their stupor, even if they had thundering headaches.

Because of the boat's disadvantages in armament and defensive guns, he had pushed the training schedule. The crew responded well. They were all ready for action. In the meantime, they lived a sailor's life — maintenance, train, eat and drink, and fuck.

12 June 1940
Ostend, Belgium
They had finished dinner and returned to her small house near the coast. He heard her turn off the bath. Liane came out of the bathroom naked. She was a tall woman, with light brown hair, nice breasts, and elegant movements. She wore her hair very short in a kind of pony ruffle, very un-German, of course.
"Why are you looking at me like that, you big, miserable Hun conqueror?" she smiled.
They spoke French to each other. Bergmann's father had insisted that he learn French as well as English. As he looked at her, he'd try to remind himself to thank his father, again, for making him learn French.
"I admire your Maginot Line, Cherie," he said with a devious smile as he stood up from the chair. He wore only his undershorts.
He stepped behind her, wrapping his arms around her, and lightly stroking her belly and then her vaginal area.
Kissing her neck, he whispered, "May I help, Madame? I'm an Eagle Boy Scout, always ready and always very horny."
"Mon petit cho, are you thinking only of screwing?"

she said, trying to dry off.

"Petit! Well, we'll see about that later," he smiled knowingly. "But no, now I think about flying…but when I fly, I think about screwing," he said jokingly, kissing her on her cheek and nibbling her ear. He felt her becoming moist.

She laughed, turned, and began to rub the front of his underwear. Even then he couldn't completely clear the thoughts about flying. But as she continued to rub him, then pull his shorts down, and take him in her mouth, his thoughts quickly came back to sex.

She was very oral and loved to suck him. When he was aroused, he was very wet, and the release could come quickly. But not with Liane, she could bring him to the edge of orgasms time and time again. Of all the women he had known, she knew how best to please him sexually.

After a night of intense sex, Liane snuggled next to him. She thought about her situation. What were you going to do as a young girl in a conquered country? One had to survive, and one needed a man. And Bergmann wasn't so bad for a German. He was an officer, young, tall, and handsome. He was surprisingly thoughtful, usually funny, gentle most of the time in bed, and hung, which suited her very much. It must be her anatomy, she thought, but long and thick drove her to glorious ecstasy. She turned to him. He looked entirely content asleep on his back.

Through the window, she could see it was slowly getting light. As dilapidated as the house was, she loved it very much. Her parents died in an auto accident many years ago. They left the house to her and she would never leave it. It was only about 600 meters from the coast, and, on a very clear day, she could see the English shoreline in the distance. Bergmann stirred. Let's see if my conquering Hun has any morning life in him, she thought. With very gentle touches, she began to caress him under the blanket. Very slowly, her fingers wandered over his chest, over his stomach, over his groin. She caressed him around his penis and started gently stroking it. Yes, he did have some morning life. Bergmann gave some comforting moans and, still half asleep, stretched out his legs. She felt him stiffen under her gently caressing hand. How soft his pubic hair was. She laced her fingers through the curls and plucked some apart. She pulled off the blanket, leaned over and bit his nipple.

"Ouch!" he exclaimed. "Be gentle, Cherie!" he murmured.

She licked his nipple. "Is this better?"

He pleasantly moaned. Then she took his thick penis firmly in her hand. She kissed his mouth and felt his tongue glide playfully in her mouth and around her tongue. She pulled his foreskin back and forth and felt him getting even harder. She was

171

suddenly wet and needed him now. She slipped her arm under his back and gently pulled. He moved on top of her, and she moved her legs apart. He penetrated her deeply and fully.

She was consumed with pleasure, his kisses, muscular body, and deep thrusts. Slowly she could feel it building within her. She arched her back slightly and gently sucked his nipple. Her climax gushed over her in beautiful waves. With his thrusts, he prolonged her orgasm. She could feel his muscles tightening, back arching, and penis swelling inside her. He pulled out, groaned, and erupted, drenching her belly and breasts. He collapsed in her arms and sighed deeply. She felt him relax and breathe softly.

She always appreciated the time after orgasm, the warm afterglow, and the feel of his body over her, tender lips and kisses, and the gentle tracing of her fingers over his muscles. After a while, she moved him to one side and slowly, with regret, let his flaccid penis slide out. Take a bath and wash the sheets again, she thought. She went into the bathroom to clean up with a satisfied smile.

But Bergmann didn't go to sleep, he only dozed. For some time now, sex didn't release all the tension. His brain immediately began to work, a strange mixture of a sense of duty, wild imagination, and fear of death. He was no longer in bed but imagined he was again in his plane in combat with Spitfires.

They had paid dearly for the new experiences in recent weeks, especially over Dunkirk and the Channel. The new Spitfires were almost equal to 109`s. But they couldn't dive, which 109`s could do in spades. It had saved many pilots, including him. Planes and sex, there was a lot in common. He suddenly woke. He noticed he was getting another erection. Today was not for blood-filled combat, but for luscious sex.

12 June 1940
Calais, France
General of the Artillery von Trettwitz had trouble sleeping, even after drinking almost a bottle of French cognac. What an intense trust Milch and Hitler had in his heavy artillery, engineers, and men. Emplace a cluster of guns close to the Channel, fend off the Royal Navy, and protect the invasion landing! And set it all up ASAP! What a fucking joke. Seventeen-centimeter coastal cannons against 40-centimeter ship guns. Always the same half-baked crap from these Luftwaffe air freaks. Well, perhaps if the guns were buried deep and well protected, von Trettwitz thought. That worked at the Somme in 1917. The guns couldn't reposition, but they couldn't be easily destroyed unless it was a direct hit.

He sighed and warmed to the idea. It would be a tremendous job, but perhaps the only chance against the Royal Navy's much heavier guns. Yes, it might work, if they got the groundwater under control with pumps. We're going to need some big water pumps. Tomorrow I'll put Colonel Guntermann on it. Grunting contentedly, he turned to the wall and, enjoying the warmth of the cognac, fell asleep.

June 16th, 1940 Berlin, Office of Colonel General Milch

The room was heavily impregnated with cigar smoke. Milch had let his box of cigars go around and Manstein had been the first to access it, with a friendly remark about the first-class quality of the Cuban cigars. Then the chiefs of staff from Manstein and Dönitz had also dared.

"Yes, first-class booty," laughed Milch, then he became serious.

"We assume, according to information from Intelligence, that the French will ask for a cease-fire tomorrow."

It took several seconds until calm returned to the room, so that he could continue, "Nevertheless our operation continues, because at this moment of maximum weakness of our enemies, we must exploit that to the limit.

Then he waved at Terstegen, "Get started, General Terstegen."

"Gentlemen, you all know the current state of planning. We asked you, as representatives of the army and navy, to come today to make sure that we all operate with the same targets."

Milch eyed Dönitz: "Admiral, if you want to start."

"Thank you General, first a word of praise to your previous planning," he nodded to Terstegen, "we were initially very reserved, especially in regard to our first plans last autumn, about a naval landing in England. For us as a navy this war came years too early, so that we cannot match the Royal Navy in terms of equipment. Therefore, the proposal to land first on a narrow front and primarily from the air, in view of our limited means, is the only conceivable plan anyway. Strategically, however, we must bear in mind, that the sea area off Kent is almost always no more than 25 metres deep, so that even our strongest weapon in terms of numbers, the submarines, can only be used at extremely high risk. We will therefore have to deploy the submarines mainly to the south and north of the English Channel in order to intercept units of the Royal Navy there in deeper water. In the Channel we will therefore focus on small units such as E boats. For the protection of supply ships, we have, apart from some destroyers, torpedo boats and minesweepers, almost nothing at our disposal. We assume, however, that the British think similarly to us in terms of the use of their own submarines. Therefore, the primary threat to the supply from our point of view, is the RAF, then mines and thirdly Navy warships. But they will have to come from northern bases like Scapa, Rosyth or Hull. In this case we can use our heavy units against them, if we get it approved from Führer headquarters. Anything coming from the southwest, like Southampton or Plymouth can, if at all possible, be intercepted by submarines. But please don't expect miracles, we don't have the magic wand for that. We have also decided to make Admiral Engelhardt responsible for the transport of supplies by sea, he has experience from the last war".

Milch nodded: "Thank you very much for your frank words, Admiral. General Manstein, you have the floor."

Manstein was silent for a moment to let out a ring of smoke.

"We assume that we can beat the English army, if the strategic surprise succeeds. It is also essential that we get enough tanks and heavy materiel transported and that the ammunition and fuel supply gets through, no matter how. After Dunkirk, the English army will surely be in shock for some time and the losses of tanks, artillery and vehicles were considerable and cannot be made good at short notice. But Dunkirk has also shown that our air force has to take a break in bad weather. Is there a Plan B regarding bad weather?"

Since Milch was initially silent, Terstegen took the floor: "We have had several conversations with meteorologists about this. They assure us, that in July and August the weather over the invasion area will be changeable, but generally good. We sent 3 submarines into the Atlantic to observe the weather in order to report changes in the weather conditions at an early stage. As I myself worked in London for two years, I can confirm from my own experience, that change is the right word to use. In England you can expect all weather conditions to change every hour. And typically change occurs quickly. The meteorologists explain this by the fact, that the weather there is mostly determined by a vortex system north of Ireland. Imagine a bicycle rim over Europe, with the axle north of Ireland, then the spokes over England simply stand closer together than over us further out on the spoke. We in Germany get the same weather fronts, but with a lower frequency of change than in England. On the other hand, the worst thing that can happen in July and August, based on our experience to date, is that we will not have flying weather for two or a maximum of three days. During this time the Royal Navy will dominate the Channel and we will not be able to transport supplies."

He remained silent to give Manstein an opportunity to answer.

"I am not an enemy of risky enterprises," said Manstein. "Two to three days without supplies may be damn long, but, with certain precautions, bearable. Our artillery is in the process of positioning field pieces in large numbers along the coast and especially around the take-off ports of Ostend, Calais and Dunkirk. If the Royal Navy comes within range of the guns, it will pay a high price for it. What worries me more is whether we have enough Stuka's to compensate for the lack of artillery for my troops. In the last campaign against the French that worked out very well!"

"Thank you for the praise Herr General," said Milch and then continued: "We want to improve the cooperation with the army even further. At this very moment more than one hundred of our officers are undergoing special training in order to work with their troops on site as forward observers for the Air Force. But the problem is that we will need the Stuka's urgently to reduce the English fleet. When we get that goose cooked, you will get all the Stuka's left over. Unfortunately, we only have about 400 of them, so, as Admiral Dönitz said, you shoud not expect any miracles!"

Manstein nodded thoughtfully, "Well, then we'll give the troops more mortars. Of course, that won't replace real artillery, but it's better than nothing.

Fortunately, we have already captured over 13,000 first-class Thompson Brandt mortars with plenty of ammo from the French, and there will be even more of them."

"Good," said Milch, "what recommendations or wishes do you have, what can we do over the next four weeks to improve our chances?"

"That's easy," said Dönitz, "sink any goddamn English warship you can catch with your bombers."

"We will use submarines to accelerate the mining off the English naval ports, but this is limited by the fact that we only have 7 submarines that can carry mines. That's why we also use E-boats for this." He looked at Manstein, who said: "I can only concur in that, everything that helps to secure our line of supply is very useful. It will be difficult enough, because especially in the initial phase we will have considerably fewer troops than the opponent, despite the element of surprise. But a moment of surprise is just that, a moment!"

Milch nodded, "We are aware of the risks, gentlemen, but we also see the opportunities, do you go with me there, d'accord?"

Everyone nodded in agreement.

"Does it really make sense if we leave the English alone for another 4 weeks, except for the destruction of warships, and concentrate only on preparing the invasion? What do you think, Terstegen?"

"That is not easy to answer, General. On the one hand the rest break is nothing new, after all we had the whole winter until April with the drole de guerre, where nothing happened. If I may extend the question, we must rather ask what we want the English to think, and what diversions and deceptive measures are still feasible?

Milch asked: "What have you arranged with Colonel Schellenberg and what have you and the Intelligence Department set in motion in the meantime?"

"We have something big to propose, General. We let the English win."

He waited a moment to enjoy the bewildered faces of those present, and then continued:

"Imagine we send a convoy of 30 to 40 freighters through the Skagerrak in four weeks. We requisition the freighters in Poland, Norway and Denmark. Shortly before it transits the Skaggerak we send two of them to Copenhagen with engine trouble and visibly unload 1500 men from each ship and transfer them to two other emergency requisitioned freighters. Then both replacement ships leave again and rejoin the convoy, and we leak that we plan to land with several divisions in East Anglia. We send our remaining destroyers and, if possible, our heavy vessels past Helsingborg afterwards. What is going to happen?"

He waited a moment, let the rhetorical question

float and then answered it himself. The fact that all those present looked at him in amazement did not upset him.

"There will certainly be some of our new Danish.... Uh....friends, who will inform London. Also, the Swedes will of course not be able to avoid seeing this fleet, with similar effects. The ships each have of course only 20-man crew on board, all volunteers. Moreover, we stuff every empty oil barrel we can find into the freighters to make them almost unsinkable, so that they can be used longer as a target. We let the two ships with the 3000 men disappear under the protection of the night. At the same time, we set up all the U-boats we can get in the Jade Bay in deeper water, this time with functioning torpedoes. In addition, we pull as many fighters, Stukas, bombers and all torpedo bombers as possible at short notice to Denmark and Friesland and replace them on the French airfields by dummies. The aim of the whole thing is, since the English cannot ignore us, to generate panic there and to destroy as many English warships and bombers of the RAF as possible during their attack on our bait fleet. The warships from Portsmouth and the south are a task for the Stukas, those from the north, like Scapa and Hull and so on, we feed to the U-boats, the E-boats, the bombers and the pilots of the torpedo bombers. Our warships in the vanguard will make a cowardly retreat after a few shots and lure the English in the direction of our U-boats and the convoy. Since we are within our range and, unlike the English, prepared, the chances of the operation should be very good. Then we withdraw the remaining freighters. What is left of the Royal Navy after the Luftwaffe has struck, we intercept with the heavy units of the Kriegsmarine on the way back to Scapa, provided that the heavy units are released.

In the following victory euphoria of the English, they will hopefully overlook the fact that we have plucked them hard and relax, because the damn Krauts are fended off. If they send additional troops to East Anglia and they stay there for now, so much the better. Five days later we start, with total surprise, Operation Sealion".

First it was quiet in the room, then Manstein started to knock on the table.

"Is that possible, Mr. Terstegen?" he asked.

"Yes General, we have confirmed with Captain Ohlmann, whom Admiral Dönitz kindly lent to our staff, the resources we need. All we need is about two weeks preparation time, especially for the preparation of the airfields and for the relocation of the submarines, about 1000 experienced seamen, preferably volunteers, for the freighters, and a quick decision on your part. We have also agreed on channels with Intelligence to correctly betray the operation to the English."

Now everyone was grinning.

"I am impressed, General, that sounds good. A bit like Verdun 2, but obviously more promising. General Manstein, Admiral Dönitz, do you agree?" Both nodded, obviously in the best of moods. Their chiefs of staff knocked on the table like students. Even Milch grinned broadly, he could sell it to the Führer, who liked such deceptive manoeuvres. But they should rather call it Operation Walhalla. Verdun 2 would be too obvious, but Walhalla spelt serious business.

Fact
On 17 June 1940, the French government asked the German government for armistice conditions.

Part 2: End of the French campaign

"The preparations for the invasion were completed by mid-September, within the bounds of what was possible at that time, on the basis of the order issued in July (July 16th, 1940). A decision taken four weeks earlier would have made it possible to cross the Channel by mid-August".

Erich von Manstein, then commander of the 38th Army Corps, which was scheduled for deployment in the course of the Sea Lion Operation, in his memoirs (1955:167). Manstein was probably the most capable military strategist of the 20th century.

June 17th, 1940, Stuka Squadron II 2, Airfield St. Omer

The telex rattled out the order. But Major Winkler already knew what it would say. He was angry. It was outrageous to ground them.

The leader of 1st Squadron stood next to him and pulled the paper out of the machine.

"Do you understand that, Major?" he asked.

Winkler said mechanically "No", although it was quite clear to him what this order meant.

"What is it Rudi, in any case it means that we can have a good drink tonight. Let's tell our boys."

Not that it wouldn't be necessary for the crews to get some rest. They also needed replacements. In the few days fighting for Dunkirk they had lost eight crews, more than in the entire six weeks of the campaign against France.

June 18th, 1940, Watton

The fucking French had really surrendered.

Actually, Delaney had had a good opinion of them, the French Morane, Bloch and Dewoitine fighters, who had protected them in some missions, had fought well, bravely and aggressively against the Germans and had not let them down.

But their politicians, they are the same filth as ours, he thought.

So now they were alone. And that against the damn Germans.

And that in a Blenheim.

He could still remember well what a hot rod his Blenheim had been in 1938, when they had exchanged their Hawker Hart biplanes for it. But during the last 4 weeks, even the last optimist had realized that the Blenheim was not a winner anymore.

In May, when he was in hospital with jaundice, just three days after he had had to leave Joyce, the squadron lost 11 of 12 Blenheims in an attack on Gembloux in Belgium. Only his friend Remington and his crew had survived. Had Delaney been there, he probably would have been dead by now. Messerschmidt-fodder was the current name of the men for the Blenheim.

Delaney sat next to his navigator and gunner in the pub at the counter, and a pint of bitter in front of him, and thought about what he could say to his men to cheer them up, but nothing occurred to him. Nothing at all.

Today they themselves had barely survived their Blenheim, when the left engine had given up its ghost shortly after take-off. Although he managed to accelerate the plane to a minimal margin above stall speed of 120 miles per hour, only with luck had he been able to fly half a right turn and land on a freshly ploughed field next to the airfield. The Wingco had sent them to the pub after his short report, he knew that one could hardly fly the Blenheim on one engine.

"Can't we bomb Bristol next time or Filton, the factory where this fucking thing is built?" Jameson, his pimply gunner with the big name, threw in.

"Good idea, but then I want a Ju 88, otherwise Dowding`s Spitfires will eat us alive," said his navigator, Flight Sergeant Collins.

Delaney grinned, at least they could make jokes about it, maybe there was hope after all.

"Same thing again," he said to the owner.

The next time they should try the Blenheim in low-level flight. Like all the others he wanted nothing else than to survive. Joyce waited, he knew that. He should write to her but didn't know how to start.

June 18th, 1940, Berlin

It wouldn't be an easy task. Engelhardt had had his first experience with sea landings in 1917, when the Imperial Army occupied the Russian island of Ösel. Successful, but not comparable. What Milch demanded required a completely different approach. Admiral Engelhardt cleared his throat: "Gentlemen. From the navy's point of view, there are logistically three main groups of materiel.

In the first phase, the bridgehead phase:

- Heavy equipment: tanks, 8.8 cm anti-aircraft guns and their towing vehicles.
- Gasoline and its transport trucks
- Ammunition and its transport vehicles

Light Flak and light Pak and troops can be transported by the Ju 52.

To reduce the risk of the Royal Navy or the RAF sinking our ships, we need massive air cover. We assume that we must carry out the transports during the day because there is no possibility to keep the Royal Navy out of the Channel at night. That gives us not quite 16 hours of daylight in July. We are currently working on shortening unloading times by attaching ramps to the ships, so that the tanks and tractors can leave the ship under their own power. Altogether we need one or two intact harbours and therefore we need big and fast ships, which we send over in small, well-secured convoys.

We have about 75 fast and large steamers available and we are working on an idea to unload tanks faster than we are able to accomplish now.

If you can prevent the enemy from sinking these vessels, we can supply about 30 divisions, with a daily requirement of 300 tons per division and a loss rate of one ship per crossing. We expect to have more large and fast steamers available in the coming months.

Please assume that our Navy can only provide a minimal amount of escort protection. We have had such high losses of light units in Norway that we are extremely weak. What we can and will do is to stuff the steamers with light AA guns. Thank you."

Milch stood up: "Thank you Admiral. We have made the following decisions to protect the transport steamers, Colonel Fink please."

Fink, a slender pilot with a hooked nose, began: "Since we are done without this resupply, but on the other hand do not have enough strength to shield the Channel continuously, we will proceed as follows. We will send the transports in daylight and in convoys. At first light we will search the Channel by air reconnaissance. 80 percent of the Stuka`s will be ready to destroy any Royal Navy vessels that are still in the vicinity.

Simultaneously, the Do 17 and Me 110 units, also at first light, will attack the English bomber bases in southern England and East Anglia.

For further protection of our steamers we will always have about 200 Me 109 over the Channel. To prevent the navy AA from shooting down our own aircraft, we will apply white stripes on the wings to improve their visibility."

Engelhardt said: "Good idea. If we can get a minimum of three steamers through every three days, we can guarantee the materiel needed for the first phase, provided the army reduces their requirements need to the absolute essentials. The second phase will come when the Royal Navy and RAF are largely eliminated, then we will be able to operate virtually unchallenged in the Channel. I hope we achieve that goal!"

June 18th, 1940 Wilhelmshaven, naval shipyard

"Captain. The train is ready for departure. All hands onboard."

Captain Kröhnke threw the stub of his cigar on the tracks. It was regrettable that he could not see Monika tonight, but there was no possible going against Dönitz's direct order. He secretly admired Dönitz's thoughtfulness, even though the admiral was tinted a bit too brown in Kröhnke`s view. But since the French were now going to capitulate, there was finally the possibility to use the French Atlantic ports for the submarines. The English would soon notice that. He had been busy day and night the last week putting together endless lists of submarine spare parts and ammunition and loading the first trains, as it had been foreseeable that the French were beaten. A gigantic task, but he had made it. The navy was prepared. With this materiel two U-boat groups could be supplied for several months. He was curious about Lorient. Maybe that was even better than going out with Monika, who made more and more desperate efforts to force him into marriage.

He grinned, but then rebuked a soldier who stood casually smoking and without saluting him on the platform.

Fact
The first train of the German Kriegsmarine to France actually departed from Wilhelmshaven on June 18th, 1940.

June 18th, 1940 Puteaux Artillery Arsenal of the

French Army

It was amazing how much first-class war materiel the French had not used. Major Meyer and his staff had now been on the road in occupied France for two weeks, cataloguing only the inventory in the French arsenals already occupied.

"Gosh, Keller, 220 of the 15.5 GPF long tubes with modern mounts and completely professionally preserved, old, but not even a rust stain on it. And still mountains of ammunition. It's like Christmas and Easter in one day!"

"Yes, Herr Major. It's a good thing those pieces weren't at Sedan when we crossed the Meuse."

"You're right, my dear captain. Well, there couldn't have been such a mess with us, that's sabotage."

"We should absolutely report this find to General von Trettwitz of the Artillery Command North, Sir."

Meyer waved him off.

"Yes, you do that right away, Keller."

Meyer walked for quite a while through the large warehouse with big child's eyes and stroked one of the big guns from time to time. The GPF was over 20 years old, but still one of the best artillery pieces ever built. Only a muzzle brake was missing, to shorten the recoil.

With a well-trained crew, up to 5 shots per minute were possible, and it shot much more accurately than the K 18 from Krupp.

Since it had been decided anyway to bury the guns of the Channel blocking batteries, it was no problem to make the gun pits a little deeper in one place in order to give the large GPF cannon the necessary space for the recoil of the breech.

Tonight, he would throw a big round for his men, this just had to be celebrated.

Fact

After France's capitulation, the Wehrmacht took over 449 GPS 155 mm artillery pieces, the most advanced cannons used late in the First World War. In addition, about 1.7 million shells for it. The American further developed the GPF. The Long Tom, is a direct precursor of the cannons of this calibre still used today by NATO.

Part 3, planning the impossible

June 18th, 1940, Essen, near Krupp factory
The engineer wiped the sweat off his forehead. His workgroup had been at work for 14 hours. The hissing of the welding torches hummed in his ears.

A crazy task, to dismantle an assault gun into its component parts. The sergeant in charge of the repair workshop of Rommel's 7th Panzer Division, who had been assigned to the workgroup, lifted a part of the gearbox out of the chaos of parts with a groan.

"And watch out for the numbering of the boxes, damn it. God knows under what conditions we'll have to reassemble this thing." Sergeant Major Klinger was a Franconian, a medium-sized, broad-bodied and easygoing man who impressed the others with his enormous practical knowledge of his tank. He laid down the air filter.

"I think it's enough for today, Mr. Engineer. Come on, let's go have a beer."

The men grinned at him gratefully. They were exhausted but satisfied. Tomorrow they would have completely dismantled and packed the first StuG III. Almost 200 packages, after all, and you would need 6 Ju 52`s to transport that load. They saw that even the otherwise-stiff engineer Bergemüller grinned with satisfaction. However, assembly under field conditions would be a nightmare. Did the geniuses at the Staff really know what they had asked for?

Klinger wondered if it wouldn't be better to take a Czech-built 38 t. Could one of those smaller tanks be converted into an assault gun? How big could the cannon be?

He should work that out sometime.

Fact
Since the French army could not reach Dien Bien Phu by land in 1953, 10 American M 24 Chaffee tanks (weighing 18 tons each) were dismantled into about 180 packages and transported on C47 Dakotas by air to Dien Bien Phu, where they were reassembled. The C47 Dakota has a lift capability of 3900 kg, about the same as the Ju 52.

June 18th, 1940 Lechfeld/Bavaria, with Transport Squadron 502

Everyone could see that the lieutenant in the decoration-laden uniform was walking as if he had drunk too much. Nevertheless, the men of the squadron, even up to Major Eberle, the commander, had quickly learnt that Lieutenant Wolf of the fighters had left one leg in Poland, but that his intellect and tongue more than compensated for this loss.

They rubbed the sweat off their foreheads and looked over at the end of the runway where a Ju 52 was just about to land. They had been practicing the rapid unloading of 5 cm anti-tank guns for days. Previously it had taken them almost half an hour to unload the cannon. Now Wolf had constructed a ramp and had had people fabricate it in the workshop. The ramp was attached at two points, which had been welded below the large hatch of the Ju 52. Five minutes later Wolf had to hold on, when all the men thumped him on the shoulder because they had unloaded the Pak, which weighed almost a ton, as fast as never before. Everyone grinned until one of them asked: "But how do we get the ramp to the unloading place?"

Everyone was at a loss, then Wolf said: "Quite simply, we put the thing under the plane. In the thirties the Ju 52 was used as a bomber, there was a kind of turret for the gunner under the belly. Compared to that, the ramp is an aerodynamic showpiece!"

"And how do we move the gun on the ground when we've unloaded it," asked the same cheeky sergeant from the technical crew.

Wolf crooked his head, thought for a moment, and then said: "Get two motor bikes, weld their frames together, connect the handlebars and mount a towing bracket, and make the space between wide enough to load two 25-litre petrol canisters. Fit low-pressure heavy-duty tires. But it must be possible to get this monster through the hatch of the Ju 52. Can you do it?"

195

The sergeant, almost bursting with pride, saluted smartly and answered with a broad grin: "Almost done, Lieutenant!"

Wolf laughed. "Well, after clearing that up, we should now find out how to get 30 men into the Ju and get them out damn fast after landing."

He turned to Major Eberle, issuing an order rather than a question: "You will report to General Terstegen, sir?"

June 20th, 1940 off Vlissingen, 10:05 p.m.

The boat now made 18 knots and still left almost no wake behind. God bless the Lürssen shipyard for their ingenuity, he thought. They could always recognize the English MTB`s very quickly at night, because due to a less favourable hull shape, they had a considerable bow wave and stern sea even at low speeds, and they were much louder.

He strained to look through his large Zeiss binoculars.

"20 degrees starboard, increase speed to 24 knots." The helmsman Knoll passed his order on to the engine room and then he, turned on the new course.

Next to the bridge, a twin machinegun was now installed on each side of the bridge on custom-built mountings. They had obtained four MG 34 from an infantry unit in exchange for 2 crates of rum, and Schell had welded the mountings for them.

They had also welded some armour plates around the bridge. Georgson had once discussed this with one of the engineers at a meeting at the Lürssen shipyard. The man had bitterly complained that the Admiralty would block a lot of good ideas. Well, Meyer 2, their former skipper, had paid with his life for the stubbornness of the admirals.

"That's right!" He set the binocular down and bent over the dimly lit chart table. The new radar on Wissant had discovered a group of 3 ships that had left Ramsgate an hour ago to the north. Enemy speed 9 knots.

Now S-28 had passed the outer water mark and they did not have to watch for sandbanks anymore. The waters off Vlissingen were treacherous and Georgson had spent a lot of time in the last 2 weeks memorizing the nautical chart material of the region. They had only 1.60 meters draught and were therefore hardly endangered, but even more interesting was the chance to use the shallows to escape from larger ships.

"Increase revolutions to 32 knots, general course 280 degrees." At this speed and this course, they ought to meet the reported convoy in about 4 hours. "With a little luck, we'll be back before sunrise tomorrow morning, Captain."

Georgson looked at his helmsman sceptically.

"Knock on wood Knoll, better knock on wood. Sometimes that even helps." He put his binoculars in front of his eyes again and thought to himself: Hopefully the convoy doesn't consist of destroyers. Entirely. The deep hum of the large diesel engines had a strangely calming effect on him.

June 21st, 1940 Thames estuary, off Southend on Sea, 2:16 a.m.

Lieutenant Kirkland had only been the Third Officer of the sloop for a week. He was still struggling with bouts of seasickness but was too proud to talk openly about it. The sloop was still quite new, only 3 weeks ago it entered service in Portsmouth. They accompanied two empty steamers on their first voyage, returning after a delivery of coal to Skegness.

The low speed of the coal steamers made him nervous. When looked at more closely, he was afraid.

The helmsman was warrant officer Royston. At least he, Kirkland thought, had been in the Navy long enough to know what he was doing. With melancholy he remembered the time when he had been an accountant at an insurance company in Portsmouth. What was he doing here?

Royston suddenly shouted, "Attention, torpedo to

starboard in the water."
The torpedoe`s wake was visible in the clear night even in weak moonlight.
"Sir, what should I do?"
Kirkland stood helplessly beside him he had never experienced such a situation before. The helmsman tried on his own initiative with full rudder to starboard to avoid the torpedo, but they had no chance. The torpedo hit the rear of the sloop. Within 3 minutes only some wreckage of it tumbled lazily in the water. A second torpedo had hit one of the freighters, which was now lying dead in the water, burning, with a failed engine. Far away the deep engine hum of the running E-boat could be heard.

June 21st, 1940 U 37 approx. 8 miles off Hull
The captain had turned his white peaked cap backwards and made a quick panorama search with the periscope. The sea was nearly calm, "First-class bathing weather, nothing to see. Retract the periscope. What time?
"12 seconds", came the prompt response from the boatswain who had checked the exposure time with his stopwatch. Lieutenant Karl Huber looked again at the map of the approaches to Hull. Where had the English placed their mine barrier?

He wasn't an anxious person, but he had respect for those horned devil's eggs. He wanted to get closer to the harbour and lie in wait in front of it. According to air reconnaissance, six cruisers and ten destroyers were to be stationed here. They were his target. The batteries were full, so they could wait and probably could attach themselves to a fish trawler that would lead them through the minefields. And as a reward they would let the trawler live. He had to grin. "Go down to 20 meters, crawl along so we can listen, XO."

The shallow depth of the water worried him. It would take much deeper water to give them a chance to survive after a torpedo attack. That's why this time they carried only two torpedoes in the stern tubes, but otherwise 58 mines on board. He would put them into the main channel of Hull. Then back to Wilhelmshaven as soon as possible.

June 21st, 1940, Ju 86 high altitude reconnaissance aircraft, 12,000 metres above Hull

Despite the intense cold, Wegener sweated under his thick fur jacket. Every manoeuvre with the cumbersome machine had to be flown extremely gentle as otherwise he would lose altitude or even risk stalling.

"The Englishman just slipped off 1500 meters below us," reported the lower gunner.

Captain Wegener, a corpulent mid-thirties and former Lufthansa pilot, was relieved to let some air out of his lungs. One day the RAF would develop a fighter that could fly much higher than his old Junkers 86. Hopefully he wasn't the one who would find out.

He could see the Humber estuary and the town centre of Hull a few kilometres further in. Two more minutes, then they would be over the harbour. Hopefully the cameras were not frozen, otherwise six hours flying time would be wasted.

In front of him, but still well below his altitude, some cloudbursts of heavy AA guns appeared, so he gently turned a few degrees to the right.

"We are over the target, turn on the cameras," the navigator said.

Wegener flipped the camera switch and heard the whirring of the film rolls. A few more minutes, then we will return to France. At least they didn't have to go to Scapa, one of their colleagues worked on that today. Wegener's Royal Navy customers, six light cruisers, were, as he could see with his binoculars, all in port.

June 21st, 1940, Berlin, Staff Orange

As a number of unfortunate employees of the Reich Aviation Ministry were able to confirm, Milch had a rhetorical violence that did not yield in any way to that of Reich Propaganda Minister Goebbels.

He had skimmed over Major Schmidt's report. The man was responsible for the target planning of the Luftwaffe, a protege of Göring`s and before that the 1c of Göring`s staff.

"Schmidt, I should have you shot, as you actually work for the English and not for us. I have the impression you're getting your target information from the Baedeker."

He had turned red with anger. Major Beppo Schmidt stood at attention in front of his desk.

"Has no one yet informed you that we are not planning a strategic bombing war but want to land in England in 4 weeks at the latest. Not that we would be able to conduct a strategic bombing war, you idiot. It says here that after the good experiences from Guernica and Rotterdam you want to start immediately with a bombing of London, after you have paralyzed the RAF by a two-day bombing of their airfields and aircraft factories. Do you believe such absolute nonsense yourself?"

Milch had walked around his desk and stood very close to Major Schmidt. He could see sweat forming on the man's forehead.

Schmidt remained silent because even he knew that every answer here was wrong.

"I want to have a reasonable target plan on the table in three days, Schmidt, and one according to our strategy.

Tactics, Schmidt and finally. you better forget Douhet, that bastard was anyway only a miserable Italian.

All measures that do not have a bearing on the day of the landing and the following 7 days, have nothing to do with our planning. If I don't like the result Schmidt, you'll wish you weren't born, because we'll then reverse that. Get out of my sight."

Schmidt slammed his heels togehther smartly and turned araound and vanished from the room as quickly as possible. With a sardonic smile, Milch threw the file down. Sometimes giving an employee the axe was, like the French say - pour la encourager les autres - an effective way of ensuring excellence. Smart people those Frenchies.

He reached for the phone to call the OKH personnel office. He needed a replacement for Schmidt, and he already knew whom he wanted.

June 22nd, 1940 London, Admiralty

He sat behind his desk, literally surrounded by a

mountain of paper.

It was not even clear what kind of hint he was looking for, and several of the documents were in French, which slowed him down to some extent.

Of course, there were enough aerial photographs, showing troop concentrations and newly occupied airfields, but that was to be expected and in itself no indication of a planned invasion.

And his sources from Holland weren`t delivering any more.

Newport began to walk back and forth in his office. Was there any indirect evidence that could take him further?

Life jackets?

How could he use the French sources for this, what could they know that would be invasion-specific?

He should have a meeting with Army, Navy and RAF people, maybe they had some ideas.

He picked up the phone and called a friend at the Admiralty.

June 23rd, 1940, at Ypres

Colonel Wartmann had been to this place 22 years before. At that time living in the mud and in endless trenches. The area was covered then with shell craters and dead bodies.

None of that could be seen anymore.

He watched skeptically as his men marked the provisional airfield. They had been assigned two Ju 52s that were about to show up in a moment.

So, they could at least practice fast deplaning and movement thereafter to secure the area.

He would have liked to have had many more planes. Two aircraft wasn`t very realistic.

It was good that he at least had a free hand as far as the equipment of his troops was concerned. He had equipped the two ammunition carriers of each machinegun squad with submachineguns instead of rifles. They had learned to appreciate the firepower of the MP 40 in the last two months. In addition, he had assigned three additional machinegun troops to each company.

Then he was finally able to do something about resupply. Eliminate all the inessentials, but ammunition as much as possible and one-time rations for four days.

That was the requirement set by staff, and he hoped that resupply would come through by the time that initial load had been used up.

He had learned the storm troop method from General Hutier, who had been a good teacher. And tomorrow the obstacle course would be finished. Then the sifting began. He would only take the fittest. His people would curse, but he had always been a fan of Suworow - easy training, hard war and vice versa.

June 27th, 1940, Berlin

He wondered how they had found him.
Albert Berkow had lived near Folkestone for
several years, with his beloved wife Maggie.
But Maggie had died 5 years ago and since it was
clear to him that he would always be considered a
foreigner by the townspeople, he had sold the
house, left England and moved back to Hamburg.
His captain's pension was big enough to afford it.
He was now 67, but his memory was still first class,
and he had always been proficient with maps.
The staff officers were very excited about his
knowledge.
The many strolls with Maggie over the Kentish
downs had left him with a very vivid memory of the
meadows and farms there.
They hadn't said it clearly, but he had quickly
realized, that they were looking for possible
airstrips.
He thought of the year 1919, when he had been
Second Officer of the battlecruiser *SMS
Hindenburg*, and they had sunk the magnificent
ship into the mud of Scapa Flow, so that it did not
fall into the hands of the English. He wouldn't mind

if the Tommies lost this time.

He would help the good German cause in any way he could.

And the best of it was, the most suitable place lay on the grounds of that old Wilcox, a German-hater and firebrand who had always behaved abominable when he met him in the pub. Praise the lord, there is justice, he thought when he left the impressive RLM building.

June 28th, 1940, Vichy

Secret Additional Protocol to the Compiegne Armistice Agreement of June 25, 1940

....

3. The German government agrees to release all French prisoners of war by 31.12.1940 at the latest in four equal release groups on 1.10., 1.11., 1.12. and 31.12.1940.

4. The French government is obliged in return to deliver the following military equipment beginning on July 1, 1940:

a) All Dewoitine 520, Bloch 151, 152, 155 and Curtis H 75 fighters located in France and North Africa and the spare parts available for them.

(b) all LeO 450, Bloch 174, Breguet 690 et seq., Martin Maryland, Potez 630 et seq. bombers of the types LeO 450, Bloch 174, Breguet 690 et seq., located in France and North Africa and the spare parts available for them.

(c) all transport aircraft located in France and North Africa and the spare parts available for such aircraft.

d) All tanks of the types Somua 35, AMC 35, Panhard AMD 178, Hotchkiss H 35 and H 39, Char B 1, Renault R 35 and the spare parts available for them.

(e) all anti-aircraft guns up to a calibre of 100 mm and spare parts and ammunition and their respective tractors.

(f) All anti-tank guns up to a calibre of 100 mm and spare parts, ammunition and their tractors.

(g) All artillery pieces from 100 mm calibre, spare parts, ammunition and associated tractors. All mortars with their ammunition, regardless of calibre.

(h) A number of inland waterway and coastal vessels and boats to be specified.

(i) All available sea mines.

5. The items described under paragraph 4 shall be handed over to the German Wehrmacht at the following places in a fully serviceable and refuelled condition or shall be taken over by the German Wehrmacht together with the following depots:

......

Vichy, 28 June 1940

signed: Laval, von Witzleben.

June 28th, 1940, Above the Brussels airport
Keller was sweating. The force to control the overloaded Ju 52 on the manual steering was enormous. A crazy idea to transport a dismantled 8.8 cm AA gun. One could transport this 5-ton colossus only if you reduced the fuel load by half, in order to get the Ju in the air at all. This artillery major and his men had worked hard. Keller thought the artillery major was a piece of shit but was still impressed by the man's enthusiasm. He laid the Ju in a left turn for a new approach. They were practicing takeoff and landing and quick unloading and assembling of the mighty cannon. That still took 2 hours. Since they used the Wolf ramp, it was at least easier to get the parts in and out of the plane. He could only hope that the RAF bombers would give them the time needed. How could he be so stupid as to volunteer for such a task?
Maybe it would go better if they limited the fuel load to the absolute minimum they needed for the return flight. Kent, it could only be Kent, even if nobody said anything. So fuel for 100 kilometres, maximum 150 kilometres counting the reserve. Therefore, they would be able to take off with a another 1000 litres less and accordingly much less

weight. That could make quite a difference. He would have to talk to the Wingco once again.

June 28th, 1940, St Omer, Northern France

The concrete runway of the St. Omer airfield flickered before Berger's eyes in the heat of the midday June sun.

The Gnome Rhone engines of the Breguet sounded a bit awkward and hoarse during the run up but stabilized after a few seconds.

Berger had taped a note next to the throttle with an arrow forward, to remember that he had to push the throttle and not pull, as with German machines. If you pull, you don't take off.

Major Berger waved to Mueller in the second machine and then gave him the starting signal with his thumb raised.

The German crosses on the fuselage still looked completely new.

At the end of May he had been ordered to Saarbrücken-Ensheim, together with about 40 other French-speaking air force officers. Their order was to prepare the takeover of French aircraft, in particular Bre 693, Dewoitine 520, and LeO 45 bombers. He still wondered today about the enormous self-confidence of the bureaucracy and their unusual degree of foresight, since on this day the battle for France had been won, but by no means ended.

Now, after almost four weeks of hard work, the time had come. He and his men had managed to make the first group of 18 Breguet 693 dive bombers combat ready.

With a little threatening and a lot of bribery, they had managed to persuade some mechanics of the French ground personnel of the Armee de l`Air to continue working for them.

The Breguet 693 was a much better dive bomber than the Ju 87 that Berger had previously flown above all it had the same range, was almost as fast as modern fighters, and was much more agile than the modern Ju 88.

The French had used the plane rather conventionally and with little success as a horizontal bomber or as a low-attack aircraft, but Berger and his colleagues had found out very quickly that the plane could also perform 70° dives and was almost as accurate as the Ju 87, which from the pilots' point of view was actually only flying junk, as they had little chance of survival even against the lesser French fighters such as the Morane 406.

It had not been easy for him to warm up in such a short time with a new aircraft, but he had quickly learned to appreciate the small and fast Breguet, which, well flown, could almost take on a fighter.

His gunner was the Private Menzel.

"Gunner, all right?"

"Sure," Menzel's Franconian dialect came over the on-board speakers.

After a short period of braking, Berger pushed full throttle as the white flare ball rose to signal launch clearance.

The English had stationed a large group of cruisers outside Stuka range in Hull. They would experience a surprise today. Each of the aircraft carried in its bomb bay an armour-piercing 500 kilo bomb equipped with a special ship catching.

June 28th, 1940, Berlin

Terstegen could not clearly recognize whether Milch, who as always came into his office without knocking, was in a good or bad mood.

He looked at him questioningly.

"The Russians have invaded Bessarabia. Now they are only 80 km away from the Romanian oil wells of Ploesti. That changes the rules of the game!"

Since Terstegen was very familiar with the army's precarious supply of oil and gasoline, it took him only a few seconds to grasp the possible alternatives.

"So, either very fast or not at all against England. Against the Russians we must fight anyway in the foreseeable future. Then better get rid of the English cancer now, before it gets too big with the Empire's resources."

Mich grinned: "Bravo General, it took Halder half an hour this morning to come to this conclusion. The Führer was almost as fast as you were, and he agrees with you. But he has ordered OKH to start now with a massive troop reorientation to the east."

"Absolutely right, we won't need the mass of the army against the English at all, as long as we make the first 37 kilometres."

"Yes, Terstegen, the first 37 kilometres are the big problem, but with your help and God's, we can do it."

Terstegen was able to hide a laugh. To be compared to God by Milch was better than a marshal's baton.

"May I bring the General up to date now?"

Milch nodded, he seemed as impatient as usual.

"From the Italians we get 70 Pipistrello transport planes that ..."

Milch, who knew the Italian equivalent of the Ju 52, said only "Pray for them, they would be helpful, but don't rely on it, go on."

"I have asked Major Tresckow to think about camouflaging the operation. He says, "In a nutshell, we're not going to have strategic surprise. The reason is that every church warden in southern England is already on stanby at the belltower to ring out the invasion. What is feasible is tactical surprise as far as the landing site is concerned. But he hopes that the English will overestimate our possibilities in the current confusion. He has also developed some suggestions for deception."

"Tresckow, I do not know him. How good is he?"

"First Class, General, he is currently working for Manstein!"

"Then requisition him for our staff, I want to hear his proposals as soon as possible myself!"

"General Halder thinks he's a future candidate for the head of the General Staff, he won't give him up!"

Milch grinned, "Terstegen, we have carte blanche from the top, just do it! Who is Halder? Fortunately, we don't have to deal with such retards for once! But we need Manstein, so go through the petty official channels and borrow him, temporarily."

Milch, who had raised the German Lufthansa out of bankruptcy and within a few years to a wor enterprise with worldwide status, did not even know how to write concern, thought Terstegen.

Milch was halfway gone, when he remembered something:

"Oh Terstegen, one of your prodigies, Lieutenant Wolf, more than halved the unloading time of the Ju 52 with a ramp he constructed and he also improvised an antitank gun tractor consisting of two motorbikes. Ingenious this man. Make him captain, decorate him with something nice around his neck, and instruct him to immediately introduce his solution to the other air transport units. Keep going!"

June 29th, 1940, Rome
Secret agreement between Italy and Germany, excerpt:

... Germany supports Italian sovereignty over North Africa, Egypt, Sudan and Palestine. Control of the Suez Canal will also be assured to a future Italian protectorate.

...

To support its Italian brothers in arms the German government sends three divisions, two of them armoured, to Libya, where they will fight under Italian supreme command. The commander of this German corps is General Günter Kluge. The troops are due to arrive in Tripolitania in October 1940.

...

Italy supports the fight of the German Reich against England. It sends troops for this purpose:
a. Five batteries of heavy artillery allocated to Calais, time of arrival July 15, 1940.
b. 70 transport planes SM 81 to Northern France, time of arrival July 10, 1940.

c. 12 MAS E-boats, time of arrival July 18, 1940 in Saint Nazaire.

d. A battleship (*Littorio*), four light cruisers and ten destroyers as fleet in being to Saint Nazaire, France. Time of arrival August 15, 1940.

The units mentioned under items a, b and c are under German supreme command. All units are supplied with food and fuel by the German Army, the Luftwaffe and the Kriegsmarine.

.....

Rome, 29 June 1940
signed: Ciano, Ribbentrop

June 30th, 1940, Berlin

"Good news sir, the Navy reports that it has finally solved the problem with its torpedoes."

"Well, about time, Terstegen. What do you think of Kesselring's suggestion to take the ME 110 fighters out of the bomber escort role and use them mainly as fighter bombers in low-level flight?"

"This was already suggested by some pilots after the Polish campaign, but always blocked by Marshal Göring. What was not thinkable, wasn´t possible. I also think that this solution is better. For the destroyers it is much easier to destroy a Spitfire on their airfield than to shoot it down in air combat. This nominally reduces the number of available fighters, but airplanes that aren't able to hold their own against Hurricanes and Spitfires wouldn't have helped us anyway."

Mich nodded, "And on the other hand we strengthen the attacking units, I can live with that. How far along are the preparations for Operation Walhalla?"

"Everything is running on schedule, the logistics preparations for the transfer of the squadrons involved are almost complete, in a week's time we will be relocating the first planes and start replacing them with dummies at the current airfields in France.

The Navy has also done its job, 32 freighters are already assembled in Rostock, more will follow. Submarines and E-Boats are currently being collected in the North Sea ports and prepared for departure. We have the green light from the Führer's headquarters to deploy all surface units. On the intelligence side, the preparations have been made, the selected agents are just waiting for information to leak out."

"Very nice, I think I should take a vacation," said Milch laughing.

"Well, General, we've had worse times." Terstegen grinned now broadly.

"What are the Royal Navy and RAF doing? "

"We have all important ports observed daily by our high altitude reconnaissance aircraft, as well as a sporadic look at airfields in the South and Central England. The RN has three battle groups in Scapa, Hull and Plymouth, but at the moment they are hardly moving out of the harbours and therefore not accessible for Stukas and torpedo bombers. We tried Hull with captured ex French Breguet 693 but with mixed results. The Stuka units are still out of the fight for the next two weeks, we don't need them until Walhalla goes on stage."

"I see you have everything under control. By the way, congratulations, Lieutenant General Terstegen, with immediate effect you have been promoted!"

Now Terstegen, too, was amazed, after only two years as colonel, that was an enormous ascent.

He shook Milch`s outstretched hand, then saluted smartly.

Fact

After 29th of June 1940, the Admiralty prohibited the daytime use of destroyers in the Channel. Dover was also abandoned as a destroyer station. The losses caused by the Stuka`s had been too severe in the weeks before.

July 1st, 1940, near St. Omer

Major Winkler had plundered the Baron's wine cellar. With glassy eyes he, Steinmann, and Lieutenant Jeske sat in the armchairs of the salon. The large manor house had been accommodating the pilots of StG 2 for several days. The previous owner had left France a few days ago for North Africa. They drank his excellent red wine, a Chateau Lafitte from 1933, in silence and full of respect.

"I gave the Baron, God bless his soul, a receipt, with best regards from the German Air Force", Winkler laughed with a resounding voice, "Everything must be in order, mustn't it?

Lieutenant Jeske ran his hand through his pomaded hair.

"These French plutocrats are not badly off, I think I would like to be a baron," he said, without looking at anyone.

There was a certain lethargy in the air. Lieutenant Steinmann had been unapproachable for days, because the group was still banned from any operations and only interrupted his enduring silence sometimes with a monotonous "Shit, they have no idea how to win a war," without specifying exactly whom he meant.

But Winkler thought of his wife and his two children, whom he had not seen for two months. The twins had certainly grown quite a bit in the menatime. His wife was angry, because he had so rarely visited, but that didn't bother him further. He didn't have much need to talk to her anyway, but of course he couldn't divorce her, that was impossible as an officer and even more so because of the children. A few months ago, after he had made a suggestion in the casino, the group commander had almost torn off his head. Divorce would be unworthy of a German officer, the usual balderdash. The group commander was not even a Christian, but a dashing and devout Nazi. Winkler was angry, but then he grinned to himself and made a toast: "To our great generals and leaders, gentlemen, and to the Party, which always knows what is right, cheers". After another 3 bottles they lay snoring in their armchairs, only Jeske knelt beside the armchair and had his head on it, to prevent himself from getting too dizzy.

Fact
Strength of the RAF Fighter command, 1ˢᵗ of July 1940

Typ	Planes	Ready to fly
Hurricane (single-engine)	463	347
Spitfire (single-engine)	286	160

| Defiant (single-engine) | 37 | 25 |
| Blenheim (two-engined) | 114 | 59 |

Len Deighton: Luftschlacht über England, 1982:131

July 1st, 1940, Stavanger Sola, Southern Norway, KG 30, Air Fleet 5

"I don't want this navy shit anymore. The detonator mechanism doesn't work. 2 weeks ago, I hit a cruiser, and nothing happened. I insist, General, that we only use the torpedoes with impact detonators."

"Now calm down, my dear Lindemann. The T-Office has assured us that the proximity fuse works perfectly and..."

"The T-Office is not in my plane. The T-Office wasn't in Gerken's plane either, when he was shot down by the destroyer he had just sunk with the T-Office Torpedo. But the English didn't notice it. I flew only a few meters behind Gerken, Herr General. That was a hit, exactly amidships, and nothing happened."

"All right Lindemann. Make a report about the Gerken affair. I will talk to the GFM. I understand that the Navy has set up a commission to solve the problem and they seem to have a solution, but I do not have precise information."

"Thank you, General."

"Dismissed .... and - Lindemann - initially no fuss over the torpedo. You simply fly the next missions as a battle test of the old airdrop torpedoes."

"I understand, General."

"Too late for Gerken," Hans Lindemann thought, "but maybe not too late for us." The sun dazzled him as he stepped out of the flight control shed at Stavanger Sola. He automatically put on his sunglasses and got into his Mercedes to drive to the armoury.

Three hours later, at 3:10 p.m., the 18 Heinkels of his squadron started. Each carried two air torpedoes with impact fuses under the fuselage. In low flight, only five meters above the waves, they flew on a course of 240 degrees. The sun was still powerful, but at a cruising speed of 380 km/h it didn't get very warm in the planes. Lindemann had ordered radio silence. He ordered his gunners to check their machine guns.

A sea reconnaissance aircraft had observed a Royal Navy group leaving the Firth of Forth in the morning. As a result, they had immediately received clearance to attack from Berlin, because of the warships.

Four cruisers and 6 destroyers on a southern course

were reported. Lindemann was waiting for new target information from the second long-range reconnaissance aircraft. Immediately after the sighting report they had sent a Ju 86 high altitude reconnaissance aircraft from Bergen.

"Mainzer, take the wheel for a while."

He felt the pressure from Mainzer's hands at the wheel and leaned back. You shouldn't perform low level flying when you're already 33. The plane flew quietly above the water and Sergeant Lüders, the ventral gunner, constantly observed whether wake towing occurred when they flew too low. The sea was very calm. Unusually smooth for the North Sea even in August. In one week they would move to Gilze-Rijen in Holland. Also, good. Meisjes and creamy windbags; he was thinking of his belly, against which the meisjes would be better.

The radio operator gave him a note.

"Anton 24's radio message", that was the long-range reconnaissance aircraft:

"10 warships sighted off Norwich at 4:32 p.m. One City-class cruiser, the rest destroyer. Course 165 degrees, speed 20 knots." He gave the note to Mainzer.

"I'm taking over again, calculate bearing!"

Twenty seconds later he turned to the newly calculated heading. The other machines followed their leader´s aircraft in a long queue.

"About 20 minutes to target," Mainzer announced.

Lindemann nodded and took off his sunglasses. Shortly before the English group would come into sight, with a flate pistol he gave the order to swarm out and separate. One group would attack at an acute angle from the west and the other at the same time from the east. Hopefully all Spitfires were really in southern England. The sun was already very low. They would attack from the sun. Mainzer was the first to see the English ships.

"Full throttle now. Radio operator, order: Attack! The engines howled under full load, Lindemann pushed the Heinkel even lower towards the water. One mistake, one hit and half a second later they would all be gone. Still about 4000 meters to the goal. The English heavy flak fired sporadically, but already too late. Lindemann noticed that two somewhat larger airplanes were circling over the formation and were now turning towards the Heinkels.

"Arm torpedoes!"
Another 2000 meters, about 15 seconds. Mainzer armed the torpedoes. With minimal lateral course corrections, the Heinkel turned on a cruiser with two smokestacks. The light flak started firing. The air was filled with the smoke of the tracer bullets. Lüders shouted, "Günter was hit and went in immediately."
Five men gone. Still about 1000 meters. Lindemann

now had only the cruiser in his field of vision.
" Anti-aircraft hit left surface outside!"
The bow gunner started shooting with his MG FF.
The first course adjustments and an increase in
speed now became evident in the convoy. Much too
late. He pressed the release lever for both torpedoes,
corrected the trim and kept heading directly for the
cruiser. At only about five meters height they flew
over the looming stern of the cruiser. Quite a new
ship. Could be the *Edinburgh*. Some light flak hits
made the engine tremble. Only 10 seconds later and
almost out of range of the flak he pulled the Heinkel
up a bit and then went into a slight right turn. Both
torpedoes hit the cruiser in the forward third of the
ship. Lüders howled with enthusiasm into the on-
board intercom. Passing their Heinkel, the white 10
with the second group of bombers in its wake shot
towards the English formation, which had become
considerably scattered in the meantime. Tactical
control was no longer possible. Everybody had to
look after himself whether he wanted to see home
again.
Lindemann circled araound again at safe distance.
Several ships were on fire. Above the cruiser stood
a tower-high column of smoke. That ship would not
survive the night. A Blenheim tried to lock on
behind Lindemann`s craft, but the Heinkel, now in
light mode without its torpedoes, shook it off after a
few minutes. Between 8.30 pm and 9.10 pm 14

planes landed in Stavanger, another one performed a crash-landing on the Norwegian coast.

Lindemann and his crew went to pee on the tail wheel after the landing, glad that they had made it. The strong flak of the English had been impressive. Maybe it would be a good idea to have at least 2 Me 110 per ship to suppress the flak. The firepower of the Me 110 with its strong armament of 2 cannons and 4 MG`s was impressive and could certainly do something against the weakly protected British AA guns. Most of the time the English hadn't provided the light AA guns with protective shields. And the range of the 110 was sufficient. Since it was not clear to the English that the Me did not carry a torpedo, they would nonetheless need to initiate evasive manoeuvres, which made them slower and their course more predictable for the torpedo carriers.

Always good, forcing the enemy to react. He would have to talk to the general.

Fact
The superiority of airplanes over warships had already been demonstrated by General Mitchell's experiments in 1920/21. The sinking of HMS Repulse and HMS Prince of Wales off Malaya, the

success of the German Luftwaffe in the battles for Crete, are only two examples from the early years of the war. The Stuka`s and bombers, which sank 3 cruisers and 8 destroyers in the waters around Crete in a short time and damaged a large number of warships, are practically the same airplanes and crews, which had been stationed 9 months before in Northern France. Moreover, there were many more of them at that time and the English shipborne AA gunnery was not so strong yet. In the campaign around Crete the Luftwaffe possessed around 150 Ju 87 Stukas and 280 Bombers.
In northern France, in July 1940 316 Ju 87 and 299 Ju 88 were available. In addition, the He 111 bombers were able to fly torpedo attacks.
The difference to Crete and Malaya is, howeve,r in the possibility of the RAF to sprovide fighter protection over the Channel. A fighter protection, which however, was opposed by 850 Me 109 fighters. A lot of what ifs.

July 1st, 1940, London

Churchill sat on the couch in his bathrobe, nursing his thick cigar.
Winslow had already provided him with a whisky and was now waiting for his decision.

"I have already understood, Winslow, the aerial photos are also conclusive. Have the order issued to Bomber Command to focus on the large collection of ships and ferry boats in the northern French port. This nonsense about the strategic bombing of the Ruhr area, which in many cases they do not find at all. I have even heard that some of our bombers have flown to Denmark, that must finally stop. Maybe we will start killing kraut workers later when we have learned how to find them, but for now we have new priorities. The best thing is to talk to Portal!"

"It will be done immediately, Prime Minister. General Alan-Brook is waiting outside and is asking for an interview with you, can I call him?

Churchill grumbled: "As an old man you don't even have time to dress properly here. All right, let him come in."

July 2nd, 1940, Hull

Captain Parker was annoyed at his wife, he had not had even a slight chance to interrupt her for half an hour now.

It was of no interest to him, what was to be done with the Daimler. Since there was almost no petrol available for private purposes, they had decided to shut down the car anyway.

His wife had found a workshop where she could park the car and had been agitated for exactly 37 minutes - he had as always inconspicuously looked at his watch - that the owner of the workshop demanded so much money for parking it.

"Darling, would you excuse me, please?" he interrupted her in the middle of the sentence, "I have to get to the ship."

"Again, you just arrived this morning!"

Concerned, she remained silent for a moment. Silently she asked: "When will you leave again?"

He gave her an unfriendly look, because she wasn't supposed to ask and should not know anything about that.

And he didn't know either. The gods of the Admiralty had ordered him to get the *Manchester* ready to leave harbour as quickly as possible and above all to stock her with additional anti-aircraft ammunition. They worried the same as he did. Otherwise everyone waited to see whether the Germans would actually try to land. And then it would become unbelievably constricted and dangerous in the Channel. He had read the reports about the ship losses during the evacuation of Dunkirk. Stuka`s had sunk almost a dozen destroyers without great loss to themselves. Since *Manchester* and the other cruisers had not been deployed there, because they feared too heavy losses in that cramped and shallow area, there had been no capital-ship losses.

What if there was no choice in the event of an invasion? Stuka`s made him nervous. And the torpedo pilots and the submarines of the Germans had particularly targeted the cruisers of the Navy. *HMS Norfolk* and *HMS Enterprise* had been sunk in the last two weeks. Parker had lost good friends on both ships.

He contemplatively touched his now completely grey hair. He was just 38 years old.

Fact
During the daylight attacks of 14. and 18.12.39 on German warships on Schilling Reede near Wilhelmshaven, RAF Bomber Command had losses of 62%. The British aviation ministry then prohibited all further daylight operations with Whitley, Hampden, and Wellington bombers (the strongest and most numerous aircraft of Bomber Command). The causes of this high loss rate were the German experiments with prototype radar in this area, and the equipping of the German fighters with 2 cm cannons with greater effective range and effect than the 0.303-inch rifle calibre machine-guns of the British gunners.

Beginning in June 1940 the Germans had installed a Freya radar system at Wissant.

As Bomber Command would discover in the next months, the navigation aids available at that time were not suitable to find the target at night even by a wide margin. On 19 March 1940 Hörnum on Sylt in the North Sea was to be attacked. Later it was discovered that the target had not been hit. One pilot had even managed to bomb the Danish island of Bornholm, 400 kilometres further east in the Baltic Sea.

In order to be able to attack effectively, Bomber Command was therefore dependent on daylight. Over the Channel and the French coast, however the bombers were within the range of the German day fighters, who had no range problems in this region. Apart from that, the German fighters in July 1940 were numerically stronger than the English, and their cannon armament was, as already had been shown in December 1939 off Wilhelmshaven, much better suited for shooting down bombers than the rifle calibre machineguns of the RAF Spitfire and Hurricane fighters.

July 2nd, 1940, Belfast, Northern Ireland

He would never forget Sean's eyes. It had been three Black and Tans. They had arrested Sean and taken him to an empty farmhouse. They had hit him, burned his skin with glowing cigarettes, sodomized him, and finally drowned him in a bucket of water like a filthy cat. Lochlin had found him the day after. Sean had been a little boy, 14 years old, his brother. Twenty years now he had lived with hatred for all Englishmen. He had killed several. But that was not enough. He would hit the English now, and grievously. Churchill would surely come to the funeral of his old friend Professor Lindemann. And his German friends had provided him with the necessary weapons. Tomorrow he would travel to Dublin and then take the ferry to England.

July 2nd, 1940 Above the Channel near Dunkirk
Flying low between Liane's breasts and over the dark tanned smooth plain to the magic jungle. Much too poetic, Lieutenant Bergmann, he thought.
Most certainly there are distinct similarities between airplanes and women. Younger means better curved, smooth and more beautiful, the more beautiful and racier the more dangerous. He had never understood how the French in the 1930's had

been able to build such abysmally ugly planes.

His 109 wasn't exactly a beauty either, she was called Bump by the attendants. Liane was much prettier. She gave the word of God, who lives in France, the necessary splendour. Cardinal Richelieu is said to have enjoyed himself in the four-poster bed of the castle. Hopefully not the same mattress.

"Bergmann watch out ... break left."

He pulled his Me down and to the left into a curve. A frustrated Spitfire was surprised by the violent flight movement and passed Bergmann, still firing. Only with difficulty, Bergmann managed to turn left onto the Spitfire. He reduced the curve radius of his Me with five degrees flap position.

The Spitfire tried to curve even tighter, but Bergmann increased the flap position to 10 degrees, which made his plane vibrate, but also enabled him to fire a 2 second burst from an ideal shooting position.

The Spitfire was hit in engine and cabin. A white glycol trail came out of the engine, the canopy was pushed back, and the English pilot jumped out.

Bergmann philosophized involuntarily about the connection between victory and orgasm with adrenalin-restricted veins, and then went down to sea level with a red fuel-level indicator.

Four minutes later he landed in Denain. Before he could reach the evening and Liane, he had to fly another mission over the Channel to push the

English, who were becoming increasingly curious, away from the ports. He had just lost 2 kilograms of weight. Nevertheless, every operation where you could walk away from your plane was a success.

Fact
July 3, 1940. A British naval task force attacks the French navy in the harbour of Mers el Kebir in North Africa. 1297 French sailors die.
On July 4, 1940, the Vichy government cuts off relations with Great Britain.

July 3rd, 1940, near Brussels

"Lieutenant Mertens, wake up.
Lieutenant, Lieutenant Mertens, please wake up!"
The GvD, the orderly on duty, was relentless, it was cold in the room, 1 o'clock in the morning.
"Lieutenant, wake up, you have to fly."
"Damn, I'm awake."
The lieutenant slowly stood up and pushed his feet over the edge of the bed.
Not a tall man, almost squat. Not necessarily Aryan, but as Mertens often remarked, neither was the

234

Leader.

He put on his watch and then looked at it, 2 minutes after 1 o'clock am.

"You lunatic, why don't you let me sleep?"

The corporal stepped apprehensively from one foot to the other, "They ordered you to wake up at 1 o'clock. Command executed."

"All right, get out, GvD."

The door slammed behind the GvD, a barrack door on this run-down Belgian airfield.

He heard his observer Sergeant Klein wake up three rooms down.

They had been stationed at that airfield for a week. Actually, it was still unbelievable how fast that had gone. On the faces of the Belgians, who one saw in the evening in the city, one recognized a similar surprise, numbness, as one still felt the unrealty of it. They never spoke to you, which made Mertens and his comrades somewhat insecure, but at least Germany had won this war, at least against the Belgians and the French.

Tonight, they would fly against England, alone. The third night in a row. Some wise guy on the staff had probably thought it up. Disruptive attacks in East and South England. Even Jericho sirens, as had previously only mounted on the Ju 87 Stuka`s, had been installed on their Ju 88 in order to increase the entertainment value for the Englishmen, as Klein said.

Theoretically his 88 and the other 5 crews of the group were supposed to keep the English awake and unsettled.

He put on his felt boots - at 6000 meters height it is very cold even in July.

The door opened. Klein, his observer, entered.

A senior sergeant of the old sort, he had previously been in Spain. Mertens knew him from the flying school in Schleißheim, when he himself had been a corporal.

Klein was good, he had shot down 2 Hurricanes over Dunkirk, otherwise they wouldn't be here now.

"Morning, Lieutenant."

"Morning Erwin. Pretty cold this morning."

He set fire to his morning cigarette and then gave Klein the pack.

"What's the weather like?"

"Clear sky as predicted, we can fly in any case", Klein smiled. He knew how reluctantly Mertens got up early.

"What about Wilhelm?"

"I heard him grunting earlier in the bathroom."

Mertens took his little bag: "Let's go."

It was very quiet.

The English had attacked Berlin last night, but they had difficulty finding it, because some bombs had fallen all the way up at Neubrandenburg. Then Major Schröder had made it clear to them once again that they had to navigate particularly well in order to increase their accuracy. They didn't want to make the Luftwaffe the laughingstock of the English press.

This baboon, what did he know what it looked like at night in a bomber when you flew over a darkened country?

They marched silently for 5 minutes across the airfield to the control shack, their operations centre. It was a starry and moonlit night. They would have to watch out for night fighters. They hadn't met one of them yet, but it didn't have to stay that way.

July 4th, 1940, near Ostend

Remington flew second in the formation. The upper gunner was firing with his Vickers K but suddenly fell silent. The impacts of the German 2 cm projectiles sounded like hammer blows. He placed the Blenheim in an abrupt right turn. From the corner of his eye he saw Perkins, his navigator, collapsing. Blood ran out of his mouth. The Blenheim vibrated as he brought it into a shallow dive. The instrument panel in front of him splintered. In the rear-view mirror he saw the German as a weak sickle-like shape with flashing machine-guns behind him. He felt physically how the Blenheim disintegrated. He was now 400 metres high.

He wanted to say "shit", but he couldn't. A bullet had penetrated his neck, but he felt nothing. Blood splashed fountain-like on the instrument panel and cabin glazing. Remington saw the waves of the North Sea approaching. The Blenheim struck, but he didn't feel it. He was sitting at his steering yoke as the Blenheim sank deeper and deeper, and strangely enough it kept flying. It was dark around him, he could no longer see the dashboard, the German in the rear-view mirror was also gone now.

July 6th, 1940, U-37, 25 miles northeast of Hull

You could hear the whirring of those screws in the boat for a long time.

For an unknown reason the English convoy had not left until the late evening, shortly before sunset, so that they were able to keep up with the 15 knots on the surface, hidden in darkness.

Meanwhile they were three miles ahead of the formation, consisting of a County class cruiser and two destroyers.

The water depth was about 50 metres, not as much as Huber would have wished, but still better than in the shallow water area close to the port of Hull, where it was less than 20 metres. There he could not have risked an attack.

The commander whispered, "Up periscope XO," just as if the English could hear his voice.

As he had practiced a thousand times before, he took a quick look around through the periscope, then he began to scall out the target coordinates. If they wanted a chance against the destroyers at that shallow depth, they had to be as far away from the target as possible and force them to expand the search area. So, a long shot, better still a fan. He automatically estimated the angle of attack and his own speed required to reach the optimal position in this three-dimensional game.

At least the torpedoes, which had failed in the Norwegian campaign, worked now. Apparently heads always had to roll before anything worked. At least he hoped that the torpedoes would work now. "Clear on tubes 1 through 4, clear on rear torpedo tubes."

Within seconds the all-clear messages came back. He stayed longer than usual at the periscope, because they had a good chance to remain undiscovered with the low visibility with a distance of 2400 metres.

"Heavy cruiser, county class, lowered quarterdeck, speed 15 knots, bearing 130 degrees, heading north, distance 2450 metres constant." Unconsciously he almost heard how the helmsman entered the new values in the forward control calculator.

"Firing solution is calculated, ready to fire," came from the helmsman.

Huber took a deep breath: "Fire 1, fire 2, fire 3, fire 4." He felt the boat, now almost 8 tons lighter in front, rising slightly, but the XO immediately compensated with the front trim cell.

"New course 35 degrees, go to 7 knots, maintain periscope depth," He briefly retracted the periscope while the helmsman announced the time needed for their fish strike.

The message "Enemy increases screw speed," came from the listening room at 15 seconds.

Huber raised the periscope again and turned around to adjust for the boats new direction away from target. The impact of the first torpedo, at the location of the first 20.3 cm turret, was good to see and clearly felt. A few seconds later the second torpedo slammed into the cruiser at engine room location. He had the impression that the hull of the cruiser rose slightly out of the water during the explosion of the torpedo, and broke. That would be enough for this lightly built, almost unarmoured ship.

Almost immediately the two destroyers increased speed and turned with an enormous bow wave towards the submarine. Even from a distance of almost three kilometres it was a terrifying sight.

"Clear at stern tubes."

Huber was now calmness itself. With unhgurried

deliberation he provided the necessary data to the XO, who entered it into the calculator. When the firing solution was calculated, he gave the order to fire. The two destroyers were now 1500 meters away.

"Full speed ahead, new course 70 degrees, go to 45 meters" he said, and pray that we have enough juice in the batteries for what is coming now, he continued thinking quietly.

When the depth of 45 metres was reached, he gave the order to crawl and go on a parallel opposite course to the destroyers.

They could already hear the destroyers clearly in the boat.

Everyone waited apprehensively for the depth charges, when there was a torpedo explosion, which was drowned out seconds later by another, much stronger explosion. Then you could hear the breaking of metal

"That was the ammunition chamber," whispered the XO,

Huber turned around to Gerbert, the acoustics mate, who strained to tune his device.

"What's the matter, Gerbert?"

"The second destroyer breaks off sir!"

Huber closed his eyes and, strangely enough, thanked God in whom he hadn´t believed in for a long time now.

Two hours later they surfaced on an empty sea and were ordered to proceed to Wilhelmshaven as soon as possible.

July 6th, 1940, Rotterdam

He could sleep standing in place.

The Siebel ferry, the first experimental type to be built, hit the quay wall with a rumble when he put in a little too much throttle. Chief Petty Officer Kröger, the captain of the number 1 Siebel ferry, wiped the sweat off his forehead. He grinned at his buddy at the rudder.

"Gee Hein, I'm glad we're finally here. Last night I thought we were going to be herring fodder when that shitty Tommy bomber hit the water next to us."

"Yeah. Let's get off this self-drowning junk, man, see what kind of girls there are here". Hein Paulsen switched off the diesel supply to the engine. The small diesel turned over a few more times and then remained silent.

Kröger ordered: "All hands on deck!"

With black, soot-smeared faces the two engine petty officers came up, and the gun crew of the 2cm Flak pulled a tarpaulin over their cannon. Lürsen came from the foredeck and signalled, "Everything fixed."

"Good men, shore leave until tomorrow morning till wake up, and watch out for the Genever, that's nasty stuff, the same as Gin. Let`s go."

Kröger was the last to cross the plank. He looked over his shoulder again at his ship. Makes nearly 10 knots, on a good day, hopefully nobody will get the idea to send us to England with this thing. Kröger, who had a captain's license for the Baltic Sea in civilian life, had been a sailor for 30 years. He had drunk and fought with enough English sailors to take them seriously.

Next to him a Citroen with Lieutenant Commander Ebert, who was in charge of the flotilla, stopped.

"Moin Kröger, did everything work out?"

"Sure, sir, slowly but steadily."

"Well, then pack your gear, I have a special order for you."

Kröger was astonished at first and took off his cap to scratch his head.

"What's up?"

"You leave immediately, have to be in Rostock tomorrow evening, and take over a freighter there, only for a short time, then you get your Siebel ferry back. It's a sort of suicide mission, by the way, but I volunteered you for it."

"Well then, thank you very much sir, I don't suppose I'll be asked anymore."

"You are absolutely right, my dear Kröger. Here are your papers, I`ll wait until you have packed and

then take you to the station."
Kröger just nodded and went to get his belongings.
He had long since found out that there was no point
in debating with the navy.

July 7th, 1940, near Calais, Heavy Artillery Unit 13

The effort was enormous. Only with the help of the
Todt Organization and the workforce of an entire
infantry division had they been able achieve it.
Colonel Altmann looked up at the flattened clay
wall, which still overtopped his head by almost one
meter. That old Trettwitz was quite a fox. At his
command they had buried the pits for the 15.5 and
the 17-centimetre cannons so deep that only a direct
hit could destroy them. The camouflage net above
his head didn't let too much sun through, but he still
sweated.

They hadn't equipped the position yet. The guns
would only come at the last moment, which would
considerably reduce the chances of the English
bombers. He smiled: They had spread the word that
foundations for defensive bunkers would be
excavated here, and had even ordered large volumes
of concrete from some local companies, with a
delivery date at the end of September. The

accountants at the French suppliers would have to cancel a lot of hires.

"And deepen the ammunition supply tunnels even further, that won't help much against 40 centimetre hits, but it'll keep your people qccupied. And make sure that at least one reserve water pump is available in every battery." He thought of his father, who had fought in the first war not far from here, near Ypres. The memory of the tales of mud and rain and death made him sick to this day.

"Yes, Colonel."

Only the too-small number of available heavy cannons worried him. But perhaps there was some truth to the rumour that they would get a lot of heavy artillery pieces from French arsenals. In any case, he would exchange two K 18`s for one GPF at any time. No matter what was said about the French, their red wine and their heavy cannons were first class.

However, they would have to take additional experienced gunners out of the artillery training units. But since he planned a central fire control, so that all guns of a large battery fired at one target, it would also be possible to work with not-yet-fully trained gunners.

"And remember to bury the permanent cable to the fire control unit at least one metre deep!"

The prompt confirmation of his subordinate was for him again and again a satisfaction. The only thing even better would be being a general himself.

July 7th, 1940, Ramsgate

He woke up knowing the alarm was about to ring. He switched it off with one swift wipe. Sally lay snuggled up to him and breathed calmly and evenly. He got up slowly so as not to wake her. It was still dark outside. With quick movements he washed himself and dressed. Only the oily smell of his Clyde sweater made it clear to him that the nightmare of the day would now begin again. He went into the nursery to take another look at the twins. It was raining as he pulled the door shut and locked it. In less than two minutes he was at the Seaside Hotel, where the flotilla staff was housed. The yeoman of the guard greeted him.
"Morning, sir, would you like a cup of tea?"
"Yes, please Kenley, with milk. Fetch me a sandwich please."
"Sure, sir, I'll have it done." Kenley put the Admiralty's telexes in front of him, all those that had arrived that night and who concerned him. Through the window came the first glimmer of the day. Slowly he began to see the contours of his boats, the 4th Motor Gunboat Flotilla, under the command of Captain John Hurst. He was proud of

his command, but quite desperate about how little he could do against the Germans at the moment. On the boats he could see sailors already manning the anti-aircraft weapons in the first dim light. Good.

Mechanically he bit into the sandwich that the orderly had brought, and cursed quietly as he read in the Admiralty's first letter that he should turn two good lieutenants over to other ships. How could he wage war if his best people were constantly assigned elsewhere? He felt his stomach cramping. Like his father, he was worried about his stomach. These cramps were a real family heirloom. Sometimes he even spat blood. Sally hadn't remarked that he had lost much weight yet, but he knew he had lost 14 pounds since March, when they were in Ramsgate.

July 8th, 1940, The Hague Holland

The major was proud of his men.

In the last three weeks they had managed to recover over 200 of the Ju 52`s shot down over Holland. With these parts they were able to make 55 planes airworthy again.

Unfortunately, Dutch AA guns and fighters had been pretty successful in the few days they had fought.

Especially, the AA guns had plucked off the extremely slow-flying Ju 52 droppinh the paratrooper at low altitude. And nobody had done anything against the AA guns!

During these weeks the major had seen too many crash spots with impact fire and charred remains of corpses; he did not sleep well. Actually, he was from the technical troops and normally never had had anything to do with the real fighting. Nevertheless, he made sure that the remains of the crews had been recovered and buried with military honours. He had refused to allow anyone to excuse him from lending a hand himself, but now he found he was constantly washing his hands. Maybe Genever would help against it, they had plenty of that.

Now for the report he still owed Terstegen, whom he knew from the air war school.

Perhaps he should say a few words about the Ju 52's vulnerability to anti-aircraft guns. These planes were so slow that you could almost run alongside one, a good anti-aircraft crew could hardly miss. It would be a splendid idea if someone could take care of the AA guns during the approach.

Yes, he could get Terstegen to endorse these ideas!

July 8th, 1940, Alencon airfield

They built planes out of wood, canvas, paint and nails. Soon they were so good that at a distance of about 30 metres it was impossible to tell which was the real He 111 and which only looked like it. As machine guns they had used black painted broomsticks.

Then they had had their own reconnaissance aircraft fly over the airfield and take photos of the field, with the satisfying result that even the best analysts could not tell the difference between real planes and deceptions.

For days several Heinkels had been flown into the hinterland every morning, being replaced with dummies which were pushed into the sandbag-reinforced shelters. At night the aircraft were often rearranged so that the airfield always offered a varying picture from above.

The men from the technical section didn't know why the real Heinkels were replaced by dummies, but the grin and wink of their supervising Officer had been enough to make them realize that a lot of fooling the enemy was going on here. It was also a greater pleasure to build dummies than to service engines smeared with oil.

Gradually most of the mechanics had been flown out on Ju 52 transporters without anyone saying a word about where they were going, and they hadn't come back either.

What the men did not know was, that something similar was happening at the time on all the bomber, destroyer and fighter airfields in northern France.

July 9th, 1940, Rostock harbour

The launch swayed considerably on the choppy waters of the Trave. Kröger ducked under the tarpaulin when a gush of water came over.

The ship in front of them was an older freighter, whose overpainted name - *T. Kosziousko* - was still visible, but on the poop flew the Reichs war flag.

With a little effort Kröger climbed up the slippery ladder.

An older boatswain's mate received him upstairs. "Morn´, Captain. My name is Sven Kruse, I am the XO."

Kröger saluted laxly and then shook Kruse`s hand. "Give me a status report, what's up?"

Kruse pointed with his hand to more than two dozen other freighters, some of which lay in double packs on the Trave.

"They all belong to our group, we are supposed to

leave in a few days, but no exact date is known, and where to we do not know. A briefing for the officers has been announced for tomorrow."

"What about the ship, what cargo do we have?"

"We are, with your arrival, now an 18-man crew, all old merchant navy, the engine is in good working order, fuel oil is, on the instruction of the commanding admiral, half full bunkered. No load so far".

"Does this ship have a name?"

"We are AT 16, whatever that means!"

July 9th, 1940 approx. 80 miles SE from Scapa Flow

The heavy cruiser with its three escort destroyers ran with 18 knots on a south easterly heading.
The North Sea had one of its better days, which Charles Pearson, the captain of HMS Berwick, grimly noted. Good weather helped both the German pilots and the submarines. The airplanes could take off without problems and had best visibility. And the submarines could hear well without being disturbed by the sound of the waves. He hoped that his destroyers were on their guard, at least the lookouts had a good chance to discover a periscope.

He turned to the first officer: "Have the anti-aircraft guns brought up to full combat readiness."
Satisfied, he heard the men running to the AA guns, and after 65 seconds the readiness message came.
"Well done XO. And no sign of the RAF, whoever they are."
He could not know that a submarine, which monitored the access to Scapa Flow, had already sent a message to the Officer Commanding Submarines three hours ago about the course and the speed of its unit.

July 9ᵗʰ, 1940, over the North Sea

This time Lindemann had been successful. The general had provided them with 4 Me 110. They had already trained the pilots of the Me110 for a week on where the large English warships had positioned their anti-aircraft gunships. The whole course went together with about 40 hours low-flying training on sea level.
Lindemann was highly satisfied with his men. As usual, he left Mainzer to steer the approach and checked the position continuously. Within the next ten minutes the English had to come into sight. He only fervently hoped that the cruiser reported by the U-boat had no air cover. Spitfires could really spoil

your day.

He clicked on the on-board intercom: "Radio operator, report to the squadron, arm torpedoes, estimated arrival in about 5 minutes! Group 2 deploy as planned."

Satisfied, he could see the second group moving to the right, led by 2 of the Me 110 destroyers. He was eager to see how the English would react to the new hammer and anvil tactics they were using.

He touched Mainzer, "I'll take over."

Were there columns of smoke to be seen?

Then came the message from one of the Me110: "Enemy in sight, four ships."

Lindemann felt the usual pulling in the stomach area, but he was not distracted.

"All hands, attack to plan 2."

Resolutely he pushed the throttles fully forward. He was pleased to see the two Me 110s moving away with their significantly higher speed. They had clear indications to take care of the biggest ship. He could already recognize the cruiser clearly, County class, 3 chimneys, large airplane hangar, as already the first explosive clouds of the heavy flak before them burst in black puffs. He began to move the Heinkel back and forth with slight shearing movements to make it heavier for the Flak to pinpoint him.

Almost four thousand meters left. He could see that the two Me 110 destroyers reacted with violent flight movements to the light flak.

Now they would find out whether his idea worked.

July 9th, 1940, approx. 90 miles SE Scapa Flow
Captain Pearson cursed, the heavy anti-aircraft gun
had reacted damn late, the German torpedo pilots
were almost within reach of the light anti-aircraft
guns. Now it would turn out whether the new
quadruple PomPom would prove itself. "Did you
request fighter protection CO?"

"Yes sir, but it'll take at least twenty minutes for
them to reach our position!"

"Much too late as usual."

Then everything suddenly went very slowly, he felt
the Berwick incline strongly as the helmsman
initiated the commanded course change, and he saw
the two foremost attackers opening fire. But they
weren't bombers. What were Me 110 doing with the
torpedo pilots?

Suddenly he heard the screams of the PomPom
operator, who, a few meters behind him, positioned
at the rear edge of the bridge, went down next to
their gun with grotesque movements. In the air
around the quadruple mount a light red blood mist
floated. Then he felt a violent blow against his

stomach. Only with difficulty did he turn towards the helmsman, but he was lying in a pool of blood next to the XO, who lay there headless.

Pearson wanted to say something, but there was nobody there, so he tried to walk to the mouthpiece, but strangely enough his knees gave way and he fell on the deck.

The last thing he noticed was an enormous blow that threw him up, then it got dark.

July 9th, 1940 over the Ling Bank, North Sea

Lindemann was as euphoric as some comrades when they had taken Pervitin, a stuff he personally didn't believe in.

Only one of the squadron's machines was hit, showing a slight trail of smoke behind its right-hand engine, but was still able to keep up. That had been a walk in the park. After the preliminary attack by the Me 110 only the few light anti-aircraft guns of the escort destroyers had still fired, but they were too far away from the cruiser, as they needed sea space to avoid torpedoes. The cruiser was history after four torpedo hits, also one of the escort destroyers had broken apart after a hit.

After that he immediately gave the order for the return flight. The English fighter protection would come too late, but they would come, so why risk being still around?

"Mainzer you take the wheel, go to 20 meters, radio operator, the rest should hang on to us. Gunners, don't fall asleep, keep an eye on fighters from behind."

Satisfied, Lindemann relaxed his cramped leg muscles and shoulders; couldn't someone invent something like a power support for the controls.

July 10th, 1940, Boscomb Down, photo evaluation group

Cheryl Baines was only 19, but with her sharp eyes the best photo evaluator of group 11. She worked the night shift and tiredly rubbed her red eyes. She put her magnifying glass away for a moment to stretch, then she shouted, "Lieutenant Kearns, please come over, I have something strange here." The lieutenant, a young but rather grievous Scotsman, came limping to her. Since a plane accident a year ago he wasn't allowed to fly anymore because his knee was damaged.

"What is it Baines?"

"Look here, sir, these are photos of construction work at Calais. 3 weeks ago, I already had a picture of this place, there was an untouched dune

landscape. And now there are over 30 big shadows, probably pits and a lot of trucks." He grunted, "Do you know exactly where the older photo is?"
"Excuse me sir, but the other photo was not kept at that time because there was nothing concrete to be seen on it. But I'm quite sure." She shyly knocked down her eyes, but already smelled the alcohol in his breath.
Kearns turned red.
"What am I supposed to do with this nonsense Baines, you think I'm going to Wingco with such an unfounded message and hold my head out for your blooming young girl fantasy. O no Baines, I will not do that." He threw the photo on the table and went back to his office. He should drink less she thought and put the picture resignedly on the NO ACTION stack.

July 10th, 1940, Cherwell Manor house
Lochlin had thought long and hard about how to reach Churchill. The man was simply very incalculable and, since he was prime minister, well protected. Then his German friend had given him a tip. Churchill always attended funerals of friends, the guy was not the youngest person anymore, so that happened quite often. They had found out that regarding his friends, Professor Lindemann was the

simplest to kill. Predictable, single and carefree.
It hadn't been so easy to get enough gasoline. Hard
times! Ten litres of petrol on the carpets of the
Cherwell Manor House hall would suffice.
 Standing in the door, he lit a cloth soaked in oil
with his new Zippo and threw it into the room. The
gasoline ignited with a hissing sound. He ignored
the haggard corpse of the professor; he had seen
enough corpses.
Burning houses are a frightening and melancholic
sight at night, but Lochlin enjoyed it. Then he
walked across the meadow to his motorcycle.

July 11th, 1940, Alencon, France

Merkle could only concentrate with great effort.
His skull hurt with every movement.
The evening before, they had discovered and
decimated the casino's wine supply.
A sideways glance showed him that his comrades
were no different.
In front stood Major Keller and, as always, bobbed
his feet, although it was obvious that he was not
feeling very well. Besides, Keller hadn't drunk less
the day before than he had.
"Gentlemen. The transfer to Alencon was
completed very quickly. Colonel Stahlmüller

praised us especially. It also helped that the French bequeathed us this beautiful airfield without any damage," he said with a smile and his men also laughed.

"Our first task is to be outlined in a few words", Captain Keller, who had become a professional officer in order not to have to become a teacher like his father, stood with the pointing stick at the blackboard and felt uncomfortable in this role as always.

"Our first task is it, to decimate the bomber units of the RAF. Since the chance to catch these gentlemen in the air at the moment is small, we will visit them at home. And this essentially in low flying mode, because we got the tip from intelligence that the English radar has problems with the detection of low flying planes. So, as we don't want to end up as fish food in the North Sea, we'll have to come up with something." Now nobody laughed any more, because they had already experienced the ease with which the English Spitfire and Hurricane fighters had shot down three of their comrades during the fighting at Dunkirk. Only one of the comrades had been rescued from the canal after several hours of severe hypothermia.

"Do we finally get the 210 Herr Hauptmann," Merkle asked, who, as usual, was the unofficial spokesman for his comrades.

A few days earlier Keller had had an intensive

conversation with Colonel Kern of the General Aircraft Master's staff and knew that the Me 210, the promised replacement of her old 110, could not be expected before the middle of next year. In addition, a whole series of serious accidents had occurred during the flight testing of the 210.

But he was not allowed to tell this to his men. They still lived on the hope that the Me 110, which they meanwhile called fuel-eating scrap metal, would soon be replaced by a much better aircraft.

It was also frightening for him, how far the morale of these men, who had been the elite of the Luftwaffe a few months ago, had dropped. Göring's pampered destroyer elite, only they had noticed over France and around Dunkirk that their plane was not suited for the intended task. And they had paid dearly for it.

Shitty fuel guzzling scrap, he thought quietly.

"At the moment it doesn't make sense to convert to the 210 because we are still in the middle of an operation. We wouldn't be ready for operation for months if we had to convert. We will therefore make better use of our existing potential by changing our tactics."

His 24 pilots looked at him expectantly, it was very quiet in the room.

"In the future we will carry out our attacks in very low altitude and attack either very early in the morning or very late in the evening. This makes it much harder for the English to spot us.

Probably it will come to an invasion in England, thinking anything else would be rather weak-minded. This will probably require two tasks from us. On the one hand, the protection of our invasion fleet, thus escorting bombers, we already know that game.

Secondly, it is possible that we will be used to catch the RAF bomber squadrons on the ground before the damage can be done. That means low-flying. We will therefore practice low-flying over land and sea and night take-offs and landings over the next five days."

He looked directly at his men and saw some biting their lips in tension. Everyone knew how difficult night take-offs and landings were. They had all lost comrades and friends at the flight schools during this training phase.

July 11th, 1940, London

They had killed Lindemann. Winston Churchill sat beaten in his armchair. Lindemann had been his friend. The day after tomorrow was the funeral. Of course, he would go. He was not afraid of any stinking communists or Irish. He had already experienced something completely different. He thought of his ride over the Veld in 1902.

"Fred, bring me another Lagavullin with water."
He was afraid that his black dog would attack him
again. No, he couldn't afford that now. He had
promised them blood, sweat and tears - with regard
to the Germans - but nobody had noticed his joke.
The calcified whiners of his own party had even
dared not to applaud his speech. Sometimes he
wondered if these Englishmen were worth saving
from the accursed Huns. It was a real pity that
Göring was dead, now it was to be feared that the
Luftwaffe would fall into competent hands.

July 11th, 1940, near Cherbourg

Squadron Leader Delaney flew at about 30 meters
altitude towards Cherbourg, not alone, but
accompanied by 3 other Blenheim`s of his
squadron. It was shortly before 10 o'clock in the
evening, the sun would set in a few minutes. It was
already quite dark.

"Arm bombs".

The harbour of Cherbourg appeared in the evening
haze. An anti-aircraft position opened fire but had
reacted too late. The projectiles followed the four
Blenheim`s harmlessly. The outer pier of Cherbourg

came into sight. The anti-aircraft guns were now wide awake. Russel`s Blenheim who flew in front of him turned onto a coastal freighter of about 2000 tons as Delaney`s Blenheim got hit. Russell flew about 100 meters in front of Delaney. His bomb bay was open, the bombs fell out and he continued flying without changing direction. "What a stubborn goat this guy is," thought Delaney, who was glad about the delay fused bombs. Russell's bombs hit. Delaney threw his bombs at another group of coastal freighters right next to the disintegrating coastal freighter Russel had hit. He saw German soldiers shooting with machine-guns and pulled the plane up to leave the port over which hundreds of anti-aircraft smoke trails now crossed with a left-hand bend. On the outer pier, two quadruple 2cm flak had taken up position. The visible hits of the 2cm flak wandered from the bow to the stern of Russell's plane, which now turned its blade curve into an inverted flight and abruptly crashed 200 meters behind the mole into the sea. He had lost sight of the other Blenheim`s.

Squadron Leader Delaney's plane landed safely and was the only one to return to its base.

July 11th, 1940, Rennes, France

Lieutenant Herrmann was scared. He didn't dare to look up and meet the major's eyes. He had no hope anymore.

The major offered him a cigarette, but he just shook his head. He had always been a non-smoker and wouldn't start now, it was simply too unhealthy, and the Führer didn't smoke either.

Why had he not been able to keep his mouth shut? To tell Janine of all people something like that. He didn't even know her, except bedding her. He looked at the non-commissioned officer and the two soldiers who were sitting there tied up on their chairs. Suddenly the door blew open with a loud noise. A lieutenant reported to the major with slamming heels.

"Herr Major, everything is ready."

The major, nervously pulling his cigarette again, then kicked the stub out and turned around.

"Gentlemen, come on."

The guards almost had to drag the trembling sergeant out. Herrmann saw how the bottom of the trousers and the legs of the man's trousers turned wet and dark. He, too, was now led outside on unsteady legs. They were taken to a large barracks yard and placed in front of a wall. He saw a large crowd of soldiers lining up in the square. A sergeant came to give him a blindfold, but he shook his head. The sergeant and the two soldiers were blindfolded.

Only with half an ear did the lieutenant notice how the major read out the verdict and the execution order. Apparently, all units of the Western Front had ordered delegations here. Herrmann, who until a few minutes ago had not even wanted to believe that he would really be shot, began to tremble. He saw the firing squad marching up. They were men from his own company. The command had been given to Fritz Müller, a friend with whom he had drank many evenings.

Terstegen, who stood at the side of the regiment as an observer, painfully clenched his teeth as the volley cracked and the four men tipped to the side. This was one aspect of Milch's approach that he did not like, even though he rationally understood why Milch had ordered such a rigorous approach to these treacherous crimes. Courager les autres, as always.

No one would doubt Milch's determination anymore to go all out.

July 11th, 1940, Ramsgate.
The hotel swayed like when in an earthquake when the Stukas bombed the port of Ramsgate.
The guests in the bar hid under the tables and looked around in fear. Commander Hurst had taken

his bitter with him and finished drinking it under the table. Obviously, the Germans were not aware that the Command of the Light Naval Forces had its headquarters in this hotel, because after three minutes and a whole series of further explosions the Stukas flew home after spending their bombs.

"Simply no professionals, this master race peoples." Captain Hurst knocked the dust off his uniform and put his empty glass back on the counter. Curiously, everyone pushed their way to the door and out through the hall, crunching shards of glass, to see what the German bombardment had done.

Hurst saw at first glance that the torpedo workshop was ablaze after a direct hit. One of the boats was also missing. He walked the few meters to the edge of the harbour basin to make sure.

Where Miller's boat had been, only some wooden parts and an oil barrel floated. Every trace of the crew was missing. Hurst turned to Lieutenant Allenby, who limped towards him.

"How long are we going to last, Allenby? That's the third boat we've lost to air raids." He looked up at the sky as two hurricanes flew at low altitude over the harbour towards France.

"And the damn RAF always comes too late!" He threatened the two flyers leaving for France angry but impotent with his fist. "Allenby, you first take care of the torpedo workshop. I want to know what materials we have left in an hour at the latest".

"At your command, sir. By the way, I have found a storage facility for our parts. About 2 miles outside on a small farm. Should I have the spare parts sent there?"

Hurst thought for a moment: "Do that Allenby, here the damn Stukas are just destroying everything." With one movement of his hand he sent Allenby away.

July 11th, 1940, Copenhagen

The Danish tug captains towing his ship understood their craft. Kroeger's expert eye did not fail to notice that the fishermen on the pier were watching his ship closely. They had burned down two old tyres under the engine hatch, and the traces of fire were clearly visible even further away.

Slowly they approached the quay wall.

"Clear with lines fore and aft", Kröger ordered and saw with joy that his people were performing a perfect line manoeuvre, as if they had been together on the steamer for years".

He turned to the colonel who commanded the embarked infantry regiment. "You can disembark your men now, Colonel."

The colonel saluted, both men grinned, they had ensured that the infantry discovered some bottles of schnapps, that would loosen the tongue of some men, enough to turn information into rumours.

July 11th, 1940 Lisbon, Rossio Square

Jan Bersin, as Leberecht called himself in Lisbon, in memory of the most dangerous and brilliant GRU agent with whom he had had to fight in Spain and who had been kindly liquidated by Stalin, sat on the edge of Rossio Square in a small cafe from where he had a good view of the statue and the fountain in the middle. It was around 11 o'clock, beautiful weather and he enjoyed the view of the many beautiful Portuguese women strolling by or busy doing their shopping. He liked this city and hoped he could stay here for quite a while.

He met Jane at his hotel at least twice a week, but in the meantime, he had also met Maria, a slim young Portuguese woman, with whom he had a lot of fun. Tensely and very concentrated he observed how Manuel, a young guy whom he sometimes paid for errands, sat on the edge of the well and laid a parcel next to him.

Then he discovered Rossiter, who walked from the righthand side and stood next to Manuel as if by chance. He couldn't hear what was being said, but obviously the agreed recognition sentence worked, because Rossiter casually took the small package and went on.

Leberecht ordered another glass of Vinho Verde and was pleased that the four months he had worked to feed Rossiter with real information about German military secrets were now bearing fruit.

Fact
When Sir Charles Portal became chief of the Bomber Command in April 1940, he had about 240 so-called "heavy" bombers of the types Wellington, Whitley and Hampden (15 Squadrons) at his disposal at that time, of which hardly more than 160 each were ready for use. In addition, there were 9 squadrons Battle and 22 squadrons with Blenheim. The light Battle Bombers were considered unsuitable since 1937 and had suffered catastrophic losses in May 1940 in France. The light Blenheim bombers were also no longer really usable in 1940, although they were still built for 2 more years in different versions (as you can see, there were plenty of examples of catastrophically inadequate leadership and decision-making everywhere, not only on the German side).

July 12th, 1940, Denmark, Esbjerg

In the meantime, eighteen E-boats lay in the port of Esbjerg.

They were all moored far from each other and covered with camouflage nets.

Georgson had not been enthusiastic. Like him, everyone assumed that the invasion of England via the English Channel was imminent.

Larsen, the mate saw Georgson just arriving on board questioning. "Anything new Captain?"

"Not a damn word, only that we must be able to leave at any time within 15 minutes!"

"So, we always keep the diesel warm, which is no problem in this weather."

Georgson just nodded.

"Are the torpedoes up to date now?"

"If I had been asked, the eels would never have gone to the front with the distance detonator!"

"Too bad they didn't ask you Larsen, then we would have painted two more steamers on the bridge."

At least he would allow a case of beer in the evening, or two if the men weren't allowed to leave the boat.

July 12th, 1940, near Lille

His men were flat standing. For two weeks they had been practicing groupwise attacks with mutual fire protection, combined with a daily 10-kilometre cross-country run and a three hour session on the training course according to storm troop patterns. But they were fit as never before.

As a lieutenant he could have avoided it, but what would such a well-trained company be doing with a boss who couldn't keep up the pace? In addition, he had made sure that the sergeants also took part in the full programme.

Now Gademann felt that he was almost 10 years older than his men.

He would have liked to know why the division had imposed such a hard training schedule, but all his contacts knew as little as he did. Even the regimental commander had just shrugged when Gademann's battalion chief had asked a question at the last meeting of the regimental staff.

Probably against England, otherwise there was no opponent left. After the battles of the last weeks he and his men had learned to take the English soldiers seriously. Not particularly well led, but tough fighters the Tommie`s were. Their weakness was the slowness with which they reacted, especially when they were cut off and no longer got any direction from higher up.

So, they had to further improve their tactics in terms

of speed.

Gademann stretched out his tired bones and called his platoon leaders to him.

The cooperation with the additional MG troops was not yet at its best because they were not fast enough to change positions!

So more repetition of the same game.

July 12th, 1940, London

The major's uniform had a badly sewn hole over the heart. Lochlin had simply obtained a MC and fastened it over it. Luckily, he had gotten the blood spatter out well. The cemetery was overcrowded. Lindemann had been a well-known scientist and Churchill's advisor. A whole bunch of politicians and officers had appeared to give him the final escort. Lochlin was not noticed at all, just as he had expected. He had a Webley revolver in his left jacket pocket and a hand grenade under his trench coat on his right arm. The army depot in Salisbury had been well stocked. Churchill stood about 15 meters away from him directly at the open grave and would pass him directly on the way after the funeral. Churchill chewed on his inevitable but cold cigar. The four Secret Service people guarding him kept in the background. Maybe in the presence of so

many high-ranking dignitaries they felt a little uncomfortable. The last English head of state to die violently had been King Charles II, but there the executioner had acted with intent. Lochlin had the impression that the secret service people were busier watching that Churchill did not slide into the open grave, than watching out for possible assassins. Next to Lochlin stood a colonel in a Highland uniform and cleared his throat several times. When Churchill had thrown a shovel full of earth at the coffin, he turned abruptly and walked towards the exit of the cemetery. Lochlin pulled the safety pin out of the hand grenade, held the hanger for a moment and then let go. 21, 22, .. .
"For Sean you fucking Englishman."
The grenade was rolling in front of Churchill's feet and exploded at the same moment as Secret Service men shot Lochlin, who had now pulled the Webley. Four people, including Winston Spencer Churchill, were killed by shell splinters.

July 12th, 1940, near Calais
They'd done it before, in Belgium, two months ago. Storm troops that landed with Fieseler storks on a few meters and attacked important positions. Chaotic but successful.

They could do even better.

They had been practicing for 2 weeks to find out how long before sunrise there was enough visibility to be able to land.

The comrades from the Do 17 long-range reconnaissance aircraft had obtained the necessary pictures of the radar installations in low flight. Four Dorniers had been shot down, interestingly all those who had not approached in low flight. They would not repeat that mistake. Especially since there was a report by Intelligence that the English Radar was having difficulties with the detection of low-flying aircraft.

One of the men had also solved the problem with the altitude measurement. Since the built-in altitude measurement was almost by 100 meters too inaccurate, a low-altitude flight below 100 meters at night, even above sea level was not possible. But Sergeant Oltmann, a quiet East Frisian who nobody thought was very bright, had found a solution. Two lights under the wings, which were adjusted so that their light beams met, when the plane flew exactly 20 meters high.

"Geometry and a dirty pig of a math teacher," Oltmann had only growled when they had asked him, how he had come up with the solution.

Lieutenant Meissner, who would lead the group against the Dunkirk radar station, was confident. They would catch the English before their morning tea. He had only 10 men available in the 5 Fieseler storks, because the pilots were usable at best as MG shooters in a support role, but that would be enough for the hardly 10 Englishmen, who served the plant per shift. And his people were well trained storm troopers with a lot of fighting experience. They also carried a lot of explosives to destroy the facility.

He had been allowed to see an intelligence report , which had provided a clear description of the English radar facilities. Together with the aerial photos they were well prepared. Since altogether 5 groups were on the way at the time of attack, it would depend on an exact adherence to the schedule, the attack had to take place everywhere at the same time.

Now they had practiced this for three days consecutively, an approach of all 5 planes on the Belgian coast 15 minutes before sunrise and landing at 5 different places at the same time.

It had cost them two planes and six dead, but it worked, with less than 20 seconds time deviation. Yes, that would work. He had no doubt that in less than 15 minutes they would be able to fight down the English and to destroy the radar aerials, because half an hour after their attack, the vulnerable Ju 52s would arrive in Kent with the first wave of infantry.

Fact
To my knowledge, the two-lamp altimeter hight finding solution was developed by Squadron 617, the Dambusters, for their attack on the Möhne Dam. Fi 156 storks were used in the attack on Belgium in May 1940 at the Niwi venture.

July 12th, 1940, Copenhagen

The German convoy was only visible on the horizon. Anders Ljungby was satisfied with himself. It had been almost too easy three German soldiers had got drunk in his pub and then they had begun to talk. It soon became clear that their regiment and the others on the transport fleet, were on their way to an invasion in East Anglia. Anders had listened with wide open ears and remembered every word. Two hours later, a fishing boat meeting at sea with a Swedish colleague had left with its report. That was certainly the most important message he had ever sent to England. He hoped that the Royal Navy would receive the Germans duly. As he had seen, two other German freighters had also arrived, probably replacing the two ships that had broken down. The Germans were apparently doing really serious business.

July 12th, 1940, Aarhus Airfield

The squadron had landed shortly before sunset in Aarhus, even the Me 109 with its notoriously short range had managed to relocate from Abbeville in one hopp. Bergmann jumped from the wing and first massaged his aching butt, which as always was the first to report after the flight. Then his bladder took its toll. Since the airport building was too far away for him, he went to the other side of the sandbag wall into which some men had pushed his plane.

Strange thing that. Actually, he had wanted to have lunch with Liane, but with only an hour's warning they had been ordered to pack their fly-bags and stow them in their planes. They had already wondered about the four Ju 52 transporters that stood in front of the hangar and were loaded by the mechanics.

It was only when they arrived in the air traffic control barracks, that the Commodore had briefly discussed the transfer to Aarhus. It was expressly forbidden for them to speak or telephone with anyone outside. Liane would be damn angry, but he couldn't change that. Only three machines would be left behind.

Now even the lame Junkers transports, who had

been escorted by the third squadron, floated in with the mechanics.

Captain Reichert, who was usually well informed, came running to him from his parking place. Bergmann looked at him questioningly, but Reichert only shrugged his shoulders, "I have no idea what this is all about!

"All right, since no one's collecting us, let's go, it looks like a main building with a tower over there."

July 12th, 1940, Watton.

Delaney was drunk, but that was hardly noticeable. He was sitting in the pub with Milton, the Wingco and FO Bailey. The Wingco had taken them with them when they appeared for the report. The last two pilots of the squadron, who were not even ready for action with broken machines at the moment. After Remington had been killed, he was the last survivor of the squadron since they were stationed in Watton. The other six crews were all new people.

"We won't get new pilots until next week. Right now, the fighter squadrons are getting all the replacements."

"And how many hours do the new pilots we're supposed to get have on Blenheim?" asked Delaney, who had seen too many new pilots come and go in the last few weeks.

"Less than 20," the Wingco said.

"That's infanticide." Bailey was only FO because he had already been demoted twice because he couldn't shut up.

The Wingco first turned red and looked at Bailey unkindly.

"Child murder is a friendly calling for that", Delaney seconded.

Milton slumped down a bit, they were at the fourth Guinness and he was already in his mid-forties, but still flew regular missions.

"You're right, but we have no choice. We can't ignore the Krauts when they attack our airfields and when they provide ships for an invasion. We have to attack. And we're losing more crews than we're retraining. We can only make up for that by shortening training."

"But inadequately trained people don't live long enough, especially not in Blenheim's..."

"Yes Sean, we are in a spin. Do you know a way out?"

Delaney shook his head and ordered a new round of Guinness.

Suddenly the host turned the radio up.

Delaney only heard something like "Churchill is dead..." then everything went down in a general turmoil.

He felt as if the floor beneath him was swaying.

July 13th, 1940, London

There was an extraordinary silence lying above the otherwise bustling city, which Vaughan-Williams had so impressively portrayed musically with an unusual symphony 30 years earlier.

The workers and officials walked quietly along their way without the usual discussions, jokes or serious conversations. Many wore a black bow on their lapels.

Winston was dead, the man who had given hope to an entire country, although he had not won a single victory during his term of office. Only the rescue of the army from Dunkirk had been appreciated with great relief as something similar to a victory.

It was not yet clear who the successor would be, the name of Halifax was often mentioned, but even more frequently, especially among women, the handsome Anthony Eden was preferred. Eden already was the most important man in Winston's cabinet as minister of war, was the desired candidate.

Winslow was not sure where he now belonged. As Churchill's advisor, he had almost been part of the household at Downing Street No. 10, although he was under the direct authority of the Admiralty.

Like the others on the staff, he clearly preferred Eden to Halifax as Winston`s successor.

As an administrator in India Halifax had proved to be a weak candidate, and as foreign minister he was an appeaser, some said he had practically crawled up the Germans' asses. Now there had been many in recent years who had been impressed by Hitler's and Mussolini's economic successes, so Halifax was in the best of company.

But now the gap that Churchill left behind was a catastrophe for England. The evening before, reports had arrived from Portugal and Sweden that the Germans had gathered a large invasion fleet in the Baltic Sea with tens of thousands of soldiers on board. The staff waited eagerly for the results of the air reconnaissance. In the morning, a Wellesley specially equipped for flights at high altitudes had taken off for a reconnaissance flight over Kattegat, Copenhagen and the German Baltic Sea ports, but had not yet returned.

He could only hope that the politicians, whom he abhorred almost all the time, would quickly come to their senses.

July 14th, 1940 Martin, near Dover
They were Martin's militia, 20 men with an old

Lewis, 6 Lee-Enfield Mk 2, 3 hunting rifles and 4 axes. After 2 hours of drill on the marketplace they went to the best of all pubs and drank bitter and ale. Exceptionally none of them spoke a word. Above the bar hung a picture. It showed the first company of the 4th Somerset Infantry in August 1914, shortly before they had been embarked to France. Everyone knew they would not be seasick this time when the battle began. If only the seasick Krauts would come. While drinking beer they became loud as usual, but it quickly became clear that they did not really believe in an invasion. Most were just happy to have a few hours to get away from their wives and drink a few beers. At least there was still Guinness.

However, the mood was at freezing point. The news of Churchill's death had been a shock, especially because no one believed that his possible successors, whether Lord Halifax or Anthony Eden, could even remotely tread in Churchill's footsteps.

July 14th, 1940, Southampton.
Sergeant Enderby was very proud. His battery had been the first to get the new Bofors 4 cm gun. The best anti-aircraft gun in the world. Fully movable with a Ford Quad Tractor as prime mover. The day

before yesterday they had also practised firing at ground targets at the Salisbury Plains training range. The armoured projectile penetrated another 30 mm of armoured steel at 1000 metres. However, he was worried that his new gun was not equipped with a protective shield. Three Spitfire flew over his anti-aircraft position in the Commons of Southampton.

July 14th, 1940, London, early morning
Labour, like two months earlier, had been the deciding factor. They would not support Halifax. Within five minutes it was clear that Anthony Eden would be the new prime minister.
He first thanked the ministers and party leaders present. Then he picked up the sledgehammer and dismissed Lord Halifax with the remark that he would be prime minister and foreign minister in one person.
That was a well-calculated move, something Churchill hadn't dared to do two months earlier, but this time the Conservatives didn't even flinch.
Eden almost had the impression that they were happy that he was doing the dirty work for them.
Halifax had stood up stiffly with his face still, had indicated a bow and had left without a word.
And there he was. At almost 21, he had been one of

the youngest captains of the army, highly decorated. Well, at 43 he was one of the youngest prime ministers England had ever had, apart, of course, from the genius Pitt, who had done it at 24.

The Show must go on, as the American ex-rebels say, he thought.

"Gentlemen, yesterday evening we received information from aerial reconnaissance that a large German naval force is gathering in the Baltic Sea, north of Copenhagen. MI 6 gave us further hints, which probably come directly from the German army, that in a very few days an invasion, possibly in East Anglia is planned. Suggestions?

Beaverbrook was, as always, the first: "Then we'll just flatten the fuckers, otherwise why did we put millions into the Navy!

Eden smiled, "thank you Max. Admiral Pound, what does the Admiralty suggest?"

Admiral Pound said, "Sir, the Home Fleet is at the highest readiness. Admiral Summerfield can anchor within 20 minutes, from Scapa it's only 400 miles to Kattegat, the fleet can do that in 20 hours. The same goes for the cruiser group in the Humber."

"Well, Vice Air Marshal Park, what is the RAF planning?"

Keith Park, a mid-size but very energetic mid-fifties man, waited a moment and then said: "We plan to move eight fighter squadrons from Group 11 and Group 12 tomorrow to Central England to shield the fleet. Bomber Command and the tactical bombers are also put on standby. We don't have to move any units here because the range of the bombers is sufficient. From Fleet Air Arm we can get two squadrons of torpedo bombers currently stationed on shore, which we will move to Hull."

Everyone looked at General Alan-Brooke, who had been commanding the home army for a few days. He said: "We have only two infantry divisions in East Anglia now, because we're assuming Kent and Sussex as the landing site. In the short term we can only move two more divisions by rail at short notice, but it will take two days for the units to be operational there. But I recommend a disposition in the rear to be able to form flexible focal points against different invasion preparations".

Eden leaned back a bit, "that sounds reasonable, gentlemen, get going right away. We'll meet again tonight at 8:00!"

July 15th, 1940 Scapa Flow

Slowly the shallow Orkney Islands went out of sight in the early morning haze. Admiral James Summerfield, a slender late fifties man with a weather-beaten face, bent over the bridge nock to take a last look at Scapa.

His battle group ran with 18 knots towards Doggerbank. The Admiralty had issued an invasion warning and ordered the Home Fleet to leave. From the Kattegat, a large German convoy of troop transporters and warships left in a south westerly direction, sighted and confirmed 3 hours ago by a RAF reconnaissance aircraft.

With his glass he had a panoramic view of his fleet. With 4 battleships, 2 heavy cruisers, 8 light cruisers and 20 destroyers not insignificant, but in comparison with the fleet, which had run out 1916 to the Skagerrak battle, only a shadow.

How many times had he approached the first Sealord with the request not to transfer any more of his ships to the Mediterranean? But no, in the meantime the damned Mediterranean fleet, or Force H as it was now called, was stronger than the Home Fleet. And who was the enemy of the Force H, the Eyties with their show ships, whereby most Italian thick ships still put on mussels in their ports.

Churchill, God have mercy on his soul, had always overestimated the importance of the Mediterranean, always spoke of the soft underbelly of Europe, as if he could let his battleships run across the Alps into the Rhine. Such a map strategist, who had just led a battalion in the first war, and he didn't want to remember Gallipoli at all.

The admiral noticed that he was gripping the holding bar at the front edge of the bridge and released his grip. Hopefully at least the new one, Eden, was worth something.

At least 6 light cruisers from the Humber group would join him in three hours.

Would it make sense to detach the fast cruisers, or should he hold the fleet together? But then they were handicapped by the slow Revenge and his Rodney. Washington cherry trees they had called the Rodney and her sister ship Nelson because she was well armed and armoured, but due to the limitation of the fleet agreement, she only ran 23 knots, and that only with tail wind.

Repulse, the old battle cruiser, was indeed faster, but the whole ship warped, if it delivered a full volley of the 15-inch main armament, so easily was it built. Maybe he should have left the service in 1935 but being at home with his wife in Kent all the time was not an idea that had inspired him.

From the 2nd watch officer came the message that they had sighted airplanes.

With a satisfied grunt he noted that the RAF had sent 20 fighters to cover the air, Hurricanes as it looked.

"Order all hands to battle stations," he said.

Fact

The Royal Navy was distributed as follows at the beginning of July 1940:
Home Fleet: 4 battleships, 4 heavy cruisers, 16 light cruisers (6 of those ancient)
Mediterranean: 7 battleships, 6 light cruisers.

July 15th, 1940, Esbjerg

"Gentlemen, let me make myself clear one more time. Our goal is the English fleet, preferably the heavy units. The protection of transport ships has no priority whatsoever. So, if a destroyer attacks the convoy and a cruiser sails three kilometres further, attack the cruiser!" The flotilla commander looked at one after the other with a stern gaze.

Georgson was at first just as shocked as the other E-boat captains and their 1st officers.

One of them even began, "Captain, we can't let the comrades..."

"Yes, you can and you will!"

Then it became clear to Georgson that the freighters were just bait, they were supposed to pluck the Navy. He looked around. It was good to see that some others had also come to this realization. But nobody said anything.

The flotilla commander nodded and left the room where the talk immediately began. After five minutes everyone knew what was going on. Then everyone went to their boats as they would leave in four hours.

Georgson did not think without unease of the large quantity of large calibre guns that the Home Fleet would bring to bear.

Everything would depend on catching the Royal Navy at the right moment!

As soon as Georgson was back at his boat from the commander's meeting, a motorcyclist drove up and delivered an order to him. Georgson signed the receipt and covered his ears as the cycle-driver made a cavalier start with his BMW.

Then he opened his orders. He was ordered to leave at 22:40 o'clock and to go at maximum speed to the Norwegian port of Egersund near Stavanger. The beacon located there would emit a light signal from 3:00 o'clock at night for a short time and he was instructed to enter the port at the first light. The other boats of the flotilla would leave in 10 minutes intervals to the same destination. He was also instructed not to reveal anything about their destination to his crew.

5 hours later they left, and he hoped that the big Mercedes Diesel engines were as reliable as ever and would survive the 7 hours high speed drive to Egersund without any problems. Breaking down with engine troubles somewhere in the Kattegatt and to be there the next day perhaps to be caught by

an English destroyer did not meet his expectations. In a swell of wind force two, it was possible for them to plough through the North Sea at full load with 38 knots.

July 15th, 1940, off the Thames estuary

The four motor torpedo boats of Hurst's group ran north at high speed. What they were supposed to do there was not clear to him. Was it really useful to uncover the English Channel so completely, as even the destroyers from Plymouth were heading north and Dover had been abandoned by the Navy, not to mention the cruisers from Hull and the Home Fleet from Scapa?

But as a commander, you just carried out orders from the admiralty. The sonorous hum of the engines was almost sleep-inducing, so he looked around to see if all the watchmen were fully alert.

July 16th, 1940, Watton, 5:15 a.m.

Although the sun had not yet risen properly, the whole airfield seemed to be a single beehive. Everywhere mechanics with lights were scurrying around the Blenheim`s and in front of every plane there was a trailer full of bombs.

Nice, Delaney thought, but which idiot builds bomb flaps into a bomber, which were opened by the weight of the bombs. It's actually a miracle that they sometimes hit something with their bombs, despite the delay caused by the flaps.

And now there was an invasion alert, it was probably a large fleet of freighters and warships in the North Sea, on their way to East Anglia, wherever they wanted to disembark.

Delaney knew the coast of East Anglia quite well by now and knew that there were few places suitable for troop landings. Maybe it was a feint and the Germans were on their way to another place.

Now the mechanics were ready with the bombs, and from the command barracks a red starlight bullet rose.

"Come on, people, get in, in ten minutes we're off!" As soon as they had gone through their checklist, the white starlight went up.

Delaney was the first to roll to the runway. He hoped that the many new and inexperienced crews wouldn't mess up at the start.

Then he pushed the power levers of both Mercury engines to full load and felt the Blenheim accelerate rapidly.

If the reconnaissance planes were right, they hardly had to fly an hour.

He could only hope that his squadron would not be the there on their own. Spitfires and Hurricanes were supposed to give them cover over the North Sea, but he would have preferred to have had a few fighters above and beside his squadron.

"Pay attention, Jamie, not everything that flies have a cockade on its wing."

Jameson just clicked twice on his microphone for an answer.

July 16th, 1940, Doggerbank, cruiser HMS Manchester, 5:25am

The Manchester ran with 30 knots almost at top speed. Behind her were the five other light cruisers of the Humber Group in a V-shaped formation. Captain Parker on the bridge of HMS Manchester felt the wind in his face and enjoyed it. Light cruisers had been built for exactly such an operation. They would approach quickly, strike hard and disappear again asap. A few minutes earlier they had received a sighting message from the German convoy with location information and would reach its probable positions in about 2 hours at the current speed. The sun was just beginning to crawl over the horizon, and he felt the first rays that brought some warmth to his face, which had been

severely cooled by the cold North Sea breeze.
In a few minutes they should also have fighter
protection, the RAF had promised three squadrons
of fighters. Parker hoped that the RAF would stick
to it. He turned around to his radio officer and said
to him: "Send a signal to Admiral Summerfield.
Indicate our current position and announce that in
about 2 hours we will be at the expected location of
the German convoy running at about twelve knots."
Then he turned around again and, as he had done
for 24 years, took his binoculars before his eyes to
search the horizon for any signs of ships.

July 16th, 1940, Skagerrak, 5.45 a.m.

The admiral took his glass to look one more time at
the outgoing battle cruiser Gneisenau, which left the
escort together with the cruiser Hipper on a north
westerly course. Even though he knew that they had
the order to destroy the remains of the English fleet
after the battle for the invasion fleet, he would have
preferred the heavy ships to stay with them. So he
had only three light cruisers, four destroyers and
seven torpedo boats at his disposal and his orders
said to bring them back.
And nevertheless, it was the biggest action of the
German fleet since 1916.

He had been present at Jutland, then a mere lieutenant on the battle cruiser Derfflinger.

At that time, he had had a much better feeling than now.

He looked at his watch, just 35 minutes since sunset.

He turned to the captain of his flag ship Leipzig and said: "Order to all ships, all hands to battle stations".

The RAF would not be long in coming, at least they had strengthened the anti-aircraft guns on all ships with 2-centimetre quadruplets, which they had borrowed from the Luftwaffe.

A lookout reported a large number of high-flying aircraft. As he could see with his Zeiss glass, the Luftwaffe's fighter protection was punctual, indeed.

July 16th, 1940 over the North Sea, 6.10 a.m.
It's a good thing that the Ju 86 was able to climb to 12,000 metres without any problems, otherwise the old crate would be dead meat for Spitfires.

Captain Wegener constantly turned his head in all directions to recognize dangers early on.

He was always fascinated how far one could see from this height. As they had already received a sighting report from a U-boat observing Scapa Flow the evening before, it was easily anticipated where the English fleet would be.

And there were also fighters to be expected.

"Watch out, gentlemen, from now on we have to reckon with Indians."

The two gunners only clicked their microphones as answer. The navigator, who sat as an observer in the glazed nose pulpit, waved briefly and continued to search the horizon with his binoculars.

Five minutes later they found what they were looking for.

From their height, even large ships looked like small toys, but the characteristic V of the wake made them clearly visible.

Since the Royal Navy, as always, sailed in well-ordered formation, the composition of the formation was clearly visible.

"Four battleships, ten cruisers and twenty destroyers sighted, course 110 degrees with about 18 knots in the plan square BEF 12", came the report of the observer, which the radio operator began to transmit immediately.

Wegener flew some cautious turns to look for fighters.

He had spotted some tiny green-brown aircraft above the formation, but they were flying at least 5,000 meters lower. They could not be dangerous to them, as none of the English fighters could climb over about 10,000 meters, and they would soon have to deal with the rest of the Luftwaffe anyway. Since they still had fuel for at least five hours, he would expand the search concentrically.

July 16th, 1940, airfield near Neumünster, 6:45 a.m.

Less than 50 minutes after sighting the Home Fleet, the Heinkels from Lindemann's squadron, each heavily burdened with 2 torpedoes, rolled to the start.

He was feeling really good and was curious whether the show they had prepared for the Home Fleet would actually work as planned. First, two squadrons would attack with horizontal bombers to force the formation to break up close escort and thereby reduce the flak density. Then there would be three squadrons of torpedo bombers, all now led by anti-aircraft supressing Me 110 destroyers. These would attack the fleet simultaneously from three different directions, together with 5 squadrons of Ju 88 dive bombers. As fighter protection they had 100 Me 109 with them, which covered them. The fighters were staggered in 2000, 5000 and 8000 meters. One hour later horizontal bombers would come again. Then again, the torpedo pilots and the dive bombers. In between, submarines would look for victims.

As always, Lindemann was the first to take off.

July 16th, 1940, above Doggerbank, 6:50 a.m.
Two full wings with Heinkel 111 bombers, almost
140 machines, flew in compact formation at about
4000 meters altitude towards the Doggerbank.
Bergmann's squadron was zigzagging about 1000
meters above them, ready to react to any attack.
Another 2000 meters above them flew another
fighter squadron.

As usual, Bergmann was constantly searching his
entire 270-degree field of view. The
ophthalmologists had attested him 120 percent
visual performance at the initial examination, so it
was usually him who first discovered enemy planes.
He took turns raising his wings in order to have a
better view downwards.

It was a wonderful day, clear, almost cloudless with
a view of almost 30 kilometres. A few minutes ago,
they had flown over the rather large looking
German convoy, fortunately the Flak had
recognized that they were own airplanes and
remained silent.

Since the sighting report of the Home Fleet was
barely 40 minutes old, the Royal Navy Association

could only have driven 40 kilometres further even at maximum speed and should be in sight at any moment.

There came a message from the squadron leader: "Swordfish Torpedo bombers, at sea level, 270 degrees, distance 1 kilometre, first group, attack, immediately".

Bergmann, who flew at the top of the formation, immediately put his plane on the left surface and went into nosedive. He was absolutely sure that his wingman and the rest of the squadron would follow him immediately.

Were the English so crazy to use these completely outdated biplanes without escort? If so, that would be a slaughter, if not.....: "Watch out if they really are without escort, flight Velbers, you stay above us and watches out for company" he said.

"Is clear", Velbers unagitated voice came over the ether.

The amazingly slow Swordfish torpedo bombers, over twenty of them, were now in fill view, but since they had over 600 km/h at the speed dial, everything was happening very fast.

Bergmann began to pull back his plane in order not to land in the North Sea. They would attack the Swordfish, what a name, from the front, which would initially keep them out of the gunner's fire. The Swordfish flew about 300 meters high, which was a serious mistake. Their chance of survival would have been better if they were 30 meters high. So it was easy for Bergmann to align his Me from a position slightly below the torpedo bombers. Then he pressed the two fire buttons for cannons and MGs, he saw the engine and cockpit of the two-decker disintegrate in a splinter rain and pulled his plane over the helplessly dropping Englishman and then into a steep right turn.

"Ten Spitfires from 40 degrees, distance 1000", Velber's voice came out of his headphone.

Bergmann reacted immediately: "All except flight Schmitt, take care of the Spitfires."

That was the moment when all order disintegrated, and a wild melee began.

When Bergmann landed in Aarhus 35 minutes later, he had 14 holes in his machine. He had shot down one Swordfish and two Spitfires into the North Sea. He pushed the cockpit glazing back and pulled his pilot's hood off his sweaty head. The mechanics were already running up to refuel and reammunition his plane. Karlsen, his first waiter gave him an apple juice bottle, which he emptied in one go.

"Look at the left wing and the tail, there was a few bangs," he said to Karlsen, who nodded and disappeared.

Bergmann closed his eyes briefly to recover for a moment.

Then Karlsen came back again, "fourteen hits, but nothing essential is broken, as it looks, Lieutenant.

Bergmann nodded: "How far are the others?
"Eight more machines are almost ready, five minutes at most until they're all refuelled."
He waited eagerly for the white starlight that would signal the next start. They had been practicing the procedure with immediate refuelling and ammunitioning without the pilot exiting for weeks and were now able to take off again about 12 minutes after landing. This allowed them to fly significantly more missions per day. He only hoped that his pilots could endure the strain. The July sun was already very hot, and he was sweating under his combination, but at 5000 metres he would freeze with less clothing.

July 16th, 1940, Doggerbank, 7:15 am

The Admiral was rigid with horror. Within a few seconds, the twenty hurricanes of his fighter protection, together with a few dozen German hunters, had turned into a wildly circling turmoil, from which constantly burning machines had fallen out.
Then the lookout reported the bombers, surely more than a hundred, which were approaching his ships like an unwavering cloud of bees, completely unimpressed by the heavy anti-aircraft gun, which

began to shoot with great roar.

"Give the order to disband the formation, execute plan 12. Demand more fighter protection immediately, with the utmost urgency," Summerfield said his flag captain and felt his flagship start turning starboard.

Then the first bombs fell in long rows of explosions. For minutes, the Nelson turned back and forth erratically and ponderously in a desperate attempt to avoid the German bombs.

Summerfield had to hold on as three close impacts flooded the bridge with huge amounts of seawater. With half an ear, he heard the first damage reports reaching the captain, then he felt the air pressure accompanying a tremendous explosion that blew one of his heavy cruisers into the air as a whole row of bombs hit him from front to back.

For a moment he wondered if he should order retreat, but suddenly the sky was empty. With a quick panorama view, the admiral screened his battle group. Two cruisers and three destroyers were on fire, but the two cruisers were still moving, while the destroyers were lying dead in the water, smouldering without any forward movement.

All ships were scattered over an area of several kilometres.

"Orders to all, return to your battle positions. Return to attack course, report damage."

He turned to his flag captain, "what do we hear

from the RAF?

"Five squadrons are on their way, but will take at least 30 minutes, sir."

"Tell them we'll need continuous fighter cover for the next few hours, or we're finished."

His flag captain looked at him with his mouth open, "Sir, at once!"

Then there came the next call of a lookout "Torpedo bombers, distance 3000, 120 degrees."

As soon as the admiral had his glass on his eyes, the next lookouts reported torpedo bombers from two other directions and another caller pointed into the sky, where dive bombers became glitteringly visible.

Summerfield let his shoulders sink, he realized that this would not be a good day for the Navy, his ships were far too far apart to support each other with their AA guns. Today at the latest it would become clear whether the future would belong to the battleship or the plane, and he had not a good feeling about it.

16th July 1940, Doggerbank, 8:10 a.m.
He'd shoot a very widely dispersed fan this time. With the shallow water depth above the Doggerbank, he wasn't at all comfortable. But better

four chances than just one, if the Home Fleet turned around, which he didn't doubt would happen quite soon. He could see that fires raged on several ships. A cruiser of the Leander class had sheared out of the formation and ran away from the formation with a very slow speed and a clear turn to the northwest. Huber ordered an 80 degree turn and let the E machines go ahead at full speed to get into a holding position. It hurt him to consume so much battery power, but the target was clearly worth 20 minutes of juice.

Twenty minutes later HMS Ajax, after three torpedo hits, was history.

This time the spacer pistols of the torpedoes had worked as planned.

July 16th, 1940, Watton 8:20 a.m.

The Blenheim, looking like a battered chicken, stood to the left of the runway in the grass. The left side of the machine was covered with holes. The upper turret was splintered, and the tail was apparently splashed with red paint. One of the tires was flat and shredded. Steam rose from the left engine, but there was no fire. The windows of the nose were covered brown-red and almost opaque.

With a shrill ringing and a strong sway in the

curves, the ambulance and the airfield fire brigade raced to the plane.

With a metallic crash the cockpit door of the bomber opened, and a man let himself fall to the ground and stayed there. The ambulance driver could see that the pilot was a Squadron Leader. This man, Delaney, moved his lips, but the doctor who examined him couldn't hear anything. His overall was splattered with blood everywhere, as if he had bathed in red. The doctor looked up briefly when he saw that the ambulance driver was withdrawing from the cockpit with a white face and shook his head.

The hot engines cracked when as they cooled down, otherwise it was completely quiet. Everyone looked at the pilot lying on the ground. The gunner on board was also obviously dead, because one of the firemen vomited behind the machine in the grass after looking into the gunner's stand.

With a croaking voice Delaney interrupted the silence. "They are all gone. Devers and Smithers were shot down by ship's AA guns over the Doggerbank. We got away well, but then a Me 109 caught us on the return flight. I think he ran out of ammo, because after 2 attacks he left us alone." He was silent for a moment and closed his eyes.

"I don't think I caught anything, but I'm completely exhausted. The trim was broken and the rudder could hardly be moved, and Tommy could not help, he was already gone after the first attack .....", in the middle of the sentence his head sank to the side. Delaney had fallen asleep lying in the grass, completely exhausted.

July 16th, 1940, Doggerbank, 8:30 a.m.

Surprised, Parker watched as the 20 hurricanes that had circled over his formation for the last hour suddenly left with an abrupt left turn towards the northwest. He turned around to his 1 WO and said, "Order battle stations."

Then the radio officer came with a message from Home fleet. Parker took the note, read it and turned pale. He turned to his officers and said, "The Home Fleet is being attacked very hard by German planes, two battleships and several cruisers are already badly damaged, that's why our fighter protection was removed. Gentlemen, it is time for us to earn our wages. Go ahead with 32 knots."

Behind him the Morse lights were clattering and passed the message on to the other cruisers. Since Parker had ordered radio silence, they were still dependent on these old-fashioned aids, which, however, based on decades of experience, worked very well. 10 minutes later they saw the first hints of smoke of the German convoy.

The few German cruisers and destroyers fired only a few dozen grenades towards his cruiser battle group and had then turned and fled after the German admiral had obviously ordered the transport ships to disperse.

The Manchester, which had not received a hit, now began to target the transports and had already forked in the second, which then disappeared within 2 minutes after a hail of 15 cm shells with a large explosion from the surface. When the German planes arrived, it was not even a dilemma for Parker, because it was clear that the German troop transports had to be destroyed. They should never get anywhere near England's coast, so he would continue the attack no matter what happened.

Half an hour later, his proud cruiser was nothing more than a broken wreck lying dead in the water, because Stukas had severely struck the ship with five hits. Parker didn't notice it anymore. He lay in a corner of his flagships bridge with a shell splinter in his intestines, bleeding to death internally. Fortunately, he quickly had lost consciousness. Only three of his cruisers reached their home port 18 hours later, loaded with hundreds of dead and wounded.

July 16th, 1940, over the Doggerbank, 0:15 p.m.
For Wegener, who slowly flew huge circles at great
heights with his old Ju 86, the events under him
were like a day in the cinema.

Due to the multitude of airplanes and ships, it was
almost impossible to keep an overview, but he
could clearly see how one ship after the other had to
endure flashing explosions, how ships lay dead in
the water and finally sank with large columns of
smoke above them. It quickly became clear that this
day would be a black day for the English fleet.

But also, the German convoy, which had tried to
turn away from the Home Fleet after sighting and
had scattered, had not remained unharmed.

A group of cruisers had hit the convoy and had sunk
several of the freighters. Also, the German security
group with its few cruisers and destroyers, which
had to defend themselves against the superior
Englishmen, had been heavily battered. At least
three destroyers were left behind and sank. Only
then had air force squadrons, which until then had
fought the Home Fleet in rolling action, turned to
the new threat. Wegener had not been able to see
anything of the Royal Air Force. He was happy
when he could start his flight home to Kiel after 5
hours, when his fuel had been used up and his butt
was hurting. Despite all that he only started to
descend when he was near Neumünster. Better be
cautious than dead.

July 16th, 1940, Doggerbank, destroyer Hotspur, 2:25 p.m.

It was incredible. He could not have imagined what happened to his ships. Of course, he had read about the American experiments of Colonel Mitchell in the years between the wars, who had sunk some old German battleships with his bombers. However, these ships had been at anchor. Also at Dunkirk a whole bunch of destroyers and other ships had been sunk from the air mainly by Stukas. But he would never have thought that these small fragile flying machines would be able to sink mighty battleships with over 12 inches of steel armour. He sat there, leaning against the rear structure of the destroyer Hotspur with a poorly bandaged deep leg wound still leaking blood. The destroyer, itself already hit several times, had taken him from his flagship together with many crew members. A hit in the front engine room of the destroyer led to the fact that it was only able to go with about three knots and so he almost had a lodge seat and could watch how his flagship, the Rodney, with chopped up superstructures, missing mast and chimney and destroyed triple turrets was slowly sliding deeper and deeper, and finally capsizing she was sinking into the grey water of the North Sea with a moaning noise. Afterwards only small wreck parts and a whole lot of corpses with life jackets were to be seen in the water. Summerfield's tears ran down his face, and he didn't even look up when the destroyer's shrill warning siren reported the next air raid.

July 16th 1940, Doggerbank, 3:10 p.m.

After Admiral Summerfield had failed and had been transported from his sinking flagship to a destroyer, the command had fallen to the captain of the Revenge. But just 10 minutes later, before he even had a chance to bring any order to his units, a Ju 87 dive bomber had sent a 500 kilo bomb through the chimney, piercing the holed plate in the duct above the boiler room that had not been built to withstand 500 kilo bombs. The bomb penetrated one of the boilers and exploded, when it was only a few inches away from the bottom of the ship. The force of the explosion killed the entire crew of the front boiler room, broke the keel and tore a huge hole in the bottom. Within seconds, the ship's now inadequate bracings gave way, and the bow and stern began to form a deadly V. Within 3 minutes the Revenge had disappeared from the surface. Only a large oil spill, wreckage of wood and corpses lined the scene of the sinking. It took another quarter of an hour until the captain of HMS Repulse realised that he was probably now the commanding officer of the fleet and who had given the order of withdrawal to all ships.

July 16th, 1940, Aarhus, airfield, 4:30 p.m.
He was so exhausted and fatigued that he wasn't even able to get up from his seat, let alone unbuckle. His first mechanic wanted to help him, but he just shook his head absently.

It took him a few minutes to get his bearings again and to get back to the real world. Only after 5 minutes he was able to loosen his belts, bend out of the cockpit and vomit out his stomach contents. Then Bergmann climbed out of the Messerschmidt with slow movements, as if he were not 21 but 81.

What a day, he had flown six missions and had probably shot down five Englishmen. The left wingtip of his aircraft was torn off, the aircraft itself had plenty of bullet holes. He remembered that he had felt a pain on his right thigh during the last mission and noticed that his overall was soaked with blood from just above the knee. But since he could move his leg without any problems, it was probably just a grazing shot. 30 m away from his plane his friend Reichert climbed out of his Me 109, which had many bullet holes similar to Bergmann's machine. Thank God the English only used machine guns with 7.92 mm rifle calibre, and plenty of them. If you were hit right, that was enough to die without any problems, but it did not have the devastating effect the German fighters had with their 20 mm cannons.

Reichert came walking over to him and said: "Drink first or sleep first".

Bergmann said: "Best both at the same time. Who bought it?"

"I have no idea. I only saw Müller going down, still smoking, shortly near the coast. I hope he managed to make an emergency landing somewhere, Reinke's machine exploded on the third mission. Otherwise, I don't know."

July 16th, 1940, 100 nautical miles west of Bergen, 10:45 pm

Like a pack of wolves, the twelve E-boats crossed the North Sea at 35 knots. They formed a V with about 100 m distance from boat to boat.

Georgson had put on his oilskin to stand up to the cold, sharp wind. It would only take a few minutes before they would meet the Home Fleet, or what was left of it. The English had, as expected, returned like a bunch of frightened chickens after the Air Force had ripped them and someone had probably given the order to hurry back to Scapa Flow on a direct course. They had received a message from a long-range reconnaissance aircraft indicating the position, course and speed of the fleet. So, it was easy to calculate when they would encounter the Home Fleet. His men were all already on battle positions, the torpedoes sharp and ready. Georgson climbed on the roof of the bridge and held on to the small mast. Just 2 meters more standing height gave him a clearly widened field of view, and he knew that also several of his colleagues did it in such a way

Yeah, there they are. A moment later, the command to swarm out came from the leading boat with a light signal. Georgson ordered a course change of 30° and told Larssen to go full speed. The sound of the three big Mercedes Diesel engines was like music in his ears. Now they would be able to show what they had to offer. The sea was only slightly choppy with wind force two, so they wouldn't have any problems launching torpedoes. Then the fleet lit up t and he held on. Now came the unpleasant part. Grenades of all calibres hit all around, next to and behind his boat and the others of the flotilla, but miraculously nobody was hit. Then Georgson instructed the helmsman to start zigging to make it more difficult for the English gunner to aim and hit. Georgson, who had now climbed down from the roof, said to his helmsman, "Make sure you don't bump into one of our boats."

Immediately the helmsman turned the wheel and changed course. About 500 meters in front of them one of the E-boats was hit and flew apart in a cloud of flying debris and a black ball of smoke. Georgson couldn't see who it was, but he shouldn't think about it now. Then they came within reach of the light AA guns of the English, who were mostly equipped with two pounders, i.e. 4 cm pompoms. The number of hits around the boat increased threateningly and he heard a lot of dull blows as other boats took hits. But so far, they hadn't been hit. He had, seconds before, picked a cruiser as his target, a relatively modern ship with two chimneys, and had shown the helmsman his target. They were still about 2000 m away from the cruiser, when Georgson ordered the launch of the torpedoes. When all four torpedoes were in the water, Georgson instructed Larssen to halve the engine power and had the boat make a sharp turn, before returning to full speed.

With clenched teeth they lived through the next 3 minutes, until they were effectively out of range of the light AA guns.

Their task was accomplished and with a bit of luck

they hadn't lost too many of their boats. Georgson, who had now looked with his binoculars aft, could see that several ships had been hit, with dark clouds of smoke hanging over the Home Fleet. But he didn't give a damn, he couldn't tell exactly if the cruiser they had aimed for had sunk.

Half an hour later the flotilla commander had collected his wolves with light balls and had noticed pleasantly that only three of them were missing.

All of them were still able to run back to Norway with 24 knots. Some of the boats had received hits and had dead and wounded sailors aboard.

July 17th, 1940, Berlin

The real sensation was that Adolf Hitler, who, as practically all leading military men and politicians of the Reich knew, was alcoholically abstinent, had invited the leadership of the army, air force and navy to a champagne reception in the Reich Chancellery. All senior officers of Milch's planning staff for Operation Sea Lion had also been summoned. The noise level rose correspondingly quickly, after several glasses of champagne had loosened the tongues of the normally rather reserved higher officers. Even the Führer could be seen with a glass of champagne in his hand, which he sometimes sipped on.

Then all present were invited into a large hall, which was darkened, so that a film and picture projection of the extensive destruction of the British Home Fleet became more visible for all present. The operation Walhalla had been, despite severe own losses, a gigantic success for the German air force and the Kriegsmarine. Three English battleships had been sunk, as had half the cruisers and at least 16 destroyers. All surviving ships had retreated to Scapa Flow, partly with severe damage and persecuted by Luftwaffe bombers and Stukas. The film and the pictures were shown for about 20 minutes. Then the lights went on and several servants entered the room with velvet cushions on which decorations lay. The Führer himself knocked on his champagne glass and explained in a few words how enthusiastic he was about the performance of the pilots and the navy. Then he awarded the Knight's Cross to ten officers who had distinguished themselves. The first name called was that of Lieutenant General Terstegen. The Führer also presented him with a donation of 100,000 Reichsmark in addition to the Knight's Cross. Terstegen, who otherwise appeared eloquent and self-confident, was in this situation almost overwhelmed by his own feelings and could only express his gratitude to the Führer with a few stuttering words. The assembled officers applauded him for several minutes. They all knew who was responsible for the success of Operation Valhalla.

July 17th, 1940, London

He had spent the whole night in the Admiralty's control room and, despite the vast quantities of strong black tea he had drunk, was now dead tired. Almost every minute, radio messages from the Home Fleet and the Humber Cruiser Group were received. One worse than the other. The only positive thing was, that the Humber cruisers had caught at least two dozen of the troop transporters and the rest had probably fled east. But at what cost. In the control room it was dead silent. Winslow had never before experienced such an atmosphere. And now the first Sealord had ordered him to instruct the Prime Minister. Winslow felt as if he had to explain to his wife that her son had fallen, which fortunately was not the case, because Tom was aboard a cruiser that was sailing in the Mediterranean. Winslow had taken his cap and left the room without another word. Actually, it would have been the task of the first Sealord to report to the Prime Minister, but he was probably happy if he could pass this inglorious task on to someone else. When he stepped outside, the sun just rose, a moment he normally enjoyed, but which now left him completely cold. Could he really present such a butcher's bill to the prime minister and destroy the expectation that the Navy would be able to fend off any invasion. Well, they had stopped the German invasion fleet and destroyed a considerable part of it, but at an unaffordable price. And if the Germans would try again, in another place?

He decided to walk to Downing Street so he could get his mind in order. The news wouldn't get any worse if it arrived half an hour later at the Prime Minister.

July 18th, 1940, Berlin

He left the parliament while the applause of the deputies of his party was still roaring.

As always after great speeches he was exhausted and sweaty. But it had to be, perhaps this was the last chance to make peace. But did Eden see it that way?

Those damn Englishmen. Any reasonable person would have initiated peace negotiations after Dunkirk. But Churchill would not. God condemn his pitch-black soul. He was still annoyed at how this arrogant bunch had cheated him in September, when they had only given him the choice between collapse and war. And they had known exactly that he could not ignore the pogroms of the Poles against the German minority. And the crazy Poles, in their delusions of great power, had relied on the guarantees of the English and French who had no real chance to support them and had remained stubborn.

Would the whole thing become a repetition of the great war? He was sometimes overwhelmed by a gnawing feeling that the English had fooled him just as they had fooled the Emperor in 1914. Like thousands of others, he had then been to the Opera Square and had cheered with joy at the announcement of the declaration of war. But at that time, it had not been clear to him how perfidiously the English had played off the German Empire against France and Russia.

Well, this time it would be different. Never had they been so close to twisting the throat of the English. If they didn't want peace, then they would be crunched!

He would watch the film about Operation Walhalla again. Valhalla, someone had found the appropriate name. There was simply nothing better than Nordic mythology, even if he found Himmler's enthusiasm for it exaggerated.

Then he sat at one more time at his desk and signed the order for the planned landing in England.

Fact
On July 19th, 1940, Hitler made a final appeal for peace to England, which Halifax rejected on July 22nd, 1940.

July 18th, 1940, London

The Prime Minister was stunned. In the newspapers the sinking of the German troop transport convoy of England was celebrated as a great victory. The invasion had been fended off. But at what cost.
He leaned back in his chair and put his arms on the desk. How long had he fought to be allowed to sit at this desk?
This desk, a massive, almost red block of iron-hard rosewood, the masterpiece of an English furniture maker who, it was said, Disraeli had brought with him during his tenure and who had somehow remained standing in the office. Eden stroked the smooth hard wood, but it didn't give him the satisfaction he had felt the first time he had taken this place at Churchill's large rosewood desk in his place. He would love to run away but couldn't.
But by now Parliament, Cabinet and parties had

319

found out that it made no sense to fire the Prime Minister at every major crisis. Not that there had been a lack of crises in the ten days of his tenure. But actually no one else was there. If he couldn't do the job, then who could?

He leaned his big head on his hands and thought. What was there to do, what could he do and wasn't it time to make peace with the damned Germans? The Home Fleet had, except three cruisers and about three dozen more or less damaged destroyers, otherwise no intact ships anymore. All others lay on the bottom of the North Sea or in the British shipyards. Two battle cruisers that had made it to Scapa Flow had to be sunk there in shallow water to prevent their complete loss. And it would take a few more days for their reserves to arrive from the Mediterranean. Air Marshal Dowding had sent him a secret report that the RAF's strength in the North Sea battles had been reduced by more than a third. The light bomber units had even suffered more than 50% losses, not even one of the Royal Navy torpedo bombers involved had returned.

At the conference at which his top military advisers had reported to him, there had not been anyone who had recommended peace or even surrender, but he had seen in their faces that they did not believe in success anymore. So, what could he do?

He could no longer ask Winston, but he knew that he would had told him never to give up. And certainly not to the Germans. He had been at the front in the great war as a soldier and officer and knew that even the Germans were only made of flesh and blood.

But he also knew that they had only been able to defeat Germany because their American friends had sent hundreds of thousands of fresh troops to France every month in 1918.

Of course, he had been delighted when the Germans had been disarmed and their fleet had been sunk in Scapa Flow by their own crews. But even then, a gnawing feeling had crept into him as to whether this peace could really endure after this humiliation.

And now for ten days he had been sitting at this desk, where Churchill had been sitting before, his friend and mentor, the one with the big mouth who could cloud everything with his cigar at any time.

And Winston was dead and could give him no more answers.

Allan Brooke had advised to put the home army on high alert. On the other hand, Pound, the first Sealord, had left no doubt that the masses of German transport ships had been sunk in the North Sea, and he did not assume that the Germans would be able to find replacements quickly enough. He had fought with hands and feet against calling back the Mediterranean fleet. Even after the losses in the North Sea, the first Sealord was still in good spirits, a typical representative of the faction of the admiralty who had already claimed in the First World War after the Battle of Skagerrak that they had been victors, although they had lost twice as many ships as the Germans. After all, after June 1916 the German deep-sea fleet had practically ceased to operate and had remained in its ports. Perhaps they were lucky this time too, and the Germans would stay in their ports. He picked up the phone and ordered a whisky from his private secretary, but with plenty of water. Then he took a report from Beaverbrook, which at least told him about good production figures of Spitfire and Hurricane fighters.

And no, no, he wouldn't give up, not yet.

Authors note:

The Operation Sealion as depicted here and the 10 months of war before that time, are a highly controversial theme, especially in England.

Therefore this book has received reviews like "the German army is infallible".

Well in hindsight, by 1945 it was not, but by 1940 it nearly was!

I will not go further into this argument, because I must surely confess that being German I have a natural bias, but will cite an American scholar who has no inbuilt bias on this topic.

The word has, Professor John Mosier, who is one of the most readable historians I ever encountered:

Mosier, John. Cross of Iron *. Henry Holt and Co.. Kindle-Version. Excerpts from Chapter 13:*

... .

The main point of this book may, I think, be summed up easily enough. In purely military terms, the superiority of the Wehrmacht lay in its institutional memory. The Germans had mastered many of the problems of modern warfare, and they preserved the essentials of what they had learned as they integrated the technologies that emerged in the next decades. Their advantage in combat thus was not a function of equipment or even training: it was conceptual, and the two key concepts were speed and integration. The German army was never mechanized to the extent that its major opponents were. But its commanders were generally quicker to move than their adversaries, whether on offense or on defense. Their speed, immensely aided by the decentralization of command, meant that the Germans generally moved inside the decision cycle of their opponents.

... .

Speed counted. It trumped mechanization. So, too, with what we now call combined-arms tactics.

....

The integration of combat engineers, heavy-weapons companies, and machine-gunners into line units, which had given the Germans such an advantage in 1914, was now widely practiced. But in the most important areas, airpower and ground-to-air defenses, the Germans were far ahead. The British and French air forces were left to wage their own wars; their ground troops lacked antiaircraft support on the German scale. And only in the Wehrmacht was airpower so clearly subordinated to the objectives of the troops on the ground. Instead of relying on heavy artillery, local commanders could call in air strikes at need, while their men were protected from enemy air strikes by the antiaircraft guns assigned to them.

These concepts could be learned. Over the course of the First World War, the Allied armies had grasped the importance of both speed and integration, just as they had begun to realize that troops armed with machine guns, mortars, and howitzers were substantially more lethal on the battlefield than units equipped only with rifles. Although in that war the Germans generally had more and better weapons than their opponents, their superiority was not simply a function of better weaponry. It was conceptual. Howitzers under the direct control of battalion commanders were much more effective than the same weapons controlled by an army corps or group. *As the war progressed, the Allies, particularly the French, adjusted, but once the war was over, they forgot what they had learned. The Germans did not. The brutal conflicts of 1919–21, in which small groups of heavily armed and mobile soldiery annihilated their numerically superior opponents, ensured that, in the Wehrmacht, speed and integration would be permanently imprinted.*

……

There was a third sense in which the Germans were superior. Although the successive German military movements into Austria and Bohemia met with no armed resistance, they gave German commanders the experience of coping with the logistical problems faced by modern armies. Nowadays, armies train as realistically as possible and work out the all-important details through intensive maneuvers. In the 1930s no one really did this, and certainly not on the grand scale afforded by the march into two neighboring countries. Transporting a mechanized division seven hundred kilometers (the distance the German Second Armored Division traveled to Vienna from its base in Würzburg) was a major accomplishment in its own right. So in September 1939, when the fighting started, the armies on both sides consisted of recent recruits, but only the Germans had dealt with the logistical problems of modern warfare. They were logistical veterans if nothing else.

Poland is a large country. In September 1939, not only were the Germans faced with a war of large-scale movement; they had to fight as well. So in May 1940, the German experience in logistics and combat gave them a decisive advantage.

.....

From early on, the belief that the basis of German superiority was the blitzkrieg became a quasi-mystical concept used in explaining every German success. Insofar as the term characterized the concepts of speed and integration learned in the First World War, it conveys a grain of truth. As generally employed, however, the word blitzkrieg does not; yet as the war progressed, it began to have a great deal of influence, mostly on the way the stories of the conflict were told. At its simplest—suggesting that one could win by hurling masses of armor against the enemy—the term never worked. At its most sophisticated—and there has been no shortage of efforts to renovate the concept—it comes down to nothing more than speed and integrated tactics.

Up to a point, explaining the German advantage and the Allied deficiency is simple. The Allies had brave soldiers, competent commanders, and excellent equipment in great quantity. By any objective measure, the two sides were evenly matched. The Allies lost because they failed to learn from their experiences in the Great War and the

Germans did not. But then again, how could they have learned anything? Their governments had lied systematically about the course of that war, claiming that while it had been a struggle between two evenly matched foes, they had ultimately prevailed on the field of battle. As time passed, this delusion was regarded as an incontrovertible fact, as indeed it is today by the vast majority of British military historians. Although the months-long debacle of September 1939–June 1940 should have led to a fundamental reconsideration of the point, it did not. Instead, both the experts and their governments, unable to hide the extent of the defeat as they had done in the earlier war, invented three reasons to explain the devastating losses. The Germans had built up an enormous arsenal, largely by cheating on the Versailles Treaty, and simply overwhelmed us. We were the victims of a cunning conspiracy to wage an aggressive war. The Germans had invented a modern form of warfare, the blitzkrieg. There is, even today, no shortage of eloquent pleading on these three points.

But as I have shown in this book (and elsewhere), they're simply not true. As I studied both wars for more decades than I care to admit, I became convinced that tactics, training, and technology were only one part of the key to the achievements of the Wehrmacht. The German army of 1914 was substantially better than the British and French and

Russian armies, and it was certainly better than the German army of 1939. Although the institutional memory that preserved the emphasis on speed and nurtured the evolution of integration of force gave it a serious advantage, it seems doubtful that this advantage, all by itself, could explain the victories of 1939–41. To a great extent, those victories were a function of the leadership of the two sides. On the one side, the Allied, the record suggests what amounts to almost criminal incompetence. The only worse spectacle than French prime minister Paul Reynaud's hysterical phone call to Churchill on May 15, 1940, is Neville Chamberlain's desperate maneuvering to stay atop the floundering British government after September 1939. Anyone who loves democracy and freedom must applaud Churchill's lonely fight from May 1940 to the end of the war.

....

But most of his military decisions were simply wrong, beginning with his plans for stopping the shipments of iron ore from Scandinavia to Germany in the fall of 1939 to his insistence on invading Italy and his reluctance to back the cross-Channel invasion. Of course, these considerations pale in the face of Stalin's abysmal performance, but the case can be made that Hitler was extraordinarily lucky in the leaders who opposed him. The mention of both names brings us face-to-face with a most unpleasant problem. *The Allied leadership at the start of the war was wretched. But Hitler intuited that. Unlike everyone else in the German leadership, he was confident that they would cut and run at the first setback. The failure to come to terms with Hitler is a major stumbling block in understanding the Wehrmacht's success, perhaps the greatest stumbling block. As I have tried to explain, it is the missing element in the equation, and the single most important one. It is Hitler who empowered the risky new strategies that resulted in May 1940 (and after), who gave Student and von Manstein the encouragement to develop their ideas and then insisted on their execution. The German high command was no more receptive to innovation in warfare than the high commands of its opponents. Similarly, it was Hitler who understood that at the first reverse his opponents would descend into hysterical impotency, lose the will to fight, and quit the war.*

... ...

Hitler was a supremely evil man. But wicked does not mean insane, incompetent, or stupid. On the contrary, the wicked are generally quite rational in carrying out their schemes—one reason why they are often so successful.

... ...

The Germans felt that there had been a systematic attempt to destroy them after 1918, that the terms of the peace treaty were constructed accordingly, and that the Allies tricked them into a surrender they could never have won on the battlefield. Again, here is an area where false ideas have dominated our discourse. Rather than admit that this fear was legitimate, that it was what people felt and that there was a grain of truth in the idea, historians have devoted their energies to ridiculing the notion, suppressing the abundant evidence to the contrary. Hitler capitalized on those feelings, but he hardly invented them.

July 18th, 1940, Alencon, France

He lay in the shadow under the wing of his machine and tried to bring clarity to his thoughts, which after reading his wife's letter meandered through his brain only in confused scraps.

At least the squadron had been put to rest for a few days to give the pilots some rest and get all the aircraft back into shape. Also, the workshop and in particular the spare parts store had got truck-loads of stuff.

Whatever there was in the fold, nobody knew anything at the moment, but some were glad that they had not been there during the battles over the North Sea.

Since he had nothing to do, in the heat of the midday sun he had laid down under a wing of his Me 110, which stood on the lawn covered with camouflage nets.

"LMF," he asked himself, "or just insecure." This letter from Ellen that she doesn't want to see me anymore, never wants to see me again, what was that supposed to be? Does this woman know at all what she is writing about, what she is doing to me, what she is doing to our child? Would I have had any chance not to go to war?

That is exactly what she accuses me of, and what she cannot cope with at all. Doesn´t she see that almost all the other young men are gone just like me and are soldiers, sailors or pilots somewhere in Europe?

Has she ever seen anything other than herself?

He shook his head, but that was of no use. Of course, it was clear to him, that he had to have his head free to increase his chances of survival. But that was easy to say. Then he closed his eyes and fell asleep.

He woke up only when Lenz kicked his boot and shouted, "Hey Merkle, wake up".

"What's the matter, is the war already over?

"No!

"Then why do you wake me?"

"The squadron commander has ordered a briefing in half an hour, sounds as if we are now finding out why they have pampered us for the last few days! Merkle stood up resignedly and followed his friend, rubbing his eyes as he stumbled along.

July 18th, 1940, Rennes, France

Lelouche was overwhelmingly proud and very sad. He thought of his brother Jean, who now lay in the belly of the sunk battleship "Bretagne" in the bay of Mers el Kebir. They would give it to the English. They were the "Brigade de `l Air de la Crosse du feu". His group had 15 LeO 45 bombers ready for action. Today the first combat mission was planned. An attack on the English airfield Debden in low flight. Colonel de la Roque had been right, the Germans did the only right thing. He approached his plane. He had called it "Mers el Kebir", the name emblazoned in white letters on the fuselage. The French cockade was no longer round but square to distinguish it better from the English emblems. He did not love the Germans, but he felt an abysmal hatred for the English. Major Claude Lelouche put up the pilot's bonnet with a routine move.

July 18th, 1940, Berlin

Milch opened the meeting by knocking on his water glass.

"Gentlemen, the Führer has given the order to launch Sea Lion."

They had all expected this, of course, and Milch could see the face of Manstein and Dönitz brightening after a moment of hesitation.

"I think, since we already had the champagne with the Führer yesterday, we can do without it today and concentrate on the essentials. Operation Valhalla was indeed, as was now confirmed by long range reconnaissance aircraft. a great success. The home fleet of the Royal Navy lies either on the bottom of the Skagerrak or in the shipyards of the English east coast. This means that we have considerably reduced the ability of the English fleet to operate in the Channel. But I do not think we should rest on our laurels. We will probably have to reckon with a substantial part of the English Mediterranean fleet being transferred back to home waters by the time our first command units in England hit the ground at the latest. At the suggestion of Colonel ... excuse me, General Terstegen, ten days ago we asked the Italians to place as many submarines as possible in a protective shield east of the Strait of Gibraltar. I think, however, that we should not rely too much on their ability to fight the Royal Navy. Admiral

Dönitz, what possibilities do you see with our unfortunately very limited possibilities to do something here?

Dönitz first thought for a moment and then said: "since we don't have more than about 24 submarines available, we effectively only have the possibility to position them north and south of the channel entrance, while as far as the northern entrance of the English Channel is concerned, we have the submarines operating in very shallow waters, which to say the least does not help their survivability very much. However, since Operation Walhalla has significantly decimated the surface forces of the home fleet stationed in Scapa Flow and south of it, I think it makes sense for us to station all submarines south of the Channel. There they operate in much deeper water and are therefore much more effective. North of the channel we have only stationed E-boats and our few surviving surface units, so here at the northern entrance of the channel we have to rely on the abilities of the air force units!

Milch nodded and viewed General Manstein with a provocative look.

Manstein put on his mischievous smile and then began: "Due to the limited range of our artillery, we have of course only few possibilities to close the channel effectively. What I am pleased to say, however, is that the artillery we provided for coastal protection did an excellent job in the few weeks it took. Any English ship that gets closer than 10-15 km to the coast will have a hell of a life. We've stationed so much artillery in these stretches of coastline that, and I'm just exaggerating a little, you could almost swing from tube to tube like the legendary Tarzan."

Everyone laughed, even the otherwise rather dry Dönitz couldn't resist.

Milch nodded to Terstegen, who looked at the clock and then began:

"We are at X-72 hours right now, we have received clear messages from all units involved from the Air Force, Navy and Army. At X -60 the first orders go out, at the same time we cancel all permissions and close all bases. We have refrained from shutting down the radio traffic in order not to warn English intelligence, because of course they monitor the German radio traffic, but we have assigned properly instructed officers to all radio stations, who take care that only completely normal and irrelevant radio messages are transmitted and no essential information can get out. At X-20, the commanding officers may open their sealed orders, and on 21 July, at 5 a.m., at first light, the landing operation in England begins."

Milch rose, and the other generals also stood up.

"Gentleman, good luck!

Everyone was saluting.

July 19th, 1940, off Vlissingen

The flotilla entered the port of Vlissingen in a keel line with 20 knots, Georgson's E-boat being the second in the line behind the flotilla leader. The helmsman reacted immediately when the command came back for a 90° right turn and full speed aback. They were barely 200 m away from the pier, when Georgson saw, that a whole row of soldiers was standing every few meters along the pier with their submachine guns hooked around them. That didn't bode well. The men had already raved all the way from Esbjerg in Denmark about how good the whorehouse in Vlissingen was and what they would do with the girls there. In the last days in Norway and Denmark, there had been no opportunity, because they had been on alert or in combat all the time. Thank God there had only been a few small strikes on Georgson's boat, but not a single wounded man, which, in conjunction with the destruction of the English cruiser, had created an almost supernatural good mood among the sailors. In their minds, everyone had probably already drunk several bottles of beer.

Georgson did not interfere in the docking manoeuvre, because his helmsman Larsen could do it better than him anyway, since Larsen was at least 15 years older than Georgson.

After the boat was moored in front and behind, he climbed up to the jetty where a young lieutenant waited for him.

Unlike Georgson, he saluted rather dashingly and said: "Lieutenant, on the orders of Admiral Ruge, you and your men must stay on board. You and the other boats of the flotilla must be ready for departure within 15 minutes. The tank tenders are already waiting for you. I may inform you from the Admiral that he is very satisfied with the performance of the flotilla in the naval battle in the North Sea."

Georgson, who despite his low rank, since he was a boat captain, was not particularly impressed by higher officers, said: "That is nice of the Admiral, but my men are actually interested in something else. Can you get us at least five crates of beer?

The lieutenant grinned and pointed behind him. "We already have, with Admiral Ruge's compliments."

Now Georgson also grinned, knowing that his people had to let off at least a little steam and a few beers were the minimum. Then even the MP`s on the pier could be ignored.

July 19th, 1940, Arras.

Bergmann's squadron had already been moved back to France one day after the huge air battle over the Kattegat. After that the pilots had been left to themselves during the day, but now at 6 pm a meeting was scheduled to which all pilots had been ordered. As always there were rumours, but nobody knew anything at all.

In one of his bright moments in the morning, Bergmann had seen a whole series of trucks arrive at the base, which, as he could see, had auxiliary tanks stored in one of the warehouses. He had thought about auxiliary tanks for a moment, was happy that someone had finally thought about the inadequate range of his Messerschmitt and fell asleep again immediately.

By now he felt somewhat refreshed. Plenty of sleep, plentiful food and drink had recharged their batteries, which had been quite low after the air battle over the Kattegat.

He sat in the back row, as he had always been used to from school, where he had a good view of the rest of his comrades and the action. When he saw the door open and the group commander started to get up and in attention, he also jumped up, as always, the pilot with the fastest reaction.

A rather young colonel, carrying a chest full of medals on his blue air force uniform, entered. With a short movement of his hand, the colonel ordered them to be at ease and sit down. Then he began: "Gentlemen, first of all I am to congratulate you on behalf of the Air Force Commander General Field Marshal Milch. He is delighted with your performance and was particularly impressed by the high number of missions their group flew on 16 July. You were the fighter group with the most missions that day. Each of the pilots involved will therefore be awarded the First-Class Iron Cross and each of the other members of the squadron will be awarded the Second Class Iron Cross. Just for your information.

You may have noticed that yesterday trucks delivered jettison able external fuel tanks for your Messerschmitt fighters. Your task tomorrow is to familiarize yourselves with the technology of these auxiliary tanks, to do some test flights with them, in order to cope with the changed flight characteristics of your aircraft, having an auxiliary tank under them. The air fleet expects you to know what you are doing by tomorrow evening.

 From tomorrow evening 6 pm your whole squadron will be on 20-minute standby. You are allowed to sleep but will leave your flying suits on so that you can actually take off at any time within these 20 minutes. Tomorrow evening at 6 am there will be another briefing at which you will receive further orders. Thank you very much. Dismissed!"

Like most others, Bergmann had not expected that things would continue so quickly after the big event over the Kattegat. As it looked, tonight would be the only chance to sleep with Liane. Hopefully she still talked to him at all after she hadn't heard from him for a whole week. But maybe she also read newspapers, because even the French newspapers had reported about the big German victory.

July 20th, 1940 Northern France, 4.45 a.m.
Von der Heyden and his men once again went through their attack plan on a model. Pioneers had built an accurate replica of the Dover fortress on a mown maize field, with dummy buildings and wooden guns.
Von der Heyden used the whistle to give the start order. From the assumed landing points of the DFS 230 assault gliders, his men ran off, some in the direction of the guns, others to the entrance of the command bunker which was built into the rocks. They carried marked backpacks simulating the explosive charges.
They had rehearsed this at least 50 times, the last ten times at night.
Even now, shortly before sunrise, it was almost pitch dark. But after only two minutes the "clear" calls of his attack groups came from all target

points. He had also deposited the simulated explosive charge at the entrance of the command bunker, and with his five men had taken cover around the corner, to avoid the blast. Since they had chosen the landing points differently for each group each time, the first test runs in the dark had been a hopeless mess, but in the meantime, it worked like clockwork.

If the pilots of the gliders, whom he had integrated into the groups as infantry in the meantime, did not mess up, the English would experience an unpleasant surprise in the fortress Dover.

On the other hand, as Clausewitz constantly wrote of occurrences he called frictions, as things rarely worked out as planned during war. That's why ten gliders were planned for the seven targets.

With two whistles trills he signalled that everyone should stay in the same place and could rest for 10 minutes until it was light enough to see, if everything had gone as planned.

He also sat at the edge of the hut with which they had rebuilt the entrance bunker, put his submachine gun into the grass and observed how the eastern sky became brighter and brighter until the top edge of the sun came out visibly. It would again be a glorious almost cloudless summer day, and although the night had been clear, the thermometer again indicated almost 20° Celsius.

He didn't know exactly when it would start, but he knew that he and his men were ready for it. And the way things evolved, it would start soon.

July 20th 1940, London, afternoon

The general was pleased. He had finally made it and was now Commander-in-Chief of the Home Army. And it had also been time to finally send old Ironside into the desert. It was good that he had the confidence of Churchill and now Eden, even though it had annoyed him to spend a considerable part of his time answering Winston's pink "action this day memos". He had to yawn. In the last few days he had barely been able to sleep. The late evening conferences in the last few days always lasted until at least one o'clock in the morning. General Alan Brooke called his adjutant: "Mayhew, let the car drive up, we have to get to Maldon tonight. I promised Connors I'd definitely come to the 2nd armoured."

The adjutant saluted diligently and went to find the driver who would not be thrilled to drive to East Anglia tonight.

July 20th, 1940 London, 8:50 p.m.

Slowly a picture emerged, even though Newport's mind was essentially running on coffee and cigarettes he kept fighting against lying his incredibly tired and heavy head on the desk.

In the afternoon, a report had come from Sweden, reporting that the Swedish Navy, found one a beached ship, one of the damaged German transporters that had drifted into Swedish waters. They had only rescued 22 men, not a single soldier and not a single piece of equipment on board.

And then there was this strange information from Paris, a telephone operator who worked for MI 6 had intercepted several conversations during which German officers had said, that they could not be there for some time beginning tomorrow.

And now Jacques from Calais, a man he had known for years, had radioed a very unusual message.

Newport read the message a second time.

Jacques, whom he had recruited himself, was a very clever ex Flic of the vice department but was now running several brothels.

The report stated that five different prostitutes, who worked near airports, army units and ports along the English Channel had suddenly lost the usual clientele of German soldiers abruptly starting since the morning of July 19th.

He could not believe that the entire Wehrmacht was suddenly on the moral path.

If the soldiers were no longer allowed to go to whores, there was usually something in the bush, and the fact that not only the army, but obviously also the navy and air force were all affected, only permitted one conclusion.

Obviously, the Wehrmacht had been put on alert with curfews to carry out a major mission.

And an operation involving both the Navy and the Air Force could only be an attack on England, an invasion.

Since it was clear to him that by aerial reconnaissance, since the Germans were quite good at camouflaging, he probably wouldn't get any information about an upcoming attack operation, and it was to be assumed that the Germans wouldn't lock up their troops in the bases for weeks or even months, he could assume that the German invasion would begin in a very short time, in a period of at most days.

On the other hand, would the statements of five prostitutes be meaningful enough to go to the Prime Minister?

Perhaps he would ridicule himself, but he had to risk that, better a warning too much than no warning at all.

He only hoped that after the naval battle in the North Sea, Eden and his cabinet were not too euphoric because they thought they had essentially sunk the actual invasion fleet.

If the report from Sweden was correct, then this German operation would have been a fake to lure the fleet and the Royal Air Force into battle. As they could not ignore the German landing ships, they had sailed out of their ports and were decimated by the Germans. That had worked really well.

He picked up the phone and called the Downing Street secretary's office and said he needed to speak to the prime minister immediately.

Then he put on his uniform cap, went to the door and murmured to himself."...five whores, that's perfect."

July 20th, 1940 London, 10 p.m.

"This can't be, we just drowned the German invasion fleet in the North Sea!" Eden looked at him with a confused expression, and Admiral Winslow leaned back with his arms crossed. "Gentlemen, I know my evidence is thin, but I'm pretty sure I'm right. The information we have from Sweden shows us quite clearly, that this so-called invasion fleet was nothing more than a deception manoeuvre by the Germans, to lure our home fleet and a considerable part of the RAF into their own territory and to finish them off in their own turf, which they did quite well. They know the loss figures of the Navy and the RAF as well as I do." Newport could see that now both were insecure. "And the information we get from France, tells us clearly that the Wehrmacht is obviously at the highest level of readiness there. Please give me one reason why this should be so, because the French surrendered four weeks ago. Against whom will the Germans in France fight now, please?"

Eden leaned back, "I know you're good Newport, Churchill definitely held you in highest regard, and you were right about both Norway and France with your predictions. But I'm sorry, I'm not convinced that the statements of five prostitutes justify triggering an invasion alert. I have no desire to ridicule myself in front of the cabinet and the press, who would certainly find out. No, Newport, I need more evidence!"

For Newport, the thought patterns of politicians were not new, although from a professional point of view, he had nothing but contempt for them. He looked at Winslow with a challenge.

"I think we should convene the war cabinet tomorrow morning at the latest, Prime Minister," Winslow said and nodded his head at Newport.

"Good Winslow, prepare for this meeting. Major Newport, I very much hope, that you are wrong this

time and I very much hope that what I am doing is right. If any of you gentlemen want to swap places with me, go ahead!"
Newport and Winslow saluted. Winslow said: "No thanks, Prime Minister, I'd rather not have that position!" Newport also shook his head.

July 20th, 1940 Bay of Biscay, U37, 11 p.m.

Even at night in the Bay of Biscay one could feel that it was summer.

The submarine lay in the water like a plank, the swell being hardly noticeable. After Huber had opened the hatch and had climbed up immediately after the tower had come out of the water, he first took a look around with the night glass, to be sure that he hadn't overlooked something before with the periscope. He could feel how the bridge guard behind him took their places and heard how the gunners at the 2 cm flak made the gun ready to fire. It wasn't a very bright night, but he could see the wake of the boat even though they were running at only seven knots. A Sunderland could do that too. "Reduce speed to three knots, clear on diesel, start charging batteries immediately." He heard the helmsman down in the boat repeat the order and the boat slowed down noticeably.

"Watch out, gentlemen, it's a lovely evening, but that´s also true for the English who are looking for us."

He was annoyed that they had to surface for battery charging, because with this minimal swell they could hear much further under water at night than they could see above water. And even the English had to be aware, that after the battle in the North Sea, where the English Home Fleet had been decimated, the Mediterranean fleet had to be brought home.

Therefore, they were now about 50 miles west of Ouessant, or Ushant as the English said. If everything had worked out, another twelve submarines would be about 10 miles to the left and right of them at about the same height, and in two days there would be another ten.

The hum of the diesel seemed incredibly loud to him in the silence of the night, but he knew from experience, that a surface ship would only hear the diesel when it came closer than about 800 meters. English submarines, on the other hand, could hear them from several miles away when they were underwater.

It was like playing chess, the English boats were supposed to be in the North Sea, where there was an invasion to be expected, but perhaps someone clever enough to counteract the Dönitz move that had set up his submarines south of the Channel and south of the Bristol Channel to intercept the Mediterranean fleet on its way home. So, in the next 3 hours, until the batteries were full again, only praying helped.

Nevertheless, he looked at his watch every 3 minutes.

July 21th 1940, Alencon, 4:48 a.m.

One-week rest had been really good for them. The start was perfect, at intervals of 10 seconds one machine after the other swung into the night sky. All flew exceptionally with full lighting. Since they would still be over France for quite a while, not much could happen. At least up to now, it seemed the English didn't even know how to write night fighter, let alone that one of them had been seen over France before. Thus, it was relatively easy for the planes starting later to catch up, and already after less than 10 minutes Lenz, who led the squadron, turned with north western course toward England. At a height of no more than 200 m the whole squadron followed him.

When the sky brightened a little in the east, that was shortly before reaching the French coastline, Lenz let his position lights flicker twice and then switched them off as a signal for the others to do the same.

Merkle, who flew with his wingman staggered left behind Lenz, followed carefully, as Lenz went deeper and settled at about 70 m height over the just still visible waves. He felt that his machine, which had two 250 kilo bombs under it, was behaving much more sluggishly than usual, but that was normal with this load. His new gunner, Sergeant Gerwald, had the task with the large Zeiss night glass to look out for other planes on both sides and above them, for this was the day. As they had been told, practically the entire German Air Force was in the air in that minute, and much of it over the channel.

He hoped that the others would be able to fly low as well, but if the eggheads of the secret service were right, the English were rather unable to detect airplanes flying well below 200 m with their miracle radar. They would find out.

And the English would also soon find out that the Me 110 destroyers now had a new task. Stuka with a costume some had been joking, but since the fighter bomber training that they had intensively completed over the former French military training area of Mailly for a week had worked excellently, he was confident that they would pave their way to Lydd Airport in the Romney Marshes. Knemeyer had also taught them some damn good tricks. The men had been thrilled, especially by the scissor flying method with which two Me 110s worked together, could the even compete with single seat fighters like the Spitfire or the Hurricane.

However, he hoped that they might not have to do so today, even better if they all caught the English fighters on the ground.

Again, and again he followed the Knemeyer pattern: Observe, assess position, make a decision and act accordingly in order to stay in an optimal position behind Lenz in the formation. This, too, was a Knemeyer tip that had brought some of the self-evident actions of flying into a systematic structure. Even Merkle, who had been sitting behind various controls for more than four years, had learned a few new things from him.

The agreed light signal came from the gunner on board of Lenz machine, now it got serious. The sun had not risen yet, but he could already see the flat line that made up England's coastline.

July 21th 1940, Sunday, 4:48 a.m., over the channel off Dover

The night wasn't completely dark. A rest of moonlight was bright enough, to give the pilot of the DFS 230 glider the necessary orientation. The sun would rise in barely 15 minutes and it was not completely dark anymore. They had released the cord connecting the glider with it's He 111 towing tug ten seconds ago, so there was no way back anyway. The lieutenant, who sat directly behind the pilot, was Karl Ullrich von der Heyden. He had been born in East Prussia in 1919, coincidentally on the same day that Germany had to sign the dictation of Versailles. His father, a Major of the Imperial Army, from the ancient nobility of Brandenburg, who had come back from the war less one foot, reminded him of this fact every birthday. Early on, he had explained to Karl Ullrich what a gigantic mistake the Allies had made in this vicious dictation. And he had made it clear to him, that he too would have to fight again, because Versailles was merely an armistice. This had encouraged Karl Ullrich to follow in his father's footsteps as early as possible. On his 18th birthday he had become a soldier. Anything else would have been unthinkable for him.

In Poland he had encountered death, in Belgium he had been one of the heroes of Eben-Emael. He had been present at the storm of the fort Eben-Emael. He wore his EK 1 with pride and often thought of his three friends, who had not survived that day.
"Another 20 seconds", the pilot shouted.
Karl Ullrich felt his ears turning red with excitement and was glad that nothing could be seen

in the dark cabin. At least his pants were still dry, which hadn't been the case in Eben-Emael.

With a hard blow the glider hit the ground, rumbled a few more meters in front of him and then stayed with the wing tilted down to the left.

"Go, get out, get out," he hissed, as everything was still quiet until now. It couldn't stay that way for long. When he stepped out of the glider with his submachine gun held up, he could see that they had landed directly and perfectly on the glacis of the citadel of Dover. He could already see five other gliders from whom storm troopers emerged.

Now they would crack the bunkers, turn off the radar, blow up the long-range guns and get the staff of the commanding admiral.

Of course, everything had started much earlier, but when the first charge went off at the entrance to the fortress, he realized that there was nothing more pleasurable than that. He was in exactly the right place.

The entrance door to the command bunker was made of solid steel. Meyer two, the explosives expert of his group, brought a hollow charge with a few holds, pulled it off, and said "Cover, 5 seconds to go".

Von der Heyden pressed against the wall two meters from the door, pulled a hand grenade out of his boot and armed it. The hollow charge exploded with a violent crash, and he could see for a second that all over the area his people were busy depositing their explosives.

He saw that the door was blown inwards and threw a hand grenade inside to be on the safe side. Then everything went almost like a ballet, as they had practiced. Wolters and Meyer two were the first to enter the bunker, then von der Heyden came with the other two men in his group, followed by the groups of Schubert, Eberwein, Marks and Fährmann. All men were equipped with submachine guns, the ideal weapon for what was in store for them in the bunker.

There was light in the passage leading down. When they reached the first branch, a tired looking Englishman stumbled around the corner with a pistol and was killed by Wolters with a burst.

They worked their way systematically through the bunker for half an hour, throwing hand grenades into every room, and destroying every radio they could find. Some Englishmen tried to resist but had no chance against the firepower of the commando troop. Prisoners were not taken.

When von der Heyden and his men came back up, it was already full daylight.

Smoke was in the air and he could see that the big guns on the front glacis with blown up barrels were out of action.

There were still shots to be heard in the old fortress, but that was what von der Heyden had expected.

The 30 men who had been ordered to take the old castle had been a rather small group, since the main target had been the underground command bunker and the heavy guns.

He sent two groups for reinforcements towards the castle, two more groups to the entrance area of the site, where one group whose job was securing the entrance against reinforcements from outside was involved in a fierce firefight.

Now the task was to hold out for a few hours until the reinforcements from Folkestone arrived.

July 21st, 1940 Dover radar station, 4:55 a.m.
Corporal Anderson, who intensively observed the reflection of the green cathode tube, rubbed his eyes. No, that was impossible. He rubbed his eyes again, because shortly before the end of the night shift, after staring into the tube for almost 8 hours, his own senses sometimes played a trick on him, and the radar wasn't exactly a pattern of reliability either.

He turned the focus adjustment knobs.

That was impossible, he had hundreds of echoes on his screen. Did the Germans have so many airplanes at all?

He turned around and called the lieutenant on duty,

who shared the night shift with him when he heard a strange noise. As if an engine had a piston seizure, followed by a short squeak.

The lieutenant had also heard something, went to the door, opened it and was thrown back into the room by the volley of a submachine gun.

Anderson had no weapon, he at least tried to pick up the phone, but had no chance to say anything to the operator, because an obviously German soldier with a funny helmet came in through the door of the barracks and pointed his submachine gun at him. Anderson still wanted to get up, but then hard blows to his chest threw him from his chair, and then everything vanished into darkness.

July 21st, 1940 near Hastings, 5:15 a.m.

Delaney didn't know what had woken him up, but it was definitely Joyce's snoring that prevented him from falling asleep again.

How short the days and nights were, tomorrow .. no today on Sunday evening, he would have to return to the squadron.

It had only been three days since he had brought home back his Blenheim with his two dead friends from the Battle of the North Sea. He hadn't even got a scratch, all the blood was from Tommy, who had been shot in the head by a Me 109.

He wondered that he could sleep at all. The difference between his fight in the bloodied cockpit of his Blenheim, and now three days later, lying with his beautiful wife in a comfortable bed in the house of his parents-in-law in Hastings, was unbelievable and not tangible.

And only three other machines from the whole squadron had come back, apart of his. At first, they had all cheered because they had assumed that they had destroyed a German invasion fleet. Then one by one it had become clear what price they had paid for it.

The Wing Commander had then given him leave until Sunday evening.

He looked out of the window and noticed that it was getting a little bit lighter. Joyce was still snoring, but some unusual noise was getting louder.

He closed his eyes again, maybe it would go away, but that didn't work either.

When it became clear to him that the deep humming that was swelling up more and more was caused by nothing else but a multitude of aircraft engines, the anti-aircraft gun started to shoot.

With a loud "damn crap" he jumped out of bed and opened the window.

In the pale moonlight, minimally brightened by the sunrise, he could see three-engined planes.

"I don't think so now," he said when he realized that

these were German Ju 52 transport aircraft. He should have recognized them from their slowly but monotonous engine sound as Junkers machines. Nothing that flew around in the sky sounded similar.

He went to bed and gently woke Joyce.

" What's going on" she asked, still half asleep.

"The damn Germans are coming."

"So, what, come to bed, you're still on vacation until tonight."

"No Darling, the vacation has just been cancelled."

Only now did she open her eyes properly.

"Oh crap!"

July 21st, 1940, London 6:10 a.m.

Anthony Eden sat at the head of the table. His Havana gave off thick clouds of smoke, which the secretary in charge of the protocol sometimes acknowledged with a dry cough. He had just received news that German paratroopers had attacked Dover and Folkestone and that all airports and railway junctions between Dover and London had been bombed.

General Dill was the first to speak after Eden had read the message to them. "Well, the Germans won the first act. Our reserves are in East Anglia. We have to bring them back immediately. But how sure are we, that the landing at Dover is the main landing?"

Eden remained silent and looked at the first Sealord, Admiral Pound.

Pound's face was marked by horror at the failure of his fleet. "We will transfer the bulk of our light naval forces that we currently have in the Western Approaches to Portsmouth on the south coast and to the Nore at the east coast. Scapa is too far away, and after the battle in the North Sea there is not too much of the home fleet left. Factually we are very thin regarding destroyers and battleships. We will then be within range of the German bombers, but we have to accept that. If we don't manage to close the channel and stop the supply of the airborne troops by sea, we've lost."

Eden looked at him: "That is, the North Sea off East Anglia and the Channel are then paved with our destroyers and cruisers".

"Yes Sir" said Allan Brooke, and then continued: "So far we have only reported airborne landings. Maybe this is just a diversionary manoeuvre, because if the Germans are serious, they have to bring troops and material by ship. I don't think the Germans will be able to get supply and landing ships through the Channel, if we concentrate the Royal Navy there."

General Chief of Staff General Dill nodded and

said, "Then we will immediately start to deploy our reserves to the front in Kent."

Dill stood up and went to the big map on the side wall: "What about our naval forces in the Mediterranean and South Atlantic. I think we need those units now and here."

Admiral Pound stood up in his seat, but the Commander-in-Chief of the Army, General Alan Brooke, preceded him: "I see that just like General Dill. We have invested millions of pounds in this steel wall off our coast. Now the Navy must prove itself. Our troops in the Empire can hold out for a while without the support of the Navy."

"And what about Malta," Admiral Pound jumped up angrily, but the Prime Minister waved reassuringly at him.

After he had laid down his cigar to die, he took the floor.

"Gentlemen, I think we can live without Malta, but not without Kent. Admiral Pound put the Mediterranean fleet and everything else we have, on the march towards the channel. This is now the decisive big game with no way out".

Admiral Pound nodded stiffly.

*****

Dear Reader

For me as an author one thing is eminently important: your feedback:

How did you like my book, what was good or not so good?

Therefore, I would like to ask for a personal favour!

Please use the opportunity offered by Amazon to rate this book and make a comment.

Of course, I prefer positive comments!

Naturally you can rate this book negatively, it's a free world, so I have acquired some Voodoo puppets and needles in preparation, ... just joking!

Please, leave a commentary!

Prehistory of the Second World War
Before the First World War, Germany was an economically prosperous country. Regarding Sciences Germany practically world market leader in most areas, as one would say today, which had already been confirmed at that time by the large number of Nobel Prizes.
The ruling families of Germany, England, Russia and Austria were related to each other in many ways and did not lie in a state of war.
Core Europe had lived in peace since the short Franco-German war of 1871. The Balkan wars between 1911 and 1913 were events for Core

Europe that took place relatively far away and had little significance.

England and France, and to a lesser extent Spain, Portugal, Belgium and Italy, had conquered a considerable part of the rest of the world in the form of colonies.

Germany had only been able to get a few and insignificant colonies, because in this imperialist race she had not only started late but also with not too much conviction.

Nevertheless, the German economy was healthier and more prosperous than its competitors, especially compared to France, England and Russia.

One would search in vain for any ideology with the serious goal of a German world domination in 1914. A book on this subject published after the Second World War, written by a former Nazi (Fritz Fischer), has more to do with the re-education measures for Germany at that time, than with the actual situation before 1914.

Fortunately, 100 years after the catastrophic summer of 1914, a number of books have now been published, especially by Clarke (The Sleepwalkers), which look at the development of the war in a realistic and differentiated light.

It simply cannot be denied that Russia was the first great power to mobilize, and mobilization means war. That France, because of the

annexation of Alsace-Lorraine by Germany in 1871, subsequently pursued an extremely revanchist policy, which absolutely wanted to reverse this annexation and that England by no means acted as a brake on the way to the beginning of the war, but was probably glad to be able to eliminate its main economic competitor, Germany, and not to have to do this alone, but to be happily able to do this together with two major military powers, France and Russia.

Even Germany with its loyalty to Austria, whose Balkan policy, by the way, was clearly better than its reputation, especially on the part of the crown prince murdered in Sarajevo, Germany with its clumsily acting and not very clever emperor, must be accused of having slowed down Austria too little here. But it was not an active warmonger, like France and Russia.

From this initial situation a murderous war evolved over four years, with which, in this intensity and duration, nobody had reckoned, and for which nobody was really prepared, although attentive observers could have predicted such a course already from the Russian-Japanese war. Both soldiers and civilians, particularly in Germany due to the Allied naval blockade that led to several winters of starvation after 1916, died in their millions.

At the end of 1916 all participants were exhausted and tired of war, in France even whole divisions mutinied and did not want to fight further.

In fact, this was a situation that could have led to an armistice.

But now the USA appears. England was closer due to economic and linguistic ties, and by an excellent war propaganda of England, which exploited such incidents, as the sinking of the Lusitania, which had loaded ammunition for England, as has been proven in the meantime, by a German submarine, to its advantage, whereupon the USA declared war on Germany to Germany in April 1917. From today's point of view not the USA had no viable reason for war and was acting clearly against their own Monroe doctrine. To ask the cui bono question here would be an interesting research approach.

This shifted the balance of power on the European theatre of war in favour of the Allies. A year and a half later, Germany and Austria had to ask for a cease-fire.

Germany and Austria did this in particular on the basis of the 14 points propagated by the American President Wilson as the basis for peace.

As it turns out in the following two years, neither Wilson nor anyone else on the allied side took these 14 points seriously. Their contents, like self-

determination of the peoples, just peace etc. were trampled underfoot.

The resulting so-called Versailles Treaty was de facto a dictate of the victorious powers, since Germany and Austria were not included in the negotiations but were merely forced to sign the treaty.

In this treaty, Germany and Austria were declared the perpetrators of the war and were practically completely disarmed. Austria was crushed and both countries were massively plundered. In fact, the last payments from this Versailles dictate were made by Germany only about ten years ago.

For the German population, this dictate was completely incomprehensible at the time; they, quite rightly, did not feel that they had caused the war and had hoped for a just peace on the basis of Wilson's 14 points.

Such a treaty/dictation as that of Versailles has never occurred in this form in the European history of the last 300 years.

The fact that the one lying on the ground, which had surrendered, was still further stepped on, was almost a novelty in European history.

People, indeed, whole societies, have a keen sense of the injustice that is happening to them. This attitude has set events in motion throughout Europe and steered them in a catastrophic direction.

The English General Fuller described 6 April 1917, the day the USA entered the war, as the blackest day in Europe. He has been right.

Some quotes on the subject of war perpetrators:

"… The signatory powers of the treaty of Versailles solemnly promised the Germans that one would disarm if Germany went first with its disarmamnet. For fourteen years Germany has waited for the keeping of this promise. During this time, a series of outspoken peaceful ministers have been active in Germany, ministers who have not stopped adjuring the major powers to finally take seriously the fulfillment of this promose. One has made fun …. Of these German ministers.

In the meantime, all countries with the exception of England have increased their war weaponry and even granted loans to Germany´s neighbours, with which these countries in turn built up massive military organizations close to Germany´s borders. Can we be surprised that the Germans have at long last been driven to a revolt against this chronoc fraud by the major powers?!

Lloyd George, 29th of November 1934, speech in the House of Commons. L. G. was Englands Prime minister during WW1

That, which would happen in the 26 years that followed Versailles would have been inconceivable without the Traty of Versailles.

"The starting point of the National Socialist movement is not Munich, but Versailles."
Theodor Heuss 1932. Heus later became the first Bundespräsident of postwar Germany

Also, the highly problematic permanent crisis in the Middle East, which shapes our lives today, is a direct consequence of the idiotic French and English politics in Versailles and Sevres, which, among other things, divided the then Ottoman Empire.

Also, over the question who caused the 2nd World War one can dispute thoroughly (but not in Germany, unfortunately, see the interesting § 130 StGB (German Penal Code), which stands in obvious conflict with the UN Charter of Human Rights).

Here are some Churchill quotations on the subject of Germany:

Winston Churchill: "We will force this war upon Hitler, if he wants it or not." - **Winston Churchill (1936 broadcast)**

"Germany becomes too powerful. We have to crush it." - **Winston Churchill (November 1936 to US-General Robert E. Wood)**

"Germanys unforgiveable crime before WW2 was its attempt to loosen its economy out of the world trade system and to build up an own exchange system from which the world-finance couldn`t profit anymore. ...We butchered the wrong pig." - **Winston Churchill, The Second World War (Book by Winston Churchill, Bern, 1960)**

"The war wasn`t only about abolishing fascism, but to conquer sales markets. We could have, if we had intended so, prevented this war from breaking out without doing one shot, but we didn't want to." - **Winston Churchill to Truman (Fulton, USA March 1946)**

"This war is an English war and its goal is the destruction of Germany." - **Winston Churchill (Autumn 1939 broadcast)**

Epilogue

I am glad that one can drink bitter in the "Pub" in Polperro and not in the "Gasthaus" Pils.
I love English houses without German Tuja front gardens and aluminium doors. The roundabout fascinates me because of its elegance; the German intersection system is annoying at best.
I think Jaguars are more beautiful than Mercedes even if the German cars were 10 times more reliable!
I like British understatement and the reserved, polite but very hospitable way you meet everywhere in England.
And what would England and the world be without the Royals; just imagine Buckingham Palace owned by an SS Obergruppenführer with face cuts - horrible.

The English have now even managed to throw out morons like Juncker and Schulz and get rid of the EU octopus. Brexit, chapeau!

On the other hand: if only a few things had been decided differently, history could have developed completely different!

What if?
It is not certain that Hitler really wanted operation

371

sealion to land in England. His behaviour at the time, was more likely to suggest a negative attitude to this topic. He did not, as usual, interfere in the preparation for sealion.

This novel describes the fictional execution of the operation Sealion, the preparation of the landing (part 1), the landing itself and the subsequent conquest of England (part 2 and then 3).
The conditions for the implementation of sealion were very demanding. The most important factor was the elimination of the RAF. This was not achieved, very narrowly, although it would have been possible. Their mistake, was to start bombing London on 7.9.40 before the RAF was completely eliminated.

This was the point in time when the Luftwaffe moved from a tactical fight against the British, for which the Air Force was relatively well suited, to a strategic fight, for which the Luftwaffe was not really suited for lack of heavy bombers and for lack of range, especially of the fighters, and had to fail as could have been anticipated.

Objectively speaking, sealion could have been successful. Only a few, even then (1940) possible conditions would have been necessary to bring sealion to success. These are:

1. The planning for sealion should have been carried out as contingency planning already in spring 1940 parallel to Plan Gelb, the plan for the Blitzkrieg in France. The landing should have started as soon as possible after the fall of Dunkirk.
2. Additional tanks for Me 109 fighters could have been produced early (technically no problem).
3. The training of several bomber units in a double role as torpedo bombers.
4. Starting to fight against the RAF infrastructure already at the beginning of July, instead of the senseless channel fight
5. Ultimate request to the Vichy Government to hand over tanks, artillery, aircraft and merchant ships to be used by the German Wehrmacht.
6. No bombing of London but destruction of the RAF and RN
7. The clear political and military will to implement sealion
8. A landing primarily as an air landing in the first stage.

My fictional story implements these prerequisites.

The book begins shortly before the surrender of France. However, some sprinklers still have an earlier date, explaining some important prerequisites for the success of the operation.

In this fictional story I also took the liberty of letting Göring die by an overdose of cocaine and having Churchill killed by an Irish terrorist, although I actually like Churchill, an ingenious war criminal and German-hater. Göring was followed by Milch, a born organizer and pragmatist, who avoids Görings mistakes, and who with his unscrupulous energy, fights down the RAF and thus establishes the conditions for the landing.

I had the idea for this book in 1986, after that relatively little happened, only in 2002 I started to write seriously. After 2004 there was another break, because I realized, that such a book doesn't fit at all into the mainstream and from my point of view I wasn't good enough as a writer to have a real publishing chance.

By 2015, after first experiences with the possibilities self-publishing offers, I have continued the manuscript then finished to about 50%, and voila, here it is.

What influenced me, from the basic style, was Tom Clancy's "Red storm rising", but he can write much better than I can.

I have also read a lot of alternative history novels in recent years, especially since about 2013 the books of Harry Turtledove, a writer I can only highly recommend.

I hope the Royal Border Control will let me ashore in the future.

As I am an older guy, I don´t enjoy paperbacks printed in 10 point fonts. Because I have difficulties reading this size.
So I let this book be printed in a somewhat larger font. This is not done to make it more expensive (actually, printing costs are higher reducing my fee), but to allow elder readers to read this book without a magnifying glass.
For anyone younger than 40: don't rejoice, this happens to practically anyone past 40.

Abbreviations

Eight eight, the German 8.8 cm cannon. Originally developed as an anti-aircraft gun, it was quickly recognised in Germany, that it was possible to use this gun with anti tank grenades for tank defence. In the Second World War this was certainly the cannon, which allied tanks had the largest respect of. The only disadvantage was the height of the gun, which was well recognizable thereby. For unknown reasons no one followed this course, neither in England with the 9.4 cm AA gun nor in Russia with the comparable 8.5 cm AA gun.

BdU, commander of the submarines, since 1938 Admiral Dönitz.

Blenheim, English three-seater and twin-engine light bomber with first flight 1935. At the beginning of the war already slightly outdated, the Blenheim was nevertheless used until mid 1942 as a first line aircraft. With only one backward firing machine gun for defense, the Blenheim was easy meat for German fighters. Some were also used as night fighters.

Bofors, Swedish armaments company. The 4 cm Flak, developed by Bofors, was licensed by

England and Germany and later used by the USA.

Eins O,/XO the first watch officer on German ships. Corresponds to the XO on American ships. This is the officer who does practically all the routine work of leading a ship, allowing the captain to concentrate on the actual ship's command.

EK 1, the Iron Cross of the First Class, is a very old German order of bravery, which was already introduced in the wars of liberation against Napoleon (1813). Until the First World War it was practically the highest award a soldier could achieve and was rarely awarded then. In the Second World War it much more frequently awarded, the step above the EK 1was the knight's cross.

Fi 156 Storch (Stork), German courier, observation and liaison aircraft, which was able to take off or land within less than 50 m. Crew maximum three persons.

FO, Flight Officer, in the RAF a pilot equivalent in rank to lieutenant..

GPF, French 155 mm cannons, introduced in 1917. A model with spreading carriage and particularly large range. Still modern during the Second World

War. The only disadvantage was the necessity to dig a pit under the breech, if one wanted to shoot at full range.

Hurricane, English fighter, at the time of the air battle over England the most frequent fighter of the Fighter Command. Well-armed with eight machine guns, popular as a stable weapon platform, somewhat slower than Spitfire and Me 109, but could, well flown, quite keep up with them.

Do, airplanes of the German manufacturer Dornier. 1940 one of the most frequent bombers was the Do 17. Somewhat underpowered and not well armed enough, to assert itself against fighters like the Hurricane or the Spitfire.

IRA, the Irish Republican Army, a Catholic Irish underground movement active in Northern Ireland and England since the 1920s. The Irish in the Republic of Ireland have never forgotten that in the 1922 peace treaty the sixth northern counties of Ireland remained with England. This resulted in a guerrilla war against the English and Protestant Northern Ireland which lasted until the end of the 1990s.

JG, fighter squadron of the German Air Force.

Usually consisting of three squadrons with about twelve aircraft each.

Ju, aircraft of the German manufacturer Junkers. In 1940 this was mainly the Ju 88 bomber, one of the most important bomber aircraft of the German Luftwaffe. Fast and well-armed, but still inferior to English fighters like Hurricane and Spitfire. Also, the dive bomber Ju 87 was from Junkers. As a bomber very accurate, but completely inferior to modern fighters. From 1941 completely outdated design. Nevertheless, Colonel Rudel, who flew the Ju 87 until the end of 1944 and was the most awarded German soldier, and destroyed 519 tanks, a battleship and 7 fighter planes. Rudel remained a convinced National Socialist until the end of his life.

KG, bomber unit of the German Luftwaffe. Usually consisting of three bomber squadrons with about twelve planes each.

K 18, German 15 cm cannon from Krupp. Good but heavy.

Matilda 2, English infantry tank. Slow, heavily armoured and only to be penetrated with the 8.8 cm anti-aircraft gun. Equipped with a 4 cm (2 pounders) cannon.

Me 109, German standard fighter until 1945 from Messerschmidt.

Me 110, twin-engine heavy fighter or, as they said in the thirties, destroyer. Designed and built by the successful designer Willy Messerschmitt. First class armament, fast and very comfortable to fly, as the English test pilot Eric Brown confirmed.
Due to her significantly higher weight she was not able to stand her ground in a dogfight against single-engine fighters. From the end of 1940 the Me 110 was used very successfully as a night fighter. The only twin-engine fighter that could successfully assert itself against single-engine fighters in the Second World War, was the American Lightning, which had clear advantages with more powerful engines and turbochargers, especially at higher altitudes.

MC Military Cross, English decoration.

MG, machinegun.

ONI, Office of Naval Intelligence, Naval Intelligence Service.

OKH, High Command of the German Army.

PZL 11, Polish fighter. Fixed landing gear, open cockpit, nimble but very outdated by 1939.

RAF, Royal Air Force, the English Air Force. Only after the First World War established as an independent military formation equal to army and navy.

RLM, the Aviation Ministry of Germany, built in the mid-1930s in the Speer style in Berlin, still stands today. Comrade Schäuble and his finance ministry now sit there. It is astonishing that such a negative development is actually possible in Germany.

RN, Royal Navy, the English Navy. 1939 beside the American fleet the strongest navy of the world.

RTC, Royal Tank Corps, the English tank weapon.

Spitfire, British fighter developed by Reginald Mitchell.

StuG, assault gun. A tank without a turret with a

cannon in a casemate. This also makes it lower than a turreted tank. Due to the weight saved, it is usually equipped with a larger calibre than the tank equivalent. First with artillery units, but later also increasingly used in the German tank units. Very successful concept.

Wingco, Wing Commander, in the English Air Force Leader of a wing composed of several squadrons.

1 WO, First Watch Officer, XO.

ZG, destroyer swing, a designation used in the German Luftwaffe. In the thirties a number of countries pursued the idea of a fighter plane with long range and strong armament, which should be able to accompany own bombers over longer distances. Only in Germany this concept came to the fore in the form of the Me 110 in more than prototype form. Göring, the Luftwaffe chief, was so enthusiastic about this idea, that he assigned the elite of pilots to the units equipped with the Me 110. Initial doubts about this concept arose during the campaign against Poland, where the Me 110 was able to assert itself relatively well against the clearly outdated Polish fighters. It quickly became clear over France and England that the Me 110 had little chance of survival against the current single-engine fighters of the French and the English, that it was fast and well-armed but clearly less agile than a single-engine fighter. Nevertheless, the Me 110 was able to assert itself as a night fighter and as a fighter bomber until the end of the war, but no longer as a destroyer or heavy fighter. This was caused among other things by enormous problems with the successor model Me 210, which should have replaced the Me 110 from 1943 on. A chapter of German armament policy, which shows, how one should rather not do it.

The Author

Harry Bold is the pen name of a German sociologist, working since 1990 as business consultant for small and medium enterprises.

Contact to the author:

debug.sealion1@clever.ms